Watercolor Skulls

Watercolor Skulls

Rebel Skulls MC Book Two

LM Terry

Watercolor Skulls

Dedication

This one is dedicated to all the dark romance readers out there. Thank you for keeping an open mind and an open heart. Without you, my passion would fall flat. Every writer needs a reader. Thank you for being mine.

Table of Contents

Chapter One

Lily

Staring out across the blue water, I recognize the beauty of the scene before me. I wonder how everyone else sees it. My gaze falls to the people around me. Most are looking at the world through a lens.

The sun is shining brightly over us. I reach up with cold, shaking hands to feel the top of my head. I smile, remembering my aunt and warm summer days spent here in the bay. My hands drop back to the cold railing. The noise from the traffic behind me seems fitting. The soundtrack to my life. Shuffled here, shooed there, always going wherever I was told. The force of my father's life paving the way for me.

A man in uniform spots me, tilting his head in concern. I quickly climb over, clinging to the side of the bridge, my feet perched on a pipe beneath me. The wind whips my hair around my cheeks, the air salty and wet. All I have to do is let go and fall backwards.

"Hey, sweetheart," a man's voice says calmly above me. "Let me help you back over and we can talk. Whatever is bothering you, it can be fixed. I promise." I glance up at him briefly. It's the officer I saw staring at me. His hand is extended over the railing, reaching out to me. A second man is standing by his side nervously.

I'm way past the point of fixing anything. Nothing can be fixed. Nothing. If I let him pull me up, he will find out who I am. My father will be angry. Benjamin will be angry. There is no going back.

I turn my head to admire the beauty of the bridge one last time. A dragonfly lands on a steel bar beside me, a sign that it's time to go. The man continues to plead with me.

I close my eyes, lean back and... let go.

My body falls at a speed I was not prepared for.

What have I done?

What have I done?

I don't want to die.

I want to live.

I want to live.

And then a pain like I've never felt before, explodes through my body.

Darkness swallows me whole as the current pulls against my battered frame. Water fills my lungs as I struggle to rise to the surface.

And then I see it...

The bright light. It shines above me. The beautiful amber glow pulls me closer and closer. The dragonfly darts back and forth between me and the light. It's like I'm stuck beneath a piece of glass. Nothing unusual there. I'm always on the other side looking out. But this time I break through.

My hands rise to the surface first and then I feel the air on my face as I gasp for breath, choking. A man in the water pulls me to him. "She's alive," he yells.

The pain I feel tells me he is correct.

I lived.

I lived.

As the coast guard loads me onto their boat, I stare at the clouds. The dragonfly makes one final appearance before darting away. My eyes follow him until he blends into the scenery.

"Do you know how lucky you are?"

I blink at the young man hovering above me.

"You're the first one I've pulled out alive," he pants from exhaustion, his wet hair dripping over my face.

I close my eyes, knowing I'm now part of the one percent. The one percent who survive.

Everything after that becomes a blur. Doctors, nurses, beeping machines… it all runs into one endless sentence.

When consciousness returns, I hear my father whispering harshly to my mother. She is crying. She never cries out loud, but I can tell by her sniffles. "Get control over yourself, Margaret."

"You know who is responsible for this. She made Lily question the path we've laid out for her. If not for *her*, Lily would have accepted her life without complaint."

She's wrong. I've never complained. Not once.

My mother hiccups, still unable to control her emotions. "What are we going to tell people?"

"We are having a press conference in twenty minutes outside the hospital. Doctor Hodges is going to announce that Lily had been taking medication for a minor illness. He's going to say that an adverse side effect caused a temporary mania, which led to her jump."

Fall. It was a fall.

"Do I have to speak?" my mother asks.

"No. You just have to stand there and pretend to be a caring mother for five minutes. Do you think you can handle that?"

She sniffles again. "Yes, of course. You know I care about our daughter. I don't have to pretend."

"Sure, whatever you say, Margaret."

The door opens. Benjamin, my fiancé, tells my father that everything is set up outside.

"Margaret, wait for us in the waiting room."

I hear shuffling and then the door opening and closing. Squeezing my eyes shut tight, I pray they all left, but I know that's not true. I feel their presence.

"What a fine mess you've made, Lily," my father says in disgust.

Watercolor Skulls

Reluctantly I open my eyes, the light in the room is bright, too bright. I blink a few times, trying to sit myself up but the pain in my ribs prevents it. My gaze falls over my dad and Benjamin. Both stand stoically in their designer suits with their hair combed back into a perfect slicked back gentlemen's style. No hint of emotion on their faces.

Benjamin, my fiancé, is almost a carbon copy of my father. Disturbing, isn't it?

I don't say anything. He didn't ask me a question, so there's no need. In fact, he prefers it that way.

"The hospital will be releasing you tomorrow, early afternoon. I've arranged a car to pick you up."

"Yes, sir," I manage to croak out. My mouth is so dry. I could use a sip of water. My eyes go to the cup and pitcher on my bedside table. My father follows my gaze and pushes the tray beyond my reach.

I close my eyes and bite the inside of my cheek to keep my tears at bay.

"Do not speak to anyone. We will discuss this when you get home." He turns and walks out of the room.

Benjamin lingers by the door. He runs his hand through his hair before settling his gaze on me. "The wedding will not be delayed. I advise you rest up." He winks before turning to leave me alone.

A nurse bounces into my room. She pushes my tray back by my side, checks my I.V. and leaves. I'm sure she has been instructed not to speak to me.

My hand unconsciously searches for the pendant around my neck, my only source of comfort. It's gone. My heart breaks as I realize it probably washed out to sea.

Gingerly I try to sit up again. My ribs scream in pain but slowly I right myself, pulling my gown up to my chin to access the damage. Bruises cover my upper thighs and around my rib cage but otherwise it looks like I'm in one piece. I lower the gown and stare at the door that is sure to be guarded by one of my father's security men.

Scouring the room for answers, my eyes land on the phone sitting on a little table by the bed. I lean over, grabbing my mid-section for support as I search the drawer for a phone book. Oh, thank god, they still have these. My finger runs down the page of transportation services. Finding the one my father uses; I make the call. When the receptionist picks up, I take the first step toward my new life.

"Yes, I need to change the arrangements that were made for Ms. Lily Ramsey's pickup tomorrow at Mercy Medical."

"Of course."

I finish the call and then lie back against the pillows.

When the nurse comes in with my supper, I take the opportunity to push my plan. "Excuse me, could you tell me where my belongings are?"

She walks over to a cabinet and pulls out a bag my parents must have brought for me and then she reaches in for my purse. Oh, thank god. "Your clothes were pretty torn up from the accident, so your parents brought you something to change into. An officer brought your purse. I guess you left it behind on the bridge." She doesn't make eye contact, her face turns pink, clearly embarrassed on my behalf. "There was also a necklace." She reaches into my purse and pulls out a clear bag to show me. "It's right here in the front pocket."

When her eyes finally meet mine, I nod. "Thank you. My father called a few minutes ago." I point to the phone. "He said my ride will be here sooner than originally planned, two hours earlier. Could you let someone know to have my dismissal papers ready by then?"

The nurse puts my things back in the cupboard. "Yes, I'll make a note on your chart." She pauses before walking out of the room. "Is there anything else I can get you?"

"No. I'm fine, thank you."

She nods sadly before closing the door.

I spend the rest of the evening alone with my thoughts.

In my mind, the dragonfly was a sign to let go and maybe it was, just not in the way I thought. Maybe it's time to let go of being my father's daughter. Maybe it's time to find myself.

My aunt had a plan. I should have followed through with it but the thought of putting it into motion without her just didn't seem possible.

Chapter Two

Lily

If I thought I hurt yesterday, it's nothing compared to today. The nurse brought my release papers in early so everything would be ready when my ride arrived. She told me the doctor had prescribed some pain medication but due to my circumstances, she was entrusting those to the security guard still posted outside my door. Great, he's still here.

After she removes the I.V., she puts my bag and purse on the end of my bed. "If you need any help just push your call light," she says cheerfully. At least this one isn't looking at me like I'm a freak of nature.

"I'll let you know when your ride arrives," she adds before walking out.

I reach for my bag, sighing when I see what my mother sent for me to wear. A bright cheerful sundress with tiny pink flowers all over it. I roll my eyes. At least it should be comfortable. I slip the dress over my head and push my feet into the matching flats.

I pull the clear bag out of my purse and dump the necklace in the palm of my hand. "I don't know where to go," I whisper to the charm. My finger brushes over the silver dragonfly.

A knock on the door interrupts me. "Come in," I say as I clasp the necklace around my neck.

My father's security guy, Rudy, steps inside my room. "The car is here." He checks his watch before narrowing his eyes on me.

"They're early," I say, not taking my eyes off his.

"They are." He runs his thumb over his eyebrow. "There must have been a misunderstanding. But it looks like you're ready?"

"Yeah." I stand, grimacing as I straighten. He rushes to my side to help me.

"The nurse is bringing a wheelchair."

"That might be best," I tell him. "Before we head to the estate, I need to pick up something I left at the bridge. Well, not at the bridge but in a locker near the bridge."

The nurse comes in with the wheelchair before he can respond.

I notice they don't take me out of the main exit. We leave the building through what looks like a service entrance. I suppose the media is still hanging around, hoping for a glimpse of the Senator's crazy daughter.

When we get in the car, Rudy stares at me for a long time. "What is it you need to pick up?"

"My bag."

He looks at the bag on the seat beside me, raising an eyebrow in question.

"This is the bag mother brought up for me. I had one with me the day I fell. I left it at Bay Storage."

He shifts awkwardly in his seat. "Okay."

He instructs the driver where to go. I watch the scenery out the window. Nothing much has changed. I'm still staring through the glass, observing everyone else live. When we pull up to Bay Storage, Rudy gets out with me. He is clearly uncomfortable being so close to the bridge.

I stop in front of locker twenty-one, searching my purse for the key. After I locate it, I open the metal door and smile. My aunt's bright blue bag is waiting for me, ready to take me on a great adventure.

I turn to Rudy. "Thanks for letting me grab this."

He shrugs like it isn't a big deal and walks me back to the car, visibly relieved to be leaving. I almost feel bad for what I'm about to do. He will face my father's wrath because of my actions.

I bite my lip as we drive. "Could we stop at a pharmacy?"

He sighs. "Sure, I'll go in for you. Make me a list."

"No, that's okay." I tuck a piece of my hair behind my ear shyly. "I need some, um, some girl items."

His face heats as he turns to tell the driver to stop at the closest pharmacy.

As we pull into the parking lot, I grab the blue bag and my purse. He eyes me suspiciously but doesn't say anything. He does, however, get out of the car with me. My pulse picks up a notch. Rudy follows me inside but when I turn down the feminine product aisle, he tells me he will wait for me by the checkout. I nod, pretending to look at the boxes on the shelf. As soon as he disappears, I make a beeline for the back. A few store employees give me a funny look when I push through the doors, but nobody stops me. When I break through to the outside world, my heart thumps a little happier.

As quickly as my aching body will allow, I get as far away from the pharmacy as I can. I'm sure Rudy is freaking out about now. As soon as I find a residential area, I open the bag my aunt left for me and find the burner phone we purchased years ago. As it powers on, I look at the number on the front of the house I'm hiding behind. When the cab company picks up, I rattle off the address, telling them to send a car as soon as possible.

When the cab arrives, I have him take me back to Bay Storage, knowing I don't have much time. When I open the locker, I drop the key into my purse and shove it inside, slamming the door shut on my old life. I rush out and head toward the bridge. Before I get there, I stop at a public restroom.

Hastily, I strip out of my sundress. I grab the sea blue hair dye out of the bag and follow the instructions on the box. It's time to change from Senator Ramsey's daughter to Lily Gladstone, the girl on my fake I.D. The one with a whole new life ahead of her.

I clip the fake piercing in my nose while the dye sets and place the fake tattoo of a dragonfly on my left forearm. After I rinse my hair, I dress in torn blue jeans and a tight-fitting black V-neck t-shirt. Pulling a pair of black chucks out of the bag, I stare in the mirror for a few seconds, wondering where I found the courage to do all this. Honestly, falling off the bridge was easier.

Okay, I can do this. I can. It's what my aunt wanted. After cleaning up the bathroom and turning the bag inside out so that it's now yellow, I shove everything back inside. I glance around, making sure no trace of me exists before stepping outside. The breeze teases my newly colored hair around my cheeks.

I keep my face turned down as I make my way to a local restaurant, then I call for another cab. This one will take me to the train station.

So far so good.

Once I'm on the train, I breathe a sigh of relief, happy to be able to sit still for a while. My body hurts so bad it brings tears to my eyes. I think about what I need to do next. My aunt told me not to stay on the train too long. At least get over the mountains she had said. I look at the map I picked up in the train station and decide I'll hop off in Reno. It's a large town and maybe I can pick up a vehicle there.

My aunt and I opened an account at a national bank chain so we could access our account from anywhere. I've been pulling cash out of my dad's account every day since I was sixteen. He didn't care. As long as I was his perfect princess, all was well. I would purposely show him a new outfit every now and then so he wouldn't get suspicious of my cash transactions. He simply thought I preferred cash over his card. I've deposited over two hundred thousand dollars over the years. I'm not sure what I'll do with it all. I only need enough to get set up somewhere new. My Aunt Jenny put some of the cash in the bag so we wouldn't have to find a bank right away.

The next step will be finding a landing spot. I don't know where I want to go. I don't know where I belong. Definitely not where I was. I rub the dragonfly pendant, praying for direction.

Seven hours later, I'm standing in the train station in Reno. A cab ride soon after and I'm in a hotel lobby, scouring the classified ads for a vehicle. And there it is, my sign. I find a light blue 1964 Volkswagen Beetle for sale. It looks rough but as long as it runs, I don't care what it looks like. My aunt always wanted a Volkswagen Bus, this is the next best thing, right?

Besides, it's just me now. I swallow down the tightness in my throat. It's fine. I'm fine. I'm alive. I'm alive. I don't have time to cry right now. I'm sure the tears will come but not now.

I call the lady about the beetle. She and her husband offer to drive it to the hotel the very next day.

I trudge back to my room incredibly tired, falling asleep the minute my head hits the pillow.

The next morning, the elderly woman and her husband show up as planned.

"I've had this car since college. Let me tell you, she's seen things," the grey-haired woman jokes.

"It's beautiful," I tell her, running my hands over the hood gently.

Her husband laughs and shakes his head. "Well, Annabelle, I think we found your baby a new owner."

The old woman smiles at him before turning her kind eyes on me. "I hope she brings you as many wonderful adventures as she did me."

I pay them for the car, and she signs the title over. I hold it to my chest. This is my first purchase as Lily Gladstone. "I love it so much!" I exclaim, bouncing on the balls of my feet. The elderly couple both shake my hand, wishing me the best of luck.

Soon enough, the beetle and I are headed down the road. I'm not sure where I'm going. I just drive. Windows down, radio up, and the wind whipping my wild blue hair around my face.

This, this is what Aunt Jenny wanted for me… for us. I wipe a stray tear away and turn the music up louder.

I drive until I need to stop for gas. The town I stop in is settled in the foothills. It's beautiful here. Inside the gas station, I notice a board with all kinds of papers tacked to it. One stands out to me. Houses/Apartments for rent, call RS Rentals. I ask the clerk for a pen and write the number down on the back of my hand.

Maybe I'll drive around and check out the town. I pull the wrapper off the stale turkey sandwich I purchased and take a bite. It's a cute little town. Seems to have everything one might need. Several businesses line the main street. I drive slowly, taking everything in.

Children and their parents are out riding bikes and walking their dogs. It looks safe enough. Nothing like the big city. My gaze falls on the number scribbled on my skin. I guess it's worth a shot. If I don't like it here, I can always move on. I pull my burner phone out and call the number. A woman answers.

"Yes, I'm calling about your rentals. I'm looking for a house to rent."

"Cool, we got a few open right now. Would you like to set up a time to look at them?" she asks.

"Well, I'm kind of needing something right away if that's possible." I glance at the time on the bank. It's still early afternoon.

"Sure thing. Give me thirty minutes to wrap up what I'm working on. How many bedrooms are you looking for?" she asks, I can hear her pop her gum over the receiver.

"Oh, I don't know. Maybe one or two."

"Okay, I'll text you an address. See you in thirty."

"Thank you so much."

"No problem," she says before hanging up.

I get a text a few seconds later. It takes me a few minutes but eventually I find the address she sent. I pull up in front of the house. It looks nice but it's right in the middle of town. I guess I envisioned myself in a more rural setting. I don't know, maybe it would be best to be in town. I tap my fingers on the steering wheel, waiting for the rental lady.

A loud hot rod pulls into the driveway and a woman steps out. Holy cow. I blink a few times, taking her in. Surely, this is not the woman I spoke to on the phone. She notices me and smiles wide. She starts toward me as I slowly get out of my beetle.

She thrusts her tattooed arm out to me, her green eyes sparkling in the sun. "You must be the one who called? I'm Jesse."

"Uh, yeah. It's nice to meet you. I'm Lily… Lily Gladstone." I push my hand out and she latches on to it, shaking my hand firmly.

I notice her gaze travels down my arm, landing on the bandage from my I.V. When I pull away, I cover it with my hand. "I had a bad fall. I've been in the hospital," I say, hugging myself.

"I'm sorry, I didn't mean to draw attention. I check everyone's arms for track marks. We have a zero-tolerance policy on drug use in our rentals."

"Well, you're in luck, I've never tried any drug."

The woman narrows her eyes on me.

I hold up two fingers. "Scouts honor."

She laughs and waves for me to follow her into the house. Her hair is jet black and hangs to her waist. She is strikingly beautiful. She walks through the house, pointing out all the details. The house is cute, but I was really hoping for something a little more remote.

"I have a few apartments open on the east side of town. If that interests you, we can go take a look." Her phone dings and she pulls it out of her back pocket. She rolls her eyes as she types a response. "Sorry, it's my husband."

"No problem. Um, do you have anything on the edge of town? I was hoping to find something more rural," I tell her, glancing around the living room. I'm trying to picture myself here, but it doesn't feel right.

"Well, I do have a place a few miles away but it's not really ready to be rented. My dad and I were always going to fix it up, but we just haven't had time."

"Is it livable?"

She sighs. "It is but I'm telling you it's rough."

"That's okay."

Her phone dings again and she shoots off another text. Her fingers fly over the screen. "Let me tell you, protective men are nice but Jesus Christ he needs to get off my dick."

My eyes go wide at her language and then they drop to her crotch.

She notices and laughs, stuffing her phone back in her pocket. "Don't worry. I don't have a dick. Just a figure of speech."

My cheeks heat at my naivety. "I didn't... ugh, I'm sorry. You could say I've lived a sheltered life."

"Nothing wrong with that," she says, offering me a kind smile. "I'll try to watch my language."

I put my hand out to stop her. "No. No, please don't. It's... it's refreshing."

"That's good, because I don't really have a filter." She laughs lightly, looking around the room. She nods her head as if making up her mind about something. "Follow me. We'll go take a look."

"Great. Thank you."

She gets back in her rusty looking rod, and I notice the skull painted on the door. This woman is unlike anyone I've ever met. She is uniquely her. I follow her out of town and down the dusty road, large trees line both sides. Now this is more like it. The tension in my chest uncoils slightly.

When the house comes into view, I almost cry out loud. The house has a small porch on the front which gives it a cozy appearance but it's the windows I notice. There are so many of them. Jesse pulls up in front and parks. I slide in behind her.

"So, what do you think? It's kind of out in the boonies but maybe that's what you're looking for?" She tilts her head, studying me closely.

"It's beautiful. I love all the windows," I say in awe, my eyes dancing over the home.

"They are new. It's the one thing we got done." She unlocks the door and steps inside. "It still needs painted and the flooring needs a little work."

I cover my mouth with my hands. It's perfect. The living room runs along the whole front of the home. Windows line all three walls. To the left, it opens to a kitchen with tall old-style cabinets. On the right, is a set of stairs, the railing made out of a crooked looking branch, perfect in its imperfection. "I'll take it."

Jesse laughs, tipping her head back, her hair fans out behind her, revealing a tattoo of a rose behind her ear. "You haven't even seen the upstairs."

"I don't need to see more. It's perfect."

"It will be a couple of weeks before I can get my guys over here to fix it up for you."

"That's okay. I can fix it up myself. I'm really needing something today if that's possible."

A flash of concern rushes over her face. "Are you sure?" She looks out the window at my beetle.

"I'm sure. Just let me know what color you want the rooms and I'll get the paint," I plead with her.

She scratches her head. "As long as you don't paint anything baby shit yellow, I'm good." Jesse rests her butt against the counter that separates the living room from the kitchen. "Are you in some sort of trouble?"

My head drops. I'm a terrible liar. That's why my aunt and I decided to use my real first name and a fake last one. We thought it would be easier for me to tell half a lie than a whole one. Maybe that's what I need to do here, half lie. "I had a bad breakup. I'm looking for a fresh start."

Her eyes go back to the band-aid on my arm before perusing over the rest of my body. She points to the fake tattoo on my arm. "Ever think about getting a real one?"

It's already peeling from my shower this morning. I laugh lightly. "Oh, I don't know."

"I've got a tattoo shop in town. Stop by sometime. I think my partner has a bad ass design of a dragonfly."

"Yeah, I'll think about it." I scratch at the stupid thing, suddenly feeling very insecure in front of this woman.

She smacks her hands on the counter before pushing herself away. "Rent is due the first of every month. I'll wave the first few months if you paint the rooms. I'll have my guys come to work on the floors. You can switch the utilities over in the next day or two, I'll get you the numbers to call them."

"Oh my gosh, thank you. Thank you so much."

She shrugs off my thanks. "Do you have a moving truck coming with the rest of your stuff? Maybe we can get the floors done before they arrive."

I tuck my blue hair behind my ear. "No, everything I own is in my car."

Her gaze goes back to the windows. "So, you plan on staying here tonight?"

I nod.

"No bed?"

"I'll be fine. Tomorrow, I'll go into town and get what I need."

She pulls her phone out of her pocket. "Let me call my husband. We have a bed at our old house. I'll have him bring it over."

My mouth falls open. This woman doesn't even know me, yet she is going out of her way to make sure I'm comfortable my first night here. "Oh, I don't want to be any trouble. I'm fine really."

Her eyebrow cocks up. "I insist."

I bow my head, letting her make the call.

"Hey, I need you to go over to the old house and pick up the bed in Rachel's room and bring it over to the house on Windflower Road." She pauses, chewing at her nail. "Yeah, I rented it to someone, and she needs a fucking bed, okay."

My mouth opens to tell her I don't need it, but she puts her hand up to stop me. I snap my mouth shut, admiring her strength. This woman is a force in itself.

"Tell Raffe to get off your sister and help or... I could call Jeremy and see if he can help me load it up." She winks at me, a wicked smile playing over her flawless face.

"See you soon, love ya," she makes a kissy sound into the phone and then hangs up.

"The guys will be here soon." She spins around, tapping the side of her head in thought. "We should get some cleaning supplies. Oh, and groceries. Have you eaten today?"

"Um, yeah."

Her eyes run down my body as mine do the same to her. She is curvy in all the right places. I am too but my parent's put me on a stringent diet so that I didn't plump up any farther... their words not mine. In fact, the gas station turkey sandwich was the first meat I've had since my aunt was alive and to be honest, it's not sitting very well. My hand rubs over my belly lightly, careful not to push too hard on my bruises.

"Let's run into town." She walks toward me and drapes her arm around my shoulders. My heart beats wildly in my chest. I bite my bottom lip to stop it from trembling. My Aunt Jenny was the last person to touch me... to really touch me. Jesse reminds me of her.

She guides us back out onto the porch, leaving the door unlocked in case her "guys" make it back before us. I'm tired but it would be nice to get a few more things done today. And honestly, a bed sounds wonderful right now. I just have to keep going. If I stop... or rather when I stop, I'll have to face the facts of everything that's happened.

Jesse will be a good distraction.

Chapter Three

Jesse

Lily has a problem. I'm not sure what it is but it's written all over her like a damn math equation on a white board.

Let's start with her ride. It's not plated which tells me it's either stolen or recently purchased. Her demeanor indicates recently purchased.

Next, let's take a close look at her person. Her nails are perfectly manicured, eyebrows painfully sculpted, flawless complexion, and last but not least her teeth are perfectly straight and blindingly white. Okay, so there's all that going on but then add a cheap box of hair dye, phony nose ring and a god-awful fake tattoo. Like what the fuck?

I can't figure it out. I can't figure *her* out. So, I simply need more time. Which is why I offered to take her grocery shopping. Well, that and there's something else.

She's lonely.

I recognize it as I would a long-lost friend.

She reminds me of a seed that blew out of a flower bed only to land randomly along the fence line. The seed is forced to watch the other flowers grow and bloom together in a mixture of texture and color. While the lonely seed sprouts unnoticed, without nurture, wilting in the summer sun.

I know because I've been there.

I watch her out the corner of my eye. She is timid, shy, but holds herself in a quiet, poised sort of way. Coming here, renting this house is big for her. It's more than just a move, it's a spiritual journey.

"So, where are you from?"

"The west coast."

She shifts the bag she brought behind her legs nervously. She gave me a vague answer. I'm assuming it's the truth, but she doesn't want to pinpoint an exact location. Interesting.

"Are you going to live at the house alone? No boyfriend? Husband? Kids?" I rattle off the possibilities, paying close attention to her reaction to each. Nope, none of the above, she didn't even flinch.

"It's just me."

She keeps her answers short, showing me that she doesn't want to risk revealing anything extra about herself.

As we pull up in front of the local grocery store, I realize I didn't learn a fucking thing about her other than she is alone, which I already figured, and that she's from the west coast.

"I'll grab the cleaning supplies while you load up on groceries."

She nods, bending over to unzip her bag. She pulls out a wad of cash, handing me the amount we agreed on for the deposit and then she shoves a few bills into her pocket. She's carrying an awful lot of cash around. I sigh out loud. This girl isn't very street smart.

When we meet up at the checkout, I notice she hardly bought any groceries. There are a few containers of fat free yogurt, some sort of grainy cereal and milk that comes from a nut. Milk should come from a cow as Gabriel's god intended.

I glance at the time on my phone, we have thirty minutes before the hardware store closes. "Let's go grab some paint. That way you can get started whenever you want."

Lily surprises me with the colors she picks. I like them. She would look at a few color tiles and then close her eyes before nodding her head and telling me which one she liked. We may have gotten a little carried away, but I can always use the leftover paint at our other rentals. We grab a few more supplies and then head back to the house.

"Are you an artist?" I ask. She has a good eye for colors.

She laughs. "No, I'm a kindergarten teacher." Her hand flies to her mouth like she revealed something without meaning to.

"Hmm, you have good taste in colors. Besides tattooing, I paint, mostly murals but I dabble in other art forms."

She relaxes when I don't mention the teacher gig. "Being an artist sounds wonderful," she says wistfully, her eyes scanning the scenery beyond the window.

"You should give it a try. Just paint something. You don't have to show anyone. Do it for yourself."

24

She smiles wide, dimples I hadn't seen before gracing her cheeks. Lily is cute as all get out when she smiles. "I just might do that."

I spot my dad's truck in the driveway when we pull in. Lily glances nervously at it as well. "My dad is here. He's the one who's really in charge of the business. He likes to meet all our tenants."

"It's a family business?"

"Yeah, well, sort of a club business. RS Rentals stands for Rebel Skull Rentals, but we found people were reluctant to rent from us if we revealed the whole name."

Her brown eyes go wide. "Rebel Skulls as in the motorcycle gang?"

Sighing loudly, I decide to answer honestly. More than likely, I made Dirk bring that bed for nothing. She is going to be running for the hills here soon.

"I wouldn't say gang, club is the better word. We've evolved over the last decade or so. We're not nearly as dangerous as we once were." I wink at her.

She drops her head and stares at her hands in her lap for a few seconds before raising her eyes to me. "Sounds interesting."

I pull my head back. Not the response I thought I would get from this timid, little mouse. I chuckle and open my door. "Oh, you're about to see how interesting."

She follows me into the house, our eyes dart to the ceiling from all the thumping and cursing going on upstairs. Dirk yells down the stairs, "What fucking room do you want this thing in, Jess?"

I laugh and jog up the stairs, Lily following slowly behind. "Chill out, she hasn't even had the chance to look at the upstairs."

Dirk, Raffe and my dad are all leaning against the bed frame in the hallway. Lily pauses on the top step, frozen in her spot. Her eyes dart over the men and her face turns a pasty white.

Chapter Four

Lily

Oh. Oh, maybe this was a mistake. What have I gotten myself into? A big guy with greying hair steps away from the bed frame and wraps Jesse up in his arms. "Baby girl, you didn't tell me you decided to rent this place out. It's not ready."

Jesse hugs him tight before kissing him on the cheek. "I didn't intend to, but she fell in love with the place. She needs it today."

He glances at me over her shoulder and smiles. He looks like Jesse. They have the same intense green eyes. "Is that so?" He steps around her, heading straight for me. I hold my ground, forcing myself not to back away.

"I'm Bill, Jesse's dad." He smiles proudly when he calls himself her dad. It makes me happy for her, yet sad for me. He thrusts a big hand out toward me, so I reach out to take it. He shakes my hand and pulls me in for a hug.

He hugs me.

Jesse clears her throat. "Dad," she says quietly.

He releases me at once. "Oh, sorry. I'm a bit of a hugger." He laughs.

"That's okay," I say, wrapping my arms around my aching ribs. Shoot that hurt.

I glance at the other two men. My heart stops. A pretty, edgy looking one winks at me in greeting. He seems harmless but the other one makes me pause. He is scary with a capital S. I take a step back. Of course, he notices and smirks.

Jesse walks over and smacks him in the arm. "Lily, this is my husband, Dirk, and our best friend, Raffe." She points to the pretty one.

"It's nice to meet all of you. I'm sorry to be a bother. Jesse insisted." I place my hand over my heart, letting them know how grateful I am.

Raffe laughs. "Jesse insisting? You don't say." He pats Dirk on the back.

I quickly look at the two empty rooms and point to the smallest one. "This room will work."

Jesse steps in front of me. "The other room is bigger."

"I don't mind the small room. I like the window in that one."

"You heard her boys," she says, clapping her hands together to get them moving.

We leave Raffe and Dirk alone to get the bed set up. Bill, Jesse, and I head back downstairs. She heads over to the refrigerator and starts to wipe it down with the cleaner she bought.

"I can do that. Please, you've done so much for me already."

"I feel bad, this isn't our usual standard of rental," she says, scrubbing away.

Her dad leans against the counter, turning his eyes on me. "Will you be looking for a job around here?"

I hop on the counter, wincing at the pain that radiates up my spine. His eyebrows pull together as he watches me. "I guess. I haven't thought much about it. Everything is happening so fast."

Jesse hollers from the fridge, her head still inside. "She had a bad breakup. She's a teacher."

"Oh," he says, pulling himself away from the counter and stretching. "Well, you probably wouldn't be interested then."

"I don't know. I'm kind of looking for something different. What were you thinking?"

"I just opened a bar in town. I'm needing another bartender. Business has been picking up and my wife and I are having a hard time keeping up. Jesse is busy with her tattoo shop and our other daughters just turned eighteen, so they are still too young to give us a hand, not that either of them would want to."

"I don't know anything about bartending," I admit honestly.

"Well, most of our customers are beer drinkers so as long as you can run a bottle opener you should be good. I'm down to give you a shot." He knocks his knuckles on the counter. "So, what do you say?"

My mind rolls it around, these people have been so nice to me and I'm a complete stranger. It just doesn't make sense. But I like them. They don't sugar coat things. They tell you how it is right from the get-go.

"Okay." I hold my hand out to shake on it.

"How old are you?" he asks as he shakes my hand.

"Twenty-five."

"Ah, same age as Jesse." He releases my hand and spins around to face her. She is standing with a wet sponge in her hand, smiling at him. She looks happy that he asked me to work for him.

"I think it's clean enough for your groceries now."

I jump down and double over. Gosh darn it. Why do I keep forgetting I fell off a bridge and fractured my ribs? It shouldn't be that hard to remember.

Bill rushes to my side, grabbing me under the elbow to help me upright. "You okay there, honey?"

"I'm... I'm fine. I had a fall last week. It's nothing."

He glances at Jesse, and she gives him a look that says don't push the subject. Just as he's about to ask me about it, Raffe and Dirk tromp down the stairs, pulling his attention away from me.

"Thank you all for your help but really, I can take it from here." I don't want to sound like I'm dismissing them, but I really need to lay down.

Jesse grabs her dad's arm and pulls him away from me. "I'll check on you tomorrow on my way home from the shop."

I nod, wrapping my arms around my mid-section. "Thank you again. You went above and beyond."

"Please, we brought a bed, and I cleaned the fridge. Hardly above and beyond." Jesse rolls her eyes and then surprises me by giving me a quick peck on the cheek.

The men wave goodbye as they head out. The scary one lingers, staring at me intently before closing the door behind him.

My hand rubs over my cheek. I watch as they drive away, the sun vanishing with them. I shove the few groceries I bought in the fridge. I'm too tired to try and eat anything. I pull a blanket out of my aunt's bag and sluggishly trudge up the stairs, exhausted. I lie down on the bed and cover myself up, head and all.

Only then do I allow the tears to come. The pain in my body… and in my mind, sucks the air from my lungs. I let out everything I've been holding in the past few days.

"I'm sorry it took me so long," I cry out to my dead aunt. "I should have done what you told me to from the start."

Soon sleep prevails and snuffs out my pain.

Chapter Five

Dirk

"So, is she our newest project?"

Jesse gives me a dirty look. "I don't like it when you call them projects. They are people."

Quietly, we both tiptoe into our daughter's room to check on her. She is sleeping peacefully just like the little angel she is. "Katie said they played hard today," she whispers.

I kiss my fingers and then press them against her soft black hair before we step out of the room.

Once the door clicks, I pick Jesse up off her feet and carry her to our room, dumping her on the bed.

"I'm tired," she says, yawning.

I flip her over onto her stomach and smack her ass. "The hell you are."

She giggles and wiggles her cute little ass in my face as I crawl over her. She rolls under me so that we are face to face. "I like her."

"She has smurf hair."

"Says the guy who looks like a psychotic, tattooed killer," she tosses back.

"At least I'm living my truth. She on the other hand is not. She's hiding something."

"She is," Jesse agrees easily. "She's hurt, physically at least. She said she fell."

I stare into my wife's eyes. Pain from her past rises to the surface.

"She reminds you of yourself?" My hand trails along the side of her face.

She nods, biting back tears.

"Okay, then she's the next project."

Jesse bites my bottom lip. "Not project. She's the next friend we help."

"You don't have any friends that are girls."

"That's not true."

"How many friends do you have that are girls?"

She thinks about it for a minute. "I'm friends with Penny."

I laugh in her face. "Penny is hundreds of miles away. It's easy over the damn phone. This will not be easy, and you know it." I tap the side of her head.

"Haven't you ever met someone, and you just know they're meant to be in your life?" she asks.

"I think you already know the answer to that." I roll my hips, pressing my hard cock against her. Her lips part slowly, releasing a tiny groan of desire. Damn, I never get tired of this.

This new girl is going to be work. But I can't say no to my wife, so here we are. Jesus Christ. One thing about being married to Jesse is that life is never boring.

She's always bringing home strays.

Her legs wrap around me, pulling me closer to her and it seals the deal.

I will definitely be helping smurf girl.

Hope she's ready for her exorcism.

Chapter Six

Lily

I open my eyes, finding the sun high in the sky. Holy cow, how long did I sleep? I glance at the clock on the phone. Shoot, it's noon. I've never slept this late in my entire life. My fingers dance over my dragonfly pendant. "It's a new day," I whisper to my aunt.

I lie in bed for a few more minutes, enjoying the thought of the day being entirely mine. My stomach grumbles, so I decide to head down and find something to eat. I grab a yogurt and plastic spoon before gravitating toward the porch. A swing dangles precariously from the rafters above. I don't think I'll chance it. My ribs can't take another blow. Perching myself on the top step, I take in the scenery around me.

The tightness in my chest eases a tiny bit more. Every day it loosens, and my heart beats a little freer. It's so beautiful here, I almost worry that I'm dreaming. The birds chirp happily, carrying my soul to higher ground. I smile as the breeze kisses my cheeks. I'm free.

I'm free.

I stand up as the realization slams into me. I spin in circles, the world swirling around me before I fall into the grass, dizzy with happiness. The sun shines brightly above me. I shield my eyes, noticing a dozen or so dragonflies darting overhead. I sit up, wiping tears from my eyes.

I'm home.

Somehow, despite everything, I found my home.

The next step is finding me.

I pull myself from the ground, feeling more hopeful than I've felt since my aunt passed.

Deciding to explore the property, I set out to look around. There's a tiny greenhouse out back along the tree line. I pull the door open, it's empty but I notice it's set up with a watering system. It even has temperature controls. I don't know anything about gardening but I'm willing to learn. I'll have to see if there is a library in town. I close the door and make my way over to a storage shed.

When I open the door, the sun cuts into the space, dust motes dancing in the rays. A glint of something shiny catches my eye. I step inside, squatting down to inspect the object. It's a window. I glance around, spying dozens of old windows lining the walls of the shed. All different sizes.

My hand brushes the dust off the frame. Jesse did say they put in new windows. These must be the originals. They are beautiful. It's sad they are out here in the dark.

"Do you miss the sun?" I whisper.

I decide to pull a few of them out, taking them inside. Surely, I can think of a new life for them. I lean them against the wall and decide I should get to work on painting. I crack open a can of rosewood colored paint and start on the living room. It's not a very bright color but I think it will reflect the natural lighting in the room perfectly.

Watercolor Skulls

Hours go by as I paint in silence. I set the paint brush down on the side of the can. It's so quiet. I'm used to that, nothing new there. Being alone is something I'm accustomed to. But in this moment, I realize I'm not liking it much. Which isn't like me at all… it's unusual and a little crazy.

My parents were never home. My dad was usually in D.C. and my mother was who knows where with her trophy wife friends. Sure, there were always other people in our home but no one who gave a care about what I was doing.

The four years my aunt came to live with us were the best years of my life. When she was around, I never felt lonely. She was my someone. Someone who had my back no matter what. Aunt Jenny is the only person in the world who saw me as more than Senator Ramsey's daughter.

I grab a granola bar and sit down on the floor. I'm happy with the progress I've made. I notice a drip of paint on the glass of one of the windows I brought in. Frowning, I set the granola bar down and pick up the window, leaning it against the kitchen cabinet by the sink. I grab a washcloth to clean the paint off. When I lift my eyes to the blob, I drop the cloth on the floor.

My heart kicks its heels up. I know what I'm going to do with the windows. I grab my keys and head into the hardware store and then to the craft store.

I'm so engrossed in all the colors of paint they have to choose from that I don't notice Jesse standing beside me.

"Boo," she says.

I jump a foot. "Holy moly! Jesse," I say breathlessly. "You scared me."

She laughs, her green eyes twinkling with mischief. "Whatcha doing?"

"Oh, I found the old windows in the shed out back and I had an idea of how to use them… if that's okay?" I ask hesitantly.

"Yeah, that's cool," she says, grabbing a few cans of spray paint off the shelf behind me.

Dirk comes around the corner, tossing a tiny little girl with dark pigtails in the air. He catches her and kisses her cheek obsessively, making her giggle. He stops when he sees Jesse and me.

Jesse smiles. "This is our daughter, Billie Rose. She's almost three and her daddy carries her everywhere. He hasn't figured out she has two feet."

"Can you say hi to our new friend? Her name is Lily." Dirk turns so she can see me.

My heart swells a little at his term for me… new friend, that sounds wonderful. The little girl waves at me shyly before tucking her face in the side of Dirk's tattooed neck.

"You have such a pretty name," I tell her. She peeks at me and giggles.

"She likes to pretend she's shy but trust me, once she gets to know you, she will talk your ear off. Not that you'll be able to understand any of it." Dirk chucks her under the chin and she tugs at the scruff on his face. He pretends to be hurt which makes her giggle even more.

They are so adorable that I find myself staring.

When I finally turn back to Jesse, I see she is staring at her little family too. A look of contentment over her features.

Jesse's focus shifts back to me. "So, I was thinking. I'm going to round everyone up this Saturday and we are coming over to help with the painting and repairs. If you need any furniture picked up, we could do that too."

"Oh, Jesse, really, I'm fine. I have nothing but time."

"Not once Bill gets you trained at the bar. He'll have your ass working all the damn time. He's a slave driver." Dirk smirks when Jesse smacks his arm.

She turns her head back to me. Her eyebrow cocked.

"Oh, okay, I suppose I could use the help."

She drops the eyebrow and smiles triumphantly. "I'll arrange everything. Plan on a bunch of bikers showing up at your house early Saturday morning."

I nod nervously. One or two bikers I can handle but a whole mess of them. I mean, I have nothing against them, it's just I don't know their culture. I worry they won't like me. I'm not sure I'll fit in.

She looks at my arm where my fake tattoo had been. It's red from all the scrubbing I did to get it off this morning. "Stop by my shop tomorrow at one. You can't miss it, it's right on main street. We'll get you a real dragonfly tattoo."

"Oh. Oh, like tomorrow, tomorrow?" My eyes wander over my virgin skin, it's a stark contrast to the two people standing beside me.

"Yep. That way you don't have time to chicken out." She runs her finger over the pendant around my neck. "Dragonflies are special to you?"

"Yes. I thought I lost this not too long ago," I whisper.

"Well, you can never lose a tattoo," she says softly.

My eyes lock on hers. "That is true. Okay, tomorrow at one."

She nods once before wrapping her arm around Dirk's waist. "I'll see you then."

Dirk tips Billie Rose into Jesse's arms. "I'll meet you at the truck."

He watches her walk away before turning back to me. "So, what are you hiding?" he asks.

I take a step back. "W-what? I'm not hiding anything."

He narrows his eyes, his eyebrow popping up just like Jesse's does. "Okay, let me lay this out for you. If you are going to be our friend... my daughter's friend, then I need to be able trust you."

My hand rests over my heart, it's thumping so darn hard. This guy is crazy, but I get it. He wants to protect his family and for that reason alone I like him. "I don't know what I could say that would put your mind at ease. I'm truly here to start a new life for myself."

"Drugs?"

"No."

"Been abused?"

"No." I drop my head, staring at the floor.

"No?" he questions.

40

I look him in the eye. "No, in fact most would say I've had a charmed life. My family is well off."

He huffs at this. "Doesn't matter how much money people have. Evil loves money."

I laugh lightly. "Yeah, I guess you're right."

"I'm always right." He looks down the aisle, making sure no one is eavesdropping. "You got a record?"

Confused, I shake my head.

"The fact you don't know what I'm talking about would indicate the answer is a no." He flips the ring in his lip with his tongue, studying me intently. "Okay, I'm going to let you in but be prepared for future interrogations. I'll see you this weekend." He grabs my hand and squeezes it. "You're not alone anymore."

I stare at him, blinking. He smiles kindly, he doesn't look nearly as scary when he smiles. He releases my hand and starts to walk away.

"Wait." I drop my head, sighing. "Wait. I am hiding something."

He walks backwards. "I know you are. I'm giving you a free pass… for now." He throws a wink my direction, then spins around on one foot and walks away.

I brush tears from my cheeks. I've never had anyone interested in my life. No one has been so willing to offer me their help and these two don't even know me.

What if they get to know me and they don't like me? What if I don't like myself? I know my dad wouldn't like the woman I've buried deep down inside.

I decide to make a quick pass by the tattoo shop so that I'll know where it is tomorrow. I'm equal parts excited and terrified. I really don't know why I agreed to get one. Will it hurt? My tummy does a little flip at the thought. It will be fine. Jesse and Dirk have beautiful artwork on their skin. I know she won't steer me wrong.

I have no problem finding it. The bright neon sign flashes Big D and Little J's tattoos. My dad would hate it if he knew I was thinking about marking my skin. Aunt Jenny had a tattoo of a butterfly on the back of her neck. One time when we were out by the pool, I caught him staring at it. I'm sure he hated it. God forbid you did anything to set yourself apart from someone else.

I thought it was cute on her and come to think of it, Aunt Jenny would be proud of me for doing this. I brush my hands together, it's settled. I'm getting my very first tattoo tomorrow.

There's one more stop on my agenda for today. The thrift shop. My aunt told me thrift shops were shopping centers for the soul. I agree. My fingers dance over the hangers on a rack of old t-shirts. Time to find my style.

I only pick out things I like. I don't think about what is appropriate, what will match my hair or eyes, I just pick what makes my heart pump faster. I'm giddy by the time I leave the store. The guy at the counter probably thought I was nuts but hey, I needed a whole new wardrobe.

There were so many old and wonderful things there. I found some real treasures and a few nice pieces of furniture that just need a little love and a new home. The clerk said he would hold the furniture till Saturday. I feel bad I'm going to have to take Jesse up on her offer to help but now I'm happy she offered.

When I pull into my driveway, I smile.

Home sweet home.

It takes several trips back and forth but eventually, I lug everything inside. My poor little beetle was packed down tight.

After digging through all my bags, I find the little am/fm radio I bought. I plug it in and turn the music up as loud as it will go. Time to get to work.

The day quickly fades into night. It's funny how fast time can go when you are enjoying yourself. I know I've been working but it doesn't feel like it. It feels like I'm… like I'm living.

Before heading to bed, I do one last thing. I hang the window I painted on a wall in the living room. The bright yellow flowers make my heart skip happily.

I've always felt I've been trapped on one side of the glass, watching everyone else live on the other side. I was stuck in a life that wasn't mine. Today, I looked beyond the glass and saw what I wanted to see. And not only did I see it, but I also created it. A field of bright and beautiful sunflowers.

Today was good. Today I feel… well, I feel a little more human.

Chapter Seven

Senator Ramsey

Jenny is responsible for this. I know she is. Everything was fine until I moved that little bitch in. Not only did she entice me, but she obviously got under Lily's skin as well. She was my one weakness. I'll never admit that to anyone but there was just something about her.

Anyhow, Lily has always been an amenable daughter. I've never had any problems with her until the day Benjamin proposed. That night she came to my office with tears in her eyes and told me she didn't want to marry him.

He is the perfect match for her. Benjamin just completed law school and he comes from a political family. I recognize the hunger in his eyes, he wants to rise to the top. We have a lot in common and I enjoy his company. He likes all the things I do, hunting, golf, fine cigars, expensive liquor, and beautiful women.

Lily knows how it works. I molded her into the perfect wife for him. She is sweet, quiet, and poised. I even encouraged her to go into elementary teaching. Having a teacher in the family is good for my image.

So, I sent her to bed that night without discussion. It was a ridiculous request. Of course, she's going to marry him. His father and I set this up when she was still in middle school. They've been dating since high school.

Now, I know it must hurt her tender young heart to see him in the media carousing with other women, but she will just have to get thicker skin. Her job is to stand by and keep this family in good light. Benjamin has a great future ahead of him. She needs to help nurture that. That is a woman's place. Like it or not, I don't care. It's my world and in my world she does as told. Or she used to that is.

I didn't ask why she jumped off the bridge. It doesn't matter. It was a stupid, stupid thing to do. My people had to work overtime to squash the rumors. And now, now she is missing.

If I could have gotten away with it, I would have put a bullet in Rudy's head myself. But I can't risk any more negative attention. It's an election year after all. My only regret in all this was that I didn't get rid of Jenny sooner. I shouldn't have let her come to stay with us at all. Doesn't matter now, the problem took care of itself. It was fun while it lasted though. She was a feisty little thing.

I run my palm over my cock, thinking about her. Jesus, I need to take some pressure off. I click the intercom on my desk.

"Can I help you, sir?" my assistant answers.

"Call John and have him send someone over. Oh, tell him to make it a blond."

"Yes, sir. Benjamin has returned, would you like me to send him in."

"Yes." I lean back in my chair and kick my shiny black dress shoes up on the desk.

Benjamin walks in, smirking at my laid-back state. "Drink?" he asks as he helps himself to my best bourbon.

I nod, patiently waiting for him to tell me what he found out.

He sets a glass on the desk in front of me before he takes a seat. He takes a long drink, letting his gaze lock on mine. "They think she jumped again."

I sigh loudly, checking my watch. I hope that whore gets here soon. "What do you think?"

He leans forward, resting his arms on his knees, his drink dangling between his legs. "Well, they found her purse in that locker Rudy told us about. She may have slipped the cameras. They told me it happens. Not every suicide is noticed."

"But you don't think she did it?"

He laughs lightly. "No, I don't think she did it. I think she ran."

Running a palm over my freshly shaved face, I think about it. "Rudy said she picked up a bag and that she had it with her when she took off. Did they find a bag?"

"Nope." He smacks his lips and leans back, staring at the ceiling. "The wedding is only two weeks away, should we postpone?"

Damnit this girl made a mess. I hope Benjamin punishes her good for this little stunt. "Let's put out a press release saying we have decided to have a private family ceremony with a reception to follow at a later date. If we don't find her by then, we will pretend the ceremony took place even if it doesn't. It shouldn't surprise anyone, especially since she just had an accident."

"So, your confident we will find her?" he asks.

"Oh, I'll find her. It's time to call in a few favors."

He taps his empty glass on his knee. "I didn't do anything to her." He runs his hand through his hair. "I mean, I've always treated her like a lady."

"Don't worry, we will get her back before she tarnishes either of our reputations." I lean forward, staring him straight in the eye. "But make sure once we get her back, she learns her lesson and learns it well."

He nods in understanding.

Chapter Eight

Lily

This might have been a mistake. I grip the wheel of my beetle tightly. I'm so nervous I think I might get sick. I couldn't even eat my lunch. The neon sign taunts me as I park. I know, I know. I want to do this. I do.

It's just Jesse, so it will be fine. If I chicken out, she won't care. It's fine. Everything is fine. I check my appearance in the rearview mirror, flipping my hair into a messy bun. I run a finger under my eyes, hoping it erases the dark circles that seem to be a permanent feature lately. No luck. Oh well, here goes nothing.

A little bell dings at my entry. I take a deep breath as I get my bearings. It's so wonderful. It smells good too. The walls are covered in paintings and there are shelves lining them. They hold all sorts of unique trinkets. Mostly skulls. Skulls are everywhere, some scary, some beautiful. Bluesy southern rock plays quietly in the background.

"I'll be right there," a gruff voice calls from somewhere in the back. My eyes dart around the room looking for Jesse. Where is she?

A big guy steps out. Oh, oh my. He fills the entire doorway.

He steps forward, coming to the counter to greet me. "You must be Jesse's one o'clock?"

"Y... yes, my name is Lily," I stutter, still thrown off by the enormous size of this man.

He sits down at the counter, pointing to the stool across from him. "I'm Dan. It's nice to meet you. Please, have a seat."

Reluctantly, I sit down, hoping Jesse shows up soon.

"Jesse had a family emergency."

My eyes go wide.

He laughs. "Let me rephrase. Her daughter fell and scratched her knee." He rolls his eyes. "She's one of those crazy helicopter moms if you know what I mean."

No, I don't know. I've never had a mom who cared. I fell off a bridge and she didn't even stay at the hospital long enough to ask me how I was feeling. His chair creaks and I realize he is waiting for some sort of response from me.

Slowly, I raise my eyes to his. My heart flips clean upside down. He has amber eyes. The same color as the sun reflected through the murky water I fell into. They pull me to the surface just like the sun did that day. I smile shyly and tuck a strand of my blue hair behind my ear. "She's a lucky little girl," I finally say.

He studies me closely. "Yeah, she is," he agrees. "So, Jesse said you were interested in one of my designs. She asked me if I could draw it up for you. Which one was it?"

"She said you had one of a dragonfly." I bite my bottom lip when he gives me a funny look. He stares at me for a long, long time. His eyes run over my hair, my face, my figure. I swallow hard and shift in my chair. Did I upset him? Does he not want his design on my body? "Um, maybe this was a mistake." I shake my head and stand.

He reaches across the counter and locks his hand around my arm. "No, don't go. I do have a dragonfly design. It's just not in the book. Jesse must have been snooping through my stuff," he says gruffly.

I stand there awkwardly, not sure if I should sit back down or leave. "I was just wanting a dragonfly. She must not have known it was special to you," I say softly, staring at his hand on my arm.

"Why a dragonfly?" he asks.

The same feeling comes over me that I had on the bridge. Climb back over the railing or let go and fall. My eyes go to the door and then they skitter over the man sitting across from me. His amber eyes are so sincere. He really wants to know why I chose a dragonfly.

My eyes drop back to his warm hand still clamped on my arm. My tummy does a little flip. He follows my gaze and seems surprised to find he is still holding on to me. He pulls his hand away, nervously running his fingers through his beard.

His hair is warm chestnut brown with a few grey hairs showing at his temples and a speckling in the very middle of his beard. His beard is full, and it looks soft not wiry like most men. His hair is cut short at the sides, the top is longer and combed to the left in perfect waves. I want to run my fingers through it and mess it up. And his eyes... oh, I've already told you about those. I could stare at them all day. They warm me up, like sitting in front of a crackling fire in the fall.

He sits forward, making me jump. "Easy now," he says in a deep voice that sparks a burning low in my belly.

I sit down… yes, I'm choosing the fall.

He smiles, lines crinkle around his eyes. I like them. I want to see them always.

"My aunt told me dragonflies have two sets of wings so they can carry angels on their backs."

He blinks at me. His lips part as if he is going to say something, but he snaps them shut and turns away from me.

I watch as he pulls a piece of paper out of a drawer. His pencil scratches across the sheet, an image coming to life with each stroke. He peeks up at me briefly before turning his eyes back to his drawing. "I do have a design of a dragonfly, but I think this one will fit you better."

"What did the other one look like?"

"It was a skull, dragonfly and roses."

"Sounds beautiful. I guess I never thought of getting a skull." My eyes dart around the room. "Will this one have a skull?"

A wicked grin spreads across his face. "Oh, this one will definitely have a skull."

I bite my lip, a bit giddy that this guy is drawing something just for me. Something dark and… well, I guess I don't know exactly, we'll just have to wait and see.

Chapter Nine

Dan

I force myself not to grip my pencil too hard. There is no way Jesse could have known. No way. She must have been looking for something on my desk and spotted my drawing.

God, it's all so fucking stupid I don't even want to think about it.

Okay, you want to know, and I see you're not going anywhere, so here it is... I drew the fucking thing when I was lonely. Okay? Shut up.

Raffe told me the same thing as her aunt told her. That dragonflies have two sets of wings to accommodate angels on their backs. See? It's silly.

I was missing home. Missing something. I don't know. And I thought to myself, wouldn't it be nice if a goddamn dragonfly brought me an angel. Fuck. I need Dirk to take me to his cabin and unfuck my head.

Ever since Jesse came into my life, I've been changing. Jesse made me soft. I don't want to be soft.

She's watching me draw. Not like some people do. No, she is intently watching my hands. She curled her legs under her so she could lean in closer. With each new line, her breathing changes. She's excited, scared, intrigued, mine. Fuck, no, she's not mine. I don't even know who the fuck this girl is. Okay, and there's that. She is young. Like Jesse's age young. She seems younger than Jess though. Maybe it's her innocence.

She is cute as all get out. I allow myself another little glimpse. Shit, she smiled at me. Two dimples greet me and guess what else they do? They wake my fucking dick up. No, no, no, this isn't happening. I've never, NEVER had an inappropriate response to a client, and I've had some pretty fucking hot chicks in my chair.

Lily reminds me of a Disney fairy. Her blue hair is piled messily on her head. Big brown eyes peek out from beneath lashes so long they brush her cheeks every time she blinks. Her skin is fair and flawless. I want to spank her just to see if fairy dust falls out of her ass. And speaking of that ass, I think it would fit perfectly in my goddamn hands.

Jesus, I can't help myself.

It's like there is an invisible pull between the two of us. I wonder if she feels it. No, of course not. She probably thinks I'm an old man. Not that I'm old. Well, it depends on what you think is old. I'm only a year older than Dirk, not even a full year. Christ, I gave him and Jesse so much shit for their age difference. I didn't get it. Jesse's like a daughter to me.

But this little creature, she makes me understand Dirk a little better.

"Where are you wanting this?" I ask.

She sits back down on her bottom, uncurling her legs. "Oh, I guess I haven't thought that far ahead."

I laugh. "Doesn't seem like you've thought much about this at all. You hadn't seen the design and you don't even know where you want it. Is this your first tattoo?"

She blushes, her skin turning a pink color that makes my cock stiffer than it already was.

"Yep. I have virgin skin." Holy hell. She walks her fingers down her arm, then she peeks at me from under her lashes. "Where do you recommend?"

I lick my lips, thinking of all the possibilities. It makes my blood pump hot. "Well, that depends. Some people don't want them visible to others, because of their job or other things."

"I'm going to be bartending at Bill's bar and I doubt he cares much about tattoos, seeing as he's covered in them."

Lord fucking help me.

She tips her head, watching my reactions with an amused look on her face. "But it's going to be special to me, so maybe somewhere more private."

"Well, you could put it on your back but personally I think it would look sexy as hell on your hip."

This makes her really blush. She covers her face with her hands.

"What? Don't like either of those ideas?"

"No, it's not that, it's just no one's ever referred to me as sexy." She drops her head to the counter with a thud. "Oh my god, I can't believe I just admitted that."

"Hip it is," I tease. "And for the record, I think you're sexy, tattoos or not." I go back to drawing, excited that I'm going to get to see her hip. Wait, Jesse is coming back. She's Jesse's client, I remind myself.

Lily's phone dings. When she pulls it out, I notice it's a cheap burner phone. "It's Jesse."

"Is she on her way back?"

Lily is furiously typing a message, her eyebrows drawn together. "No, I'm telling her I'm fine and she should stay with her daughter." She stops and looks up at me. "I mean, if your free today?"

I shake my head yes and go back to work. Focus, you big dumb fuck. Focus.

When I'm finished, I push the drawing in front of her. "It won't look quite like this. I'm thinking of doing it as a watercolor."

Her dainty fingers dance over the image. "It's beautiful," she whispers, not taking her eyes off the drawing. "I don't know what watercolor is, but I trust you to do whatever you think is best."

My eyes fall closed. She is putting herself in my hands. Oh, what that does to me. This woman is enticing me into thoughts I haven't allowed myself to have. When I open my eyes, she is staring at me.

"I'll get this worked up." I grab the drawing and take it to the back to make a stencil. My hands are shaking. Fucking shaking.

My cell rings, I glance at the screen as the stencil prints. It's Jess.

"How's Billie Rose doing?" I ask.

"She's fine. It was just a scratch, but you never know. I would rather be safe than sorry."

"Jesse, you're going to give yourself a coronary over that girl. It's okay to let her fall once in a while. It will toughen her up."

"Yeah, yeah. Hey, I'm sorry about rushing out. Is Lily doing okay?"

"Yeah, why wouldn't she be?" I ask gruffly.

"She's new to town. She moved into the house over on Wildflower. She doesn't have much and well, you know."

I laugh lightly. "Yes, I know. She's another one of your projects."

"Why the fuck do you guys keep saying that?"

"Cause it's true. You're always helping someone."

"Just. Just don't scare her off, okay?"

"I'm not going to scare her off."

"No?"

"No."

"Dan, I mean it. Be. Nice."

"Oh, I'm being very nice."

She sighs. "Maybe I should come back to town."

"We're fine. I'm just about to get started."

"Did she like your design?"

Now I sigh. "That one wasn't supposed to be for clients."

"Oh. I'm sorry, I didn't know."

"I know you didn't. It's fine. Anyway, I drew one up that fits her better."

"Oh, I'm super excited to see it. Send me a picture when you're done."

"We'll see. Give Billie Rose a kiss for me."

"I will. Love ya."

"Love ya too, doll."

Chapter Ten

Lily

I'm sitting here in my underwear. My dad would kill me. Benjamin would kill me. *Stop, Lily. They don't control your life anymore, you do.*

Dan put a screen around us for privacy, but still.

He can see me.

I secretly like that he can see me.

Except I forgot one thing. My bruises. They are a nice shade of purply blue today. Great.

He's busy getting everything ready. Oh god, I'm so nervous. My body is trembling and no matter how much I beg it to stop, it won't.

"You ready?" he asks while snapping on a pair of black latex gloves.

"N-no, I mean, yes. Yes." My teeth are chattering, I bite down hard, trying to stop it.

"Are you cold? Personally, I think it's warm as fuck in here."

"N-no, not cold. I'm sorry, I guess I'm just a little nervous."

He wheels his stool over to me, stopping between my legs. "Hey, we can take this slow. I don't have any other appointments today."

I nod, fighting the urge to squeeze my legs closed. This feels intimate.

"What has you scared? Is it the pain?"

"No, I'm not scared of the pain. I guess it's just the fear of the unknown."

His amber eyes pull me back to a calm surf. "You just tell me if you need me to stop. I promise, I'll get you through it."

"Okay." I offer him a big smile, letting him know I'm ready.

"Here, stand up." He scoots away, letting me drop to my feet in front of him. His eyes roam over my bruises, his eyebrows pinch together but he doesn't say anything. He places the stencil high on my hip, half of it covering my butt.

He's careful to avoid the bruising on my leg. "How does this look?" He points to a mirror on the wall.

"I like how you used lilies instead of roses." I shift back and forth in front of the mirror.

"A girl named Lily should have them tattooed somewhere on her body."

My eyes catch his in the mirror. He smiles, so I smile back. He is so handsome. Rugged yet refined. He pats the table, so I turn back and hop up beside him.

He helps me to lie on my side and shifts my legs to the position he wants me in. I keep my muscles loose so he can mold me however he sees fit. His hands are rough, his touch sure, and it makes me feel funny things.

"Okay, are you comfortable?"

I nod, taking a deep breath as he settles over my hip.

"Here we go. Just try to hold as still as you can and if you need to stop let me know."

I nod again. I'm too nervous to speak.

The gun buzzes and he presses it to my hip. It hurts but nothing like I was expecting. He stops after a minute. "What do you think? You doing okay?"

"Yeah, it's not so bad."

"Good." He focuses back on my leg. "So, tell me about your aunt."

A warmth spreads throughout my chest. I jump at the chance to talk about her. "She passed away five years ago."

"Oh, shit. I'm sorry."

"She was only six years older than me. She came to live with us for a few years. They were the best four years of my life. I loved her so much."

Dan continues to work but I know he is listening.

"She was a free spirit. My dad called her a crazy hippie, and she was, but I always admired her for being herself. Aunt Jenny didn't let anyone dictate who she was supposed to be." I laugh, tears springing to my eyes.

"She was the first person that told me I could be anything I wanted to be. I miss her."

"And what do you want to be?" he asks, turning his gun off to look at me.

"I just want to be me."

His gaze lingers on me for a second before he goes back to work.

My eyes fall closed as a warm feeling starts at the top of my head and rushes down my entire body. I feel like I'm floating. Maybe it's his strong hands, his warm breath over my skin, or could it be the pain? Whatever it is, I want to feel it again and again and again.

Dan

She's in the zone. You never know how someone will respond to the pain. Some of us love it and others avoid it at all costs. I've been studying the bruises on her thighs. I saw red the minute I saw them, assuming someone hurt her. Upon further inspection, I don't see any fingerprint bruising, so maybe she was injured some other way.

When she stretched her arm over her head and her t-shirt road up, I saw more bruising along her mid-section. It's not like I was being creepy, it's simply hard to miss. It looks painful. She took quite the blow. I want to ask but it's really none of my business.

Her eyelids flutter as I change position. She moans when I slide my hand between her legs to shift them slightly. My gaze darts to her face, but her eyes remain closed.

Goddammit, this girl is waking up a part of me I've tried hard to bury. I let my fingers trail lightly up her leg until I reach her panty line. Her skin pebbles beneath my touch. I pull my hand back quickly. Shit. Not appropriate. I didn't spend years building this business to have it taken away by a sexual harassment charge.

Her eyes are still closed. Not that she didn't notice. I'm sure she did. How could she not have?

I go back to work on the tattoo, keeping my mind out of the gutter. For the most part.

Mid-way through, I stop and ask her if she would like to take a break. She doesn't open her eyes, just shakes her head no.

She's so beautiful.

I shove my face a little closer to her skin, to inspect my work of course. My eyes fall closed as I inhale. She smells like spun sugar. I drag my nose along her leg, careful not to touch her. Okay, so maybe this is getting a little creepy.

You have to understand, I haven't been with a woman in a long, long time. It's not like I'm immune to the opposite sex. I've been with plenty of women over the years, but it was always awkward. Hard to explain. It's like no one "fit" me.

I mean, look at me. I'm a big guy and I've always been aware of my strength. So, I hold back. I've always held back. I don't know, it just never felt right.

Comical, right? Cause this girl is tiny, curvy, but tiny. Maybe five, five. I could break her easily. Oh, and do I want to break her. Fuck. No. I don't want to break her... but I do.

See… see what I mean? I'm all sorts of fucked up. This is why I've stayed single. I don't date. I fuck once in a great while but that's it. Makes for a lonely life but I can't complain. I have the shop, the club, and my friends. That's all I need.

But my fucking dick thinks it needs her. Not possible. Too young. Too innocent. Too goddamn delicious. She'll just end up giving me a sweet tooth.

When I wipe the final bit of ink away, I stare at the art adorning her pale skin. My mark. A little bit her, a little bit me and the one thing that brought us together… a dragonfly. Fuck me.

"Okay, sweetheart. I think we're all finished here." I pull my gloves off and reach over to brush the hair off of her face. She blinks her big brown eyes at me. Just so we all know, I'm fucked. Literally fucked.

"You're done?"

I nod, as my mind takes a snapshot of her face. She looks so relaxed, so much more than when she walked through my door.

She sits herself up with my help and twists so she can take her first look. Her hand flies to her mouth and her entire body begins to tremble. Now, I've seen lots of reactions over the years but this one, this one is different.

Her fingers hover over the colorful ink, wiggling in the air, wanting to touch but knowing she can't. Kind of how I feel about her. Now that I'm done, I can't touch her but oh how I want to.

She slides off the table to look at it in the mirror. "It's the most beautiful thing I've ever seen," she whispers.

"So, you like it?"

She walks over to me as I sit on my stool and hugs me. She hugs me tight. "Thank you for giving me a piece of my soul back," she says softly, her breath hot on my ear.

Slowly, I wrap my arms around her, hugging her back. This tiny little thing, standing between my legs in nothing but a t-shirt and a pair of panties makes the angel on my shoulder drop to his knees in surrender. The devil, however, licks his lips and whispers, *"Take her. Make her yours. You know she wants you."*

But does she?

She pulls away slowly. "I'm sorry. God, I'm so, so, sorry. I just, I'm just so overwhelmed. It's perfect. You don't know how much this means to me. And not just the tattoo, the experience. I'm alive. I'm alive." She laughs and spins in a circle in front of me.

I'm going to hell. I'm sure of it.

She stops, staring in the mirror a bit longer. "I didn't know what you meant by watercolor but this... oh my gosh, this is better than I ever imagined."

Wow, lots of compliments with this one. My chest puffs up a little more with each smile. Her eyes seem brighter, and her complexion is glowing a tad bit more than when she walked in. I did this. Me. I want to see if I can do more.

But that is impossible. She's a client. A paying client.

She shimmies into her jeans, careful to keep the wrap I put over her new tattoo in place.

After she pays me, my heart does this weird sort of nosedive right into my stomach. I don't want this to be over. I should ask her out. No, she's a client.

Client. Client. Client.

Chapter Eleven

Lily

As I'm paying, I feel the loneliness creeping back in. I don't want to leave. My eyes roam over Dan. I'm trying to memorize everything about him. He is so different than the clean-shaven suits I'm used to.

He's all man. He even smells manly. Like earth and trees. When I hugged him, I realized just how big he is and solid. I found myself fantasizing about things I haven't let myself think about for a long time. It's a part of me that I've tucked away.

Benjamin made it perfectly clear in the beginning what I was to him. I was the girlfriend that made him look good. I would eventually be the wife that stood by his side and popped out a few babies. That was it. He had sex with me, yes. I really don't want to talk about it. It wasn't good, for me anyhow. I don't know about him. No, that's not entirely true. He made it clear that he had women to give him the dirty sex he craved. I was just someone he used when it was convenient. Basically, I was there for the photo ops.

But Dan… I felt every touch of his fingers, every pulse of the needle as he drew it across my skin. It felt good. I know that's weird to say and I'd never say it out loud but it's true.

"So, what are we going to do next?" I hear myself ask. What am I doing?

He tips his head back and laughs. When his gaze drops, he pins me with a look that makes me clench my thighs together. "Ready for me again?" he asks, his voice gravelly and deep.

I clear my throat and drop my gaze to my feet. He senses my shyness and leans over the counter, chucking me under the chin with his knuckle. "Hey, I'm sorry, that was rude of me."

"No, no it wasn't." I force myself to face him head on. Big Dan excites me, and I haven't been excited in... well, ever. He's woken something up in me and I want more. I crave more of him. "I think I can handle it."

His eyebrows twitch, his mouth turning up on one side. "Well, then. I look forward to you becoming a regular. Call me once that heals up."

Slowly, I make my way to the door, I don't want to leave. My hand pauses on the handle. The tattoo on my leg stings, reminding me I'm alive. *You only get one life, Lily, and it's yours. Never forget that.* My aunt's words echo through my mind.

I spin around and catch Dan ogling me. Was he looking at my butt? I think he was.

"Dan, would you like to have a drink with me Friday night?"

His mouth falls open for a brief second, but he recovers quickly.

"I thought you would never ask." He grins at me in a way that makes my insides quiver, and not in a bad way. "Do you want to meet me over at the Grey Wolf bar at seven?"

Biting my bottom lip, I nod, then stumble out the door.

The bright blue sky greets me. I throw my hands out and take a deep breath. My little beetle waits for me, ready to take me on another adventure.

Feeling a burst of inspiration, I head to the hardware store. The young man at the counter laughs when he sees me. "You must have a big project. This is the third day you've been in."

"Point me in the direction of your power tools."

He shakes his head and leads the way.

After a brief tutorial on how to use the darn things, I'm on my way home. I look at the bag of wooden skulls I bought. I saw them yesterday and they reminded me of Jesse's club. Today, I thought of a way to use them.

My front yard becomes my work area. I want to be outside. The tattoo still stings on my hip and my mind wanders to the big man who put it there. My stomach does a little flip as I drill each fist sized wooden skull, placing one on top of the other until they are the length of a coffee table leg.

I grab the old window I brought in the house yesterday. This one is made up of six small panes. It's my favorite. I measure it and then I grab the smooth cherry wood I bought and cut it down to make a small box that I'll place the window on.

My mind puts it all together like a jigsaw puzzle. I've never used any of these tools, but everything comes to me naturally. It's almost spooky but I go with it. I'm having so much fun as the sun continues to slide across the sky. The wind and birds are my only source of music today and that is okay.

After I'm finished building my shadow box coffee table, I run inside to get my paints. I tape over the glass so that I don't get any paint on it. With Dan heavily on my mind I begin to splash over the wood, splattering all the different colors with no rhyme or reason. A beautiful, colorful mess.

I stand back and admire my creation.

I'll let it dry overnight and give it a clear coat tomorrow. All I need to do is install the hinges and clasp. As I'm cleaning up, the rumble of an engine steadily grows closer. A motorcycle pulls up with two riders. When they pull their helmets off, I see it's Jesse and Dirk.

Jesse waves a bag in the air. "Do you like burgers?"

My stomach grumbles as the smell of greasy fries wafts my way. I forgot that all I've eaten today is a yogurt cup. My tummy was so nervous before my tattoo that I didn't eat lunch. I nod and smile.

"Great." She sits on the step and pats the spot beside her, so I sit down next to her. She hands me a burger and my stomach growls loudly. I place my hand over it, slightly embarrassed. Jesse laughs. "I was worried you might be a vegetarian."

My eyes follow Dirk as he circles my coffee table. "No, I'm not a vegetarian. My parents tried to make me one but…" I let my words trail off.

Dirk squats down, inspecting my handiwork. "Did you do this?" he asks.

Jesse turns, just now noticing what has her husband's attention.

She jumps off the step to join him. "Lily, this is so cool."

I take a bite of my burger, remaining silent.

Dirk picks up the hardware that will attach the window to the top of the table. "It's going to open?"

"Yeah, like a shadow box."

He nods and then grins. "We're rubbing off on you." He points to the skulls. The satisfaction on his face makes me blush.

"My new tattoo inspired me."

Jesse straightens, turning to me. "Oh, that's why we're here. I wanted to apologize; I didn't mean to ditch you today."

"It's okay. Billie Rose needed you." I shove a fry in my mouth, savoring the taste of salt on my tongue.

"Well, let's see it," Jesse says. "Dan was supposed to send me a picture, but he never did."

I set my fries back in the bag, brush the salt off my fingers and pop the button on my jeans before realizing what I'm doing.

My eyes slowly rise to Dirk and Jesse. They both stand there, staring at me. Jesse rolls her hands, encouraging me to continue.

"Um, it's on my hip."

She spins me around, pushing me into the house. Dirk follows us in. "I don't think the birds would have minded but if this makes you feel better."

My eyes flit from Dirk back to her. They are patiently waiting. She's a tattoo artist, so I guess showing a little skin doesn't bother her. I shimmy out of my jeans and turn so they can see Dan's work of art.

Jesse drops to her knees by my side, her hands gripping my thighs. Oh. *Oh*. I'm not used to all this attention. My gaze crashes with Dirks. He smirks, his tongue teasing the ring in his lip. My eyes drop to Jesse. She is studying Dan's work intently.

"Wow, just wow. I've never seen Dan do anything like this. The lines are so fine. Jesus, it's beautiful."

Dirk crouches beside her but his eyes aren't on the tattoo. He is looking at something else. His gaze climbs up my frame and he gives me a look that makes me turn away.

"What's this from?" His calloused finger pushes on one of my bruises, making me wince. Jesse shoves his hand away and pulls him to his feet.

"Oh, it's nothing. I fell." I reach down, grabbing my jeans and quickly pull them up. Enough show and tell for today. "We should probably eat. Our food is getting cold."

He narrows his eyes but drops the subject. Jesse's gaze flits around the room. "You did a great job painting. Seems you have a talent for this sort of thing." She walks over to my sunflower window and smiles at it. "I'm happy you found a use for the old windows."

We all go back outside and finish our supper. "Thank you for this," I say, covering my mouth with my hand as I chew. "It's so good."

71

Dirk is leaning against his bike, smoking a cigarette, his gaze lazily on us.

"I'm a bit of a foodie," she admits. "We are having a grill out next week. You should come. The guys make the best burgers."

"If they are as good as this, count me in," I tease, bumping her shoulder with mine.

She smiles and pauses as if deep in thought. "I do feel bad I wasn't there today, but I guess it worked out. Your tattoo really is beautiful. It's so *you.*"

I think about it.

It is *me.*

It's like Dan saw me, really saw me. I trace the image over my jeans. It's a skull with lilies covering one side of its face, a dragonfly flying over them. But it's done in watercolor. The color is random, splashed outside the lines. It's a beautiful chaotic mess. Sweet, scary, intriguing. It's *me...* no, it's *us.*

My heart stops at the realization. I hide a smile behind my hands.

"He was nice to you, wasn't he? Sometimes, the big guy can be quite the asshole," Jesse says, waving a hand in front of my face to get my attention.

"Oh yeah, yeah, he was nice." I blush and turn way. Dan is her partner. Should I tell her about our date? I kind of want to keep it to myself. It's exciting. It's the first date I've had where the guy wants to go with me on his own accord.

"Well, I hate to eat and run but we need to get back to Billie Rose."

"Yeah, thanks for supper it was so good." I rub my stomach.

Jesse pulls me in for a hug and then makes her way over to Dirk. He swings his leg over his bike, saluting me. "See you Saturday, Smurf," he teases. She climbs on behind him, hugging his waist tight. They are a stunning yet terrifying site. I wouldn't want to piss either of them off.

Chapter Twelve

Lily

Yesterday, I spent the day cleaning and painting. My ribs are feeling better each day and so is my soul. Physically and mentally, I feel stronger than I have in a long time.

This morning, I woke up feeling wonderful but then I remembered my date.

I. Have. A. Date.

I went to the thrift store three times. Nothing feels right. I'm sitting on the floor with my legs crossed, staring at the clothes scattered everywhere. I have no clue what to wear to a bar. Just then, an idea pops in my head. Seems my creative juices are running over.

Ripping material with my teeth, I find my style.

After I shower, curl my hair, and do my makeup, I stand naked in front of the mirror in my bedroom. I allow myself a moment to stare at the woman in front of me. I'm her, she's me. We smile at each other. I grab the dress I hand stitched and hold it up against me. "It's nice to finally meet you, Lily," I whisper to my reflection.

When I step into the bar, all eyes turn my way. Oh, lord. My knees begin to tremble. Shit, maybe this outfit was a bad idea.

"Lily," Bill yells from behind the bar. "Hey, guys, this is Lily. She's going to be my new bartender." He comes around and takes my hand, pulling me farther inside. All the men sitting up at bar whistle and whoop their approval.

Oh. Maybe they do like the outfit.

"I was hoping you would stop in after you got settled." He runs his eyes up my frame before pulling a bar stool out for me.

I tuck a runaway curl behind my ear. "I'm here for a date. I mean drink. I'm here for a drink," I say nervously.

"Awe, I see. Well, I'm glad you're here. I wanted to see when you'd be interested in starting."

"Oh, anytime. After this weekend, I should be good to go."

"How about Monday?"

"Yeah, sure. I'm excited," I tell him.

"You want a drink?"

"Not at the moment. I'll wait for my friend."

He nods, grabbing a couple of empties from the guys sitting beside me. After he sets two fresh ones in front of them, he turns his attention back to me.

Bill leans against the counter. "A date, huh?"

"Drink. I misspoke."

"So, you must be meeting new people then?"

"A few."

The door opens behind me, and Bill's eyes lift over my head. A lopsided grin forms on his face. I spin on my stool and there stands the giant of a man. "He came," I say breathlessly.

"Wait. What? Dan is your date?"

I swivel to face Bill. "Drink. We are having a drink."

He laughs. "Oh, this is going to be fun."

I give him a dirty look before I can stop myself. He only laughs harder.

Sliding off the stool, I walk over to where Dan remains frozen in his spot. His eyes run up and down my body. His nostrils flare and I notice him clenching his hands into fists. His eyes pull away from me to stare at the men behind me. The look he gives them makes even my balls shrivel up.

I shake my head at my own thoughts. These people are changing me. I run my hand down my makeshift dress. Or maybe they are just giving me the space to evolve into the real me. My tongue runs along my teeth.

Dan looks good. He is in a tight-fitting pair of black jeans, and he has black boots on his feet. A chain hangs heavily at his side. The grey t-shirt he's wearing clings to his muscular frame. His hair is messy today, not combed smooth like it was at the shop. It looks like he's been tugging at it. Was he at war with himself on whether he should come tonight? My eyes lock on his amber ones.

His muscles tense, veins popping on his tattooed forearms. "Lily," he murmurs quietly.

"Dan." I dip my head, clasping my hands in front of me.

He reaches out and grabs my hand. A jolt races up my arm. My eyes fall closed as I blindly let him lead me to a booth in the back corner of the bar. I open my eyes when we stop, he is waiting for me to sit. So, I do. When he doesn't move, I slide farther down, he follows right in beside me.

Immediately, I feel trapped by his big body.

And. I. Love. It.

His warm leg brushes against mine.

"I don't like the way those guys are looking at you," he states, a tad bit annoyed.

My stomach flips a three sixty.

His glowing, amber eyes dart over my face. "You look nice," he says before turning away from me.

Bill saunters over and sits down across from us. "So…"

Dan drills him with a stare, effectively telling him to shut up.

"What can I get the two of you?" Bill finishes, chuckling lightly.

They both look at me. "Um, oh I don't know. I don't drink… much," I add quickly so I don't look like a complete lame ass. I mean butt. Lame butt.

"Beer?" Dan questions.

"Yeah, I've never had a beer, but sure."

His face softens. He likes that I'm innocent. Or at least I think that's how he's feeling. "Get us a pitcher," he tells Bill, shooing him away with the wave of his hand.

Dan

Jesus Christ, I want to corrupt her, break her innocence down bite by delectable bite. Her blue hair brushes against my arm. It's soft, so fucking soft. I want to grab a handful and rub it all over my cock. God, fucking, dammit.

I've been thinking of her and nothing else for the past two days. Counting the hours, the fucking minutes till I could see her again.

When she turned and stood up from that bar stool, I just about came in my pants. Trouble is, so didn't every other motherfucker in here.

At the shop, she was a cute little fucking blue haired fairy. Today, today, she's a hot as fuck, blue haired biker chick. One that belongs on the back of *my* bike. The angel on my shoulder has vanished. The devil is cracking his whip, ready to play.

Her hair is down today, curled in long beachy waves that stretch down her back to the tip of her tailbone. She's in a long, black rolling stones t-shirt dress, with a small, silver chain draped across her shapely hips that show off her hourglass figure. The red lips and white teeth on the front of the dress match her own. Jesus, her lips are so fucking kissable. Images of her painting my cock red with that lipstick make me almost groan out loud. Almost.

The t-shirt is ripped down the front, giving me an incredible view of her firm tits, they're shiny, reflecting the light from above. It also has a slit up the side, providing me a sneak peek at the tattoo I did a few days ago.

I scoot back so I can see under the table. The dress is riding up now, it looks like the tattoo is healing well. I probably should get a closer look before the night is over.

She has on a pair of black, fuck me, high heels to top it off. I wonder if she wore them so that she didn't feel so short next to me. Even with the heels, she's still a good foot shorter.

Her big brown eyes blink at me slowly. I wonder what she's thinking. I shouldn't have been so possessive. She probably thinks I'm a nut job.

A few beers in and I find out exactly what she thinks. Her hand wraps over my thigh as she leans toward me. "I think I'm getting a little tipsy," she hiccups.

Alcohol is like a truth serum. So far, I've found out that she's from San Francisco, she has no siblings, and her parents are assholes that are never home. They sound like Dirk and Rachel's parents. When she tells me she had been a kindergarten teacher before coming here, my dick gets hard. What? Fucking sue me. Her innocence mixed with that intoxicating sex appeal does it for me.

"Where did you get the bruises?" I ask since we're on a roll.

Her demeanor changes. She turns away from me, taking a sip of her beer. "Oh, I just fell." She waves her hand. "Hey, you haven't told me anything about yourself. I feel like I'm doing all the talking."

"You are. I like it that way."

She licks her lips and I notice she shifts her ass on the seat.

"You're not lying to me, are you?" I ask, tipping my head down, staring at her.

She blinks those fucking big brown doe eyes at me. "No," she says breathlessly.

"You fell?"

Lily nods slowly.

"Because I had a friend who told me she fell once and what really happened was someone hurt her. Hurt her real bad. If someone gave you those, tell me." I lean into her space, putting my mouth to her ear. "I'll snap their fucking head from their body."

I hear her swallow. "No. Nobody hurt me," she says quietly. "I really did fall."

Leaning back, I grill her with a look, letting her know I mean business. "I'll spank that little ass of yours if I find out you're lying."

Her pupils go wide, her lips part and her eyes bounce over my face. I think she likes me this way. Other women run. They run fast and they run far. Like I said, no one has "fit" me.

A grin spreads across her face. "Jesse warned me you could be an asshole."

"Oh, did she?" I note this is the first time I've heard her curse. She's getting more comfortable with me.

Lily nods, her chest rising and falling, the t-shirt gives me a peek of the curve of her breast as she exhales.

"Jesse has never seen this side of me. And she never will." I crowd her again. She tips her head back. My lips crash into hers. She moans quietly into my mouth. When I pull away, I keep her trapped, one arm braced on the seat behind her head and the other on the table.

A song begins to play on the jukebox. *Take Me Home Tonight* by Eddie Money. Fucking Bill. The fucker laughs as he walks over to us. Slowly, I back away from her to tell Bill to fuck off.

He's standing by our table with an amused look on his face. I reach for my wallet, but he stops me. "Drinks are on me tonight."

Lily leans around me. "Thank you, Bill. I'll see you Monday," she tells him.

Is our night coming to an end? I don't think so and what the fuck does she mean, she'll see him Monday?

Bill explains, noticing the confusion on my face. "Lily will be bartending for me, starting Monday."

I glance at her. She nods, an excited look on her face. "Remember? I told you I was going to be working here."

"No. No fucking way."

She shoves me in the back. Good luck, little girl, that won't work.

Bill laughs and slaps his hand down on the table. "I knew this was going to be good." He pats me on the shoulder and walks away, shaking his head.

"What do you mean, no way? I *am* working here."

I turn slowly in the booth to stare down at her. "Let's go."

She huffs, sending blue strands of hair fluttering around her face. "Dan."

"Lily, I'm taking you home. You've had too much to drink to drive yourself."

"I've had as many as you," she says still trying to push me out of the booth. Isn't that cute?

"Look at me and then take a look at yourself."

She glances down her tiny frame and sticks her bottom lip out in a pout. Oh, hell, that's sexy. I'm going to love giving her things to pout about.

"Let's go." I grab her arm and drag her out of the booth. I kick the door open, holding her with one hand while my other points to the men in the bar who are still ogling my girl. "Look at her again and I'll rip your eyeballs from your skulls." I shove her out the door and toward my bike.

"Wait. Wait, I can't leave my beetle here."

"Your beetle?" I question, then I spot her Volkswagen. I smile, picturing her cute little ass in the tiny clown car. She digs her heels into the dirt, pointing at the car.

"Calm down. We can come back and get it tomorrow. It will be safe for the night."

"But will I?" she asks.

My hand drops from her arm.

"Do you want to be?"

Her eyes dart around the parking lot, turmoil skewing her beautiful face. "I… I don't know," she whispers.

The back of my finger traces along her jaw line. Her big eyes search mine for reassurance. She isn't going to find what she's looking for. I don't know what will happen when I get her home. Maybe I'll drop her off at the front door with a kiss goodnight. Maybe I'll rip her clothes off and fuck her right there on the porch. It's truly a tossup at this point.

And she only has the dragonfly to blame. The dragonfly brought me an angel and I sure as fuck am not about to let her go.

Chapter Thirteen

Lily

Oh fudge. Oh fudge. Oh fudge.

What have I done? What was I thinking, going to a bar dressed like this? Like me.

My heart skips and trips and sidesteps and fucking just about keels clean over as I think about what will happen when we get to my house.

I'm not a virgin but I've never felt this way before. I've never had anyone look at me with hungry eyes like Dan is giving me. He's possessive. Benjamin was possessive too but in a different sort of way. He owned me like one would own a car or a boat. He took me out of the garage occasionally, to show me off but then he parked me neatly back inside until the next time he needed me on his arm.

Dan wants me. Me. The real me.

I want him too.

"No, I don't want to be safe. I want to be reckless, and crazy and I want someone to watch over me while that happens." I'm breathing hard. It's scary being honest with him, but I think he might be the only person I can be candid with right now.

He hands me a helmet. "I'll look after you. If you trust me."

I reach out to take it, bowing my head slightly. "I trust you."

Dan swings his leg over his bike, kicking up the stand. He nods to the seat behind him. I shove the helmet on and as lady like as I can with my dress, straddle the seat. As soon as I settle behind him, he runs his palm up my leg before pulling my hands around his torso. "Hold on tight."

Sliding as close to him as I can, which feels pretty darn good, I hold on to his t-shirt, feeling his hard muscles twitch beneath my hands. The moment he starts the bike, something shifts inside me. It's... oh gosh. Wow. I could get used to this.

He takes off slowly out of the parking lot. As he picks up speed on the open road, I wonder how the hell I got here. Oh, yeah, a little dragonfly. I rest my head on Dan's back, a small smile on my lips. This feels good. So good. It's an adventure.

I don't know what will happen when we get to my house and honestly, it's kind of exciting not knowing. Will he come in? Will we talk? Will he want to do more than talk? Will I?

A sane woman would be scared of this big brute of a man. But I'm not afraid. I don't know why. Especially, with the way he treated me back there. He literally told a whole bar full of men to keep their eyes off me as he dragged me out the door. It should have pissed me off, not warmed my heart.

I like that he is possessive, even though I'm not his. He's not mine. I wish he were, but I don't know how someone like me holds onto someone like him. I'm okay with whatever it is. Jenny told me sometimes people come into your life for a short period, sometimes, mere minutes but that doesn't diminish the importance of them.

Whatever Dan is in my life, I'll accept it. Not only that, but I'll also cherish it. It's been a great journey so far. If it ends after tonight, so be it.

Dan drives right to my house. I didn't tell him where I lived, but maybe Jesse did. He pulls up in front of the house and shuts the engine off. I slide off and hand him his helmet back. I grab my keys from my purse and head toward the porch. I listen to see if he follows. He does. My heart is beating wildly in my chest.

When I open the door and step inside, I realize he stopped at the threshold. Slowly, I turn around to find him leaning casually against the door jamb. He doesn't say anything, he just watches me as I set my purse down on the coffee table.

"Um, I don't have much… yet, but would you like to come in?" I'm suddenly nervous. This is all so new to me.

His amber eyes glow as they move across the room, taking in what little there is in my space. When they land back on me, he grins. "You should never invite a vampire into your house, silly girl, it renders you powerless."

My eyes drop to the floor, and I laugh. "Are you telling me you're a vampire?"

"No, I'm worse."

My laughter faulters, he's trying to scare me. But I think it's his own hesitation that is keeping him on the other side of the door. I toe off my heels as I think about it. "What if I want to be powerless."

He growls. Literally, growls.

It makes me shiver and not from fear. Taking a deep breath, I look him in the eye. "Would you please come in."

He glances over his shoulder once before turning back to me. "You sure this is what you want?"

I nod.

Dan takes two big steps inside and kicks my door with the bottom of his boot, slamming it shut. The noise echoes through the entire house.

My pulse kicks into overdrive. Holy shit. I mean… oh to hell with it, I mean exactly what I said, holy shit!

He takes his leather jacket off and drops it on the coffee table by my purse, not taking his eyes off me. "Do you have a bed or are we going to do this right here?"

Oh. *Oh.*

This is really happening.

My finger points to the floor above us. I'm so stunned, I can't speak. He picks me up, my legs automatically wrapping around his waist, my arms draping loosely around his neck. Dan walks us upstairs slowly, never letting me look away from him.

His hands are on my ass. On my ass. Oh my god. Oh my god.

When we get into my bedroom, he sets me gently on my feet and turns back to close the door, quietly this time.

My body begins to tremble. No. No. Not now. I'm not scared. I'm not.

He leans his back against the door, studying me closely. "Cold?"

Biting my lip, I shake my head no. I stare at the floor, watching him in my peripheral.

When he moves, I jump. Dammit. I don't want him to think I'm a scared little rabbit.

"I'm going to ask you this once, so listen closely because I'm not going to have any restraint left after this. Understand?"

I nod my head.

"Do you want me here? And by here, I mean in your bedroom and in your bed."

He's given me several chances to back out and I can tell by his tone that this is my last one. I don't want to give him mixed messages. I decide honesty is the best policy.

"I want you here." I take a few steps closer to him. "I've… well, I've only been with one person, and it wasn't…" my words trail off.

How do you tell someone you've only had obligatory sex? Benjamin only had sex with me because it was expected of us. It was humiliating and I hated every minute of it. He wasn't nice. Benjamin treated me like I was nothing more than a sex doll. In fact, that's all I've ever been to any of them. Just a stupid doll.

"It wasn't good?" Dan finishes for me.

"You're right, it wasn't good. I'm sorry. I just don't want to give you the impression that I'm experienced… I'm not."

"Are you on birth control?"

I nod.

He walks across the room and sits down on my bed. "When you say it wasn't good," he pauses, a pained look crossing his features.

"I wasn't forced," I quickly interrupt, seeing where he was going.

Dan lets out a long breath.

"It's hard to explain," I tell him.

"I'm intense, Lily. Not to mention, a whole lot older than you. And bossy. Very bossy. Maybe I'm not the right guy for you to try new experiences with."

I sit down beside him and pull his hands into mine. "I trust you, Dan. I want this. I really, really want this."

He sighs, brushing his thumb back and forth over my fingers. "You saw how possessive I was at the bar."

"I'm good with that."

"Are you? Cause most women would kick me in the nuts for that sort of behavior."

I giggle which makes him smile.

"It did things to me, Dan." I shove my face into the side of his arm, embarrassed to admit it.

His hand runs down my hair, making me shiver against him.

"Okay," he whispers, kissing the top of my head. "We go slow, and you tell me if anything makes you uncomfortable."

I nod against his arm. Still unable to look at him.

He pushes me back so he can look into my eyes. Whatever he sees must give him the green light. "Stand up."

So, I do.

He pulls me into the space between his legs. Dan unclasps the chain around my hips, dropping it to the floor. He grabs the hem of my dress and pulls it up and over my head. The moon pours in through the window, illuminating my skin, making it look paler than it already is.

Dan reaches around and with one hand flicks the clasp on my bra. It slides down my arms and I let it fall to the ground. He hooks his thumbs under the edge of my panties and slides them down my legs. My breath catches in my throat.

I struggle not to cover myself with my hands. His gaze slides over every inch of me. His breath the only touch to my skin. A shiver starts at my head and ripples all the way down my body.

Dan rolls his eyes up to mine. "Do you like it when I look at you like this?"

"Yes," I whisper.

His hand reaches out slowly. I make a demand to my feet to hold strong, *don't back away*. When his fingers wrap around my hips, I moan. I don't know why. They just feel good and they're so warm.

He chuckles and leans forward, kissing me lightly above my belly button. His kisses trail higher and higher until he pulls my nipple into his mouth. My head drops back. His mouth is fire. It's scorching, leaving a clean slate for my nerve endings to experience something new.

He pulls me onto his lap so I'm straddling him. When my bare pussy rubs against the course material of his jeans, a hiss escapes my lips. Mindlessly, I grind myself over the hard length of him. Dan groans into my mouth. His fingers wrap in my hair, giving him total control of my movements.

My body reacts in a way which seems to surprise him.

"Do you like the feel of my cock?"

"Mmhhmm," I moan into his mouth.

He stands and turns, dumping me onto the bed. I watch as he grabs the back of his shirt, ripping it over his head in one smooth motion.

I've never been much of a religious person but good god. I want to drop to my knees and worship this man.

"Touch yourself," his voice is low and demanding.

In front of him? He wants me to touch myself, now? Right here?

"Now, Lily," he growls.

My knees fall open and I gently lay my hand over myself. My cheeks must be stained bright red, I can feel the heat radiating off them.

He pulls his belt from the loops of his jeans. The sound makes me draw my knees back together, my hips rising from the mattress. A smirk falls across his mouth. He taps the belt on my knees gently, a warning. "Uh, uh, keep em open. I want to watch," he tsks.

I let them fall to the mattress. I'm so embarrassed by how wet this is making me.

"That's it, baby. I want to see how slick your pussy is."

Hesitantly, I run a finger over my clit. My head falls back, and my eyes drop closed. It's because he's watching me. I've never been so turned on in all my life.

I feel the bed dip beside me. His hair tickles the side of my leg as he moves in for a closer view. "Beautiful," he whispers.

He sits up against the headboard and spreads his legs. "C'mere," he orders.

I climb up between his legs, swallowing hard at my first glimpse of him. My cunt clenches in response. Even it knows this is going to be a challenge.

He shifts me so that my back is pressed against his chest, and he drapes my legs on either side of his thick thighs. "I'm going to drive you mad," he whispers in my ear.

"What if I'm already mad?" My chest rises and falls fast as my skin melds against his.

"Are you straight jacket mad?"

"Some would say so."

A throaty chuckle rumbles deep in his chest, making my stomach flip.

"Well, buckle up, baby."

His hands grope my breasts before one sneaks away, sliding slowly down my torso. I dip my head to watch it. It's like coming upon a snake in the grass. You freeze but it raises its head and slithers closer. You know it's about to strike, but you can't move.

When his fingers glide through my folds, my head falls back against his chest. He circles my clit ever so slowly. My hips rise to chase his fingers each time they move away.

"Oh, I think you really like this," he whispers into my ear, his teeth sinking into my ear lobe gently but effectively holding me in place.

"Don't stop," I pant.

I'm so close, so close, and then his hand is gone, running lightly up my leg.

This happens over and over until I'm so wound, I can't take it anymore. I growl in frustration.

"Is there something you want?"

"No, I neeeed it," I grind my hips upwards, crushing my pussy into the palm of his hand.

"But there's more." He runs his tongue along the shell of my ear.

I dig my nails into his thighs, whimpering for more. Give it to me. *Please give it to me.*

His finger taps over my entrance, and I freeze. Yes. Yes. That's what I need.

When he inserts one finger into me, my head presses hard against his solid chest. "Does that feel good, baby?" He slides a second one in before I have a chance to answer.

"Yes, yes, please," I beg, pressing my heels into the bed, trying to rock myself on his hand.

He lifts his knees so my feet cannot touch the mattress. "So, so, very impatient."

"It feels so good."

"Do you want it to feel even better," he teases, his gravelly voice sending my heart into arrhythmia.

"Not. Possible," I grit, so close to exploding my legs are shaking.

He curls his fingers, pressing the palm of his hand firmly against my clit. His hand pumps into me at a rhythmic pace, never taking the pressure off my clit.

Tears spring to my eyes as I fight the urge. Oh. Oh. What the fuck?

What in the fuck?!

Then it happens. My body seizes against his. I grip his forearms and scream.

Watercolor Skulls

I scream.

After a few minutes, he gently shifts from behind me. He waits patiently as I try to catch my breath. Gently, he pushes my knees apart and settles himself between my thighs. His thumbs brush the tears from the corner of my eyes. "You want more?" he asks, quietly.

His amber eyes are so sincere, so concerned for my well-being. I nod, smiling at him.

He leans back and grips his cock, giving it a few long strokes before lining it up with my entrance. We both watch as he slides in. Once he is fully seated, his eyes roll to mine. "I think we're a perfect fit." His hips pull back before pushing in slowly. His gaze settles on where we are joined.

He pumps inside me again and again, mesmerized by the sight before him. I'm mumbling words that are in no way forming complete sentences, the outside world completely forgotten.

Every now and then I crack my eyes open to study the god taking his pleasure from my body. His arms are braced on each side of me, veins bulging from the careful restraint he's taking with me. What the heck would it be like if he let loose?

His hips pick up pace, and he drops his weight on me, no longer able to hold back. He chases his pleasure and just when I think I'm done, he hits a place inside of me that cracks me clean open. He groans, bringing his lips down on mine. He kisses me through my orgasm just as his begins. As he comes, he rests his forehead against mine, staring deep into my soul.

When his eyes drop closed and his muscles tighten, I think I've died and gone to heaven. My body made this happen. Me. How wonderful.

He drops his face into my neck, his body slowly relaxing on top of me. Suddenly, he pushes himself up. "Shit, sorry, I didn't mean to crush you."

"You're not crushing me." I wrap my arms around him and pull him back down. "I like it. I like the feel of you on me. It makes me feel safe."

He stares at me for several long minutes before rolling us over. I rest my cheek on his shoulder, happily running my fingers through the hair on his chest.

His voice suddenly breaks the silence, "You okay?"

I nod. He reaches down and grips my chin, forcing me to look at him.

"Really, I'm good."

"Then why are you crying?"

I sit up quickly, wiping my eyes. I'm crying?

"Hey." He sits up too, placing his arm around my shoulders.

"I'm sorry. I didn't know I was crying. I'm okay, really, I am." I'm so embarrassed, I try to turn away from him.

"It's okay to cry. I just want to make sure you're not hurt or sad or… regretful?" he questions, keeping his arm braced around me.

"No, it's none of those things. I don't know what it is."

He dips his head, catching my eyes. "It was powerful."

I think about it. He's right. It was powerful. I felt powerful. I laugh lightly. "I thought you were supposed to render me power*less*."

"That's just an illusion. You've always held the power. From the moment I laid eyes on you." He brushes tears away with his thumbs and kisses my forehead. "I'm going to grab you some water."

Nodding my head, I watch him climb out of bed. He's so gentle with me and my fragile heart. I know that I said I would be okay with this being a one-time thing... but I think I lied.

Chapter Fourteen

Dan

I told myself I would be okay with this being a one-night stand.

Nope. Not good enough.

She is a perfect fit.

I grab two waters from the fridge, noting how little food she has. Cracking the lid on one, I take a long drink as my eyes scan her house. There is nothing here except paint cans, power tools, a ladder, and a coffee table. Oh, and she has a bed.

A bed I'll be spending a fair amount of time in if I have my way.

Holy shit, that was the best sex I've ever had. I was a little worried when she started to cry but hell, I felt like crying. It was… different. It was intense.

Fuck, she's so tiny I thought I might break her, but I didn't. Her body accepted every part of me. And I like the fact she talked to me. She might not always know what she's feeling but she does her best to communicate. That is huge. That I've never had. I don't like playing guessing games. Tell me straight up how it is.

I hear her little feet pad across the hall to the bathroom. She's so fucking cute.

I'm about to head upstairs when a painting on the wall catches my attention. It's a field of sunflowers painted on an old window. It reminds me of home. I glance up the stairs as the toilet flushes. I continue my way up the stairs, stopping to look back at the painting.

She makes a beeline, still naked, back to her bed. When I walk in behind her, she's already buried in the blankets, holding them up to her chin.

How adorable.

I hand her a bottle of water and she takes it, drinking greedily as soon as the cap comes off.

"Did you paint the picture downstairs?"

"Yeah, I found some old windows in a shed out back." She caps the water, wiping her mouth with the back of her hand.

"It gave me an idea," I tell her, climbing back into bed. I slide under the covers, my leg bumping against hers. Folding my arms behind my head, I settle against her pillows.

"What's the idea?" She looks surprised that I laid back down. Did she think I was going somewhere? Not a chance.

"An idea for our next date."

This makes her smile, and oh how that smile lifts my lonely soul. I'm going to do my best to see it every. single. day.

"So, you really want to go out with me again?" She nibbles on her bottom lip.

"Oh, you're going to have a hard time getting me to leave your side."

She blushes and lets her hair fall across her face. "I like the sound of that," she says quietly.

"Good, then get your cute little ass over here so we can get some sleep, tomorrow's not far away."

Lily sets her water on the floor and then snuggles down beside me, resting her face against my chest. Her leg curls over the top of mine and I feel her smile against my skin. She falls asleep soon after, giving me a chance to revel in the feel of her body pressed to mine. I've avoided women for so long, I almost forgot how good they smell and how soft they are. I pull her closer and she murmurs in her sleep like a little kitten, rubbing her cheek over me.

Tomorrow, I'm going to do something I've never done. I'm going to take her home with me. I know I just met her, but I want to show her who I am. What I'm really hoping, is that she will show me who she is.

When I wake up, I find the little thing sitting up, staring at me. Her eyes are running down my body, then slowly back up again. When they snag on mine, she realizes she's been caught. She quickly looks away.

I grab her hand and pull her over the top of me. "Good morning, Lily," I whisper in her ear.

She giggles as she tries to steady herself on top of me. "Good morning." She sighs, folding her hands on my chest and resting her chin on them.

"Hungry? How about we head into town for breakfast."

"I could make you something."

"With what? I saw your fridge last night, remember?"

She smiles sweetly. "I have yogurt."

"Yogurt is not breakfast. I need bacon, woman." I smack her on the ass lightly and she laughs.

"Let me shower first." She jumps off me and hurries to the bathroom across the hall.

I wait a few minutes until I hear the water turn on. Pushing the covers aside, I decide a shower does sound good, the bacon can wait.

Chapter Fifteen

Lily

Dan stayed. All night. I can't tell you how happy this makes me.

Nobody has stayed with me this long, besides Jenny. My parents came and went so fast, our home was just another hotel to them. And Benjamin stayed long enough to get points with my dad. Sure, he might take me out and show me off for a few hours but then he dropped me off without a second glance. Some evenings, he stayed long enough to make me hate my life a little more than I already did. I loathed those nights.

The door to the bathroom opens, making me jump. I watch as Dan walks in, he braces one hand on the wall behind the toilet and the other grabs his... *oh, oh, he's peeing.* In front of me! I've never seen a man pee. My face heats to an alarming level as I stare at him like he's a wild animal in a nature preserve.

One side of his mouth kicks up in a sexy smile. I turn away from him, embarrassed. God, I'm such a freaking child. I mean, come on. I'm twenty-five. Little Miss Bland, that's who I am. Why did I think an experienced, sexy man like Dan would want to be with me? I wring my hands nervously, thinking I should just cancel on breakfast. I'll never be able to keep up with him.

I mean, just look at him. I sneak another quick peek. He's definitely out of my league. Dan has a dark, dangerous look about him. I bet people give him a wide berth and women probably fall at his feet.

The shower door opens, the cool air brushes over my wet skin, making me shiver. Dan presses against my backside, walking me into the shower wall. "Why are you crying again?" he asks as my chest presses against the cool tile.

"I'm not."

He bends down, whispering, his lips brushing lightly over the shell of my ear, "You are."

"It's… it's just the spray from the shower," I say with a tiny bit of sass.

Whack. The sound of his palm slapping against my wet ass cracks loudly in the shower. "Why. Are. You. Crying?" he demands.

I drop my head to the wall, letting the tears fall freely now.

"Talk to me," he says more gently.

"It will sound crazy, and I don't want to sound crazy."

"Are you regretting last night?" he asks, insecurity laced in his words.

"No," I answer without hesitation. "I didn't expect you to stay this long. I'm not used to people wanting to spend so much time with me."

He stills behind me as he processes my words. "Does it feel like I don't want to spend time with you?" He presses his hard cock into my back.

A tiny puff of air escapes my lips. I roll my head to the side. "What do you see in me?"

His nose runs over my cheek. "I see an opportunity to experience the light."

This makes me smile.

"What do you see in me?" he counters, his hips dipping so that his cock glides between my legs.

"I see an opportunity to explore the dark."

He throws his head back and laughs, the sound vibrating through my entire body. "Well, I guess we will balance each other out then."

He squeezes my breasts in his hands as he slides into my body. Oh, god. My head falls back onto his chest. He fucks me slowly as if we have all the time in the world, peppering kisses along my shoulders and the back of my neck. "You feel so fucking good, baby," he groans.

His hand lifts my leg, his fingers gripping me tightly under the knee, driving his cock deeper inside of me.

Oh, right there. I swear he's known my body in a previous life. His thrusts begin to quicken. He is pressing into me so deeply that each stroke lifts me off my toes.

He brushes his face next to mine, so we are cheek to cheek. "Come for me, baby." He slides his hand between me and the wall, pinching my clit as he rocks into me.

My fingers curl against the tiles as I obey his wish. I convulse in his arms as he holds me tight against him. His hard body stiffens behind me as he succumbs to his own pleasure.

We stand there for a minute, unaware of the water turning cold, then it hits us at the same time. "Shit!" I squeal as we both dance around, trying to wash as quickly as we can.

"You need a bigger hot water heater."

"I'll ask my landlord to get right on that," I joke as we step out. "Oh, wait. Technically, you're my landlord."

He tips his head to the side.

"So, after you get that done, I have a few other things I need you to take a look at," I tease, backing slowly out the door.

He waits until I'm a step outside before he chases. I run down the stairs, dripping water all over the floor without a care in the world. His heavy footsteps follow close behind. "Oh, I'll take a look all right," he says as he catches up to me.

We are both laughing, trying to catch our breath as the front door swings wide open.

Dan and I both freeze as Jesse, Dirk, Bill, Raffe and two women I haven't met before, walk in. Dan quickly pulls me in front of him and wraps one of his big arms over my breasts and splays a hand over my crotch.

I finally brave a glance up to find all their mouths hanging wide open as they stare at us.

"Oh, oh shit! It's Saturday!" I squeal.

Bill starts laughing. "Oh, hell, I knew this was going to be good, but this takes the fucking cake." One of the women slap him in the chest but he only doubles over, wheezing he's laughing so hard.

My new boss just saw me naked. Great.

"I'm so…" I shake my head back and forth. "I'm so sorry, I forgot about today."

"I see why you forgot." Jesse dips her eyes suggestively toward Dan. "Impressive."

Dirk growls and pokes her in the ribs. She giggles and looks past me to Dan. "Dan, what are you doing here?" She looks a little dumbfounded that he is naked, and in my kitchen.

"Well, we were just about to go to breakfast," he says not a hint of awkwardness in his voice.

Jesse pushes two big boxes out in front of her. "Want a donut?" she asks, her eyebrow quirking up. "Go on, don't be shy," she teases.

Just then, I hear more bikes roaring down the road. How did we not hear them? Oh, yeah, the shower. Crap.

"Um, well, if you'll excuse me, I mean us…" I look up at Dan and he smiles down at me. He's smiling. Not a hint of guilt on his handsome face. Unlike me, who is acting like a kid caught with her hand in the cookie jar.

"If you'll excuse *us*, we will go put some clothes on before the whole club gets here."

Bill roars with laughter, Dirk and Raffe join him.

"Come on," the older woman says, shooing everyone outside. "Let's give them a minute."

Everyone walks out except Jesse and Dirk.

Dan taps his foot in annoyance. "Go on, you heard Mama Bear."

"I don't take orders from her," Dirk says, popping an unlit cigarette between his lips. Jesse leans into him. His eyes run up and down my body, making me shiver against Dan. My eyes drop to the floor. I don't think I've ever been more embarrassed in my whole life.

"You know, you two look sexy as hell together," he says, taking the cigarette out of his mouth to point at us.

"For the love of my goddaughter, I won't kill you but so help me, cousin, if you don't take your eyes off my girl, you're going to find my fist in a place you won't like," Dan says, his tone deadly serious.

Dirk smirks and turns around to give us a chance to dart upstairs. Jesse doesn't move. She's still smiling at us. Dirk clears his throat, and she rolls her eyes before turning around too.

"You all are no fun," she pouts.

I make a mad dash for the stairs, hearing Dan right behind me. When we get to my room, I start throwing my clothes on in a rush. "I can't believe I forgot it's Saturday," I grumble, struggling to get my jeans up over my still wet legs. I throw Dan his t-shirt as I stumble around.

Dan stops me. "Hey, chill, it's not that big of deal. So, they saw us naked."

I shake my head and sit on the bed, placing my face in my hands. "They are going to think I'm easy. I slept with you on our first date. Oh my god, what was I thinking, I'm not that sort of girl."

Dan sits down beside me. "Lily, they are going to think no such thing. They are my family. If I chose to be here with you, they know you are something special. I don't sleep around."

Peeking out between my fingers, I study his face. I drop my hands in my lap. "I didn't mean to sound like I was regretful. I'm not. I just… I've never done anything like this."

"I know. Neither have I."

My eyes bounce between his, then we both burst out laughing, the humor of the moment finally hitting us now that we are dressed.

He wraps me up in his arms. "They are going to tease us but it's only teasing, don't take it personally. The club is full of assholes."

"I'm so embarrassed. Seriously, I don't know how I forgot they were coming today."

"So, I'm assuming the club is here to work on the house?"

I nod. "She didn't tell you?"

Jesse hollers from the other side of the door, "I wrote it on the white board in the kitchen."

Dan chuckles but throws his boot at the door. "Go away," he tells her. Jesse laughs on the other side.

She doesn't go away. "Are you two fucking decent?"

"Yeah." He sighs.

Jesse opens the door, resting her hip on the door frame. "Like I said, it was on the white board at the warehouse." She crosses her arms over her chest, her eyes dancing from Dan to me and back again.

"I guess I didn't see it." He smacks his hands on his knees before standing. "Well, I guess our date will have to wait until tomorrow. Where do you want me, boss?" He pulls me to my feet, his eyes on Jesse.

"I've got a crew to finish the painting and one working on the floors. Why don't you go with Raffe and Dirk to get the furniture that Lily needs picked up?"

"Will do." He leans down and kisses me soundly on the mouth. When he pulls away, he offers me an encouraging smile before he heads out, leaving Jesse and I alone in my room.

"I'm so, so, sorry, Jesse."

She sits on my bed, pulling her long blue-black hair over her shoulder. "Lily, you don't have to apologize. You forgot. It's no big deal. Besides, it was a good laugh."

My face heats as I sit down beside her. "I didn't plan on bringing Dan home last night. It just sort of happened."

"You like him?" she asks, tipping her head to study me.

I nod, smiling shyly. "He's not like anyone I've ever met."

She chuckles, sighing as she lies back on my bed. "Dan is special." I lie down too, turning to face her. I tuck my arm under my head for a pillow. "He isn't like most guys."

"I've noticed." I wrap my finger around my dragonfly necklace. "I think my dragonfly led me to him," I whisper, knowing how silly that must sound.

"Hmm, I get you. The universe led me to Dirk when I needed him the most." She rolls to her side. "Maybe Dan can help you get over your bad breakup."

A knot forms in my throat, I've missed having someone to talk to. I miss Jenny so much.

"There really isn't anything to get over. My family sort of arranged for me to date the guy. We were only together as an obligation."

My eyes roam over the ink on her skin. It's all dark, no color is anywhere on her body. I wish I were tough like her. I bet nobody walks on Jesse. She marches to the beat of her own drum. I've done nothing but march to the beat of my dad's. I bet Jesse would have been able to save Jenny... and the others.

She props herself up on an elbow. "Is your family from another country? Because that sounds a bit archaic."

"No, my family is just wealthy, and, in their world, money marries money."

She curls her lip up in distaste. "So, even if the guy was a complete jackass your parents would have made you date him?"

I laugh sadly. "He was a complete jackass. I never argued with my dad about it until wedding plans started to take place. I told him I didn't want to marry the guy, but it was never my choice."

"So, you left?"

"Yep. I hopped on a train to Reno, bought the beetle and ended up here."

She lies back and stares up at the ceiling. "You need to name her."

"Who?"

"Your car. She's got to have a name."

I giggle. "I've never heard of naming your car."

"My rod is Sylvia. Her and I have been through some shit, let me tell you."

I think about it. "How about Blueberry," I say jokingly.

"It is blue and small." She laughs. "Blueberry it is."

We both giggle. Being silly feels good.

"So, about Dan." She wiggles her eyebrows.

"Ugh." I roll over on my back and cover my eyes. "I can't go out there and face everyone."

"Oh, no one's going to say a word to you about it. Well, maybe Dirk. Or Raffe. Okay and my dad. No one else is ballsy enough to mention it. I'm sure Dan has already threatened everyone with bodily harm if anyone upsets you."

I peek at her. "You're kidding?" She raises an eyebrow. I sit up. "No, of course you're not kidding. He is a bit protective."

"All the men in this club are. The women too."

"Is it terrible that I like that?" I whisper.

She sits up beside me, shrugging her shoulders. "Some women like their men sweet and some like assholes."

"But he's a good asshole, right?" I ask, even though I'm quite sure I know the answer.

"He's one of the best." She traces over a tattoo on her arm. "He's like a second dad to me."

"So, I'm going to take it you don't want to hear about last night then?" I tease.

Her eyes shoot to mine. "I should say no. I really should say no." She leans over, speaking in hushed tones, "But, holy cow, he's um…"

"He is *and* he knows how to use it," I finish for her.

We both fall back on the bed, giggling like a couple of schoolgirls. "Okay, okay, I don't want to hear anymore," she gasps.

Jesse stands up, wiping her eyes. She pulls me to my feet. "Ready to meet the club?"

I grab my brush and run it through my hair quick. "Ready."

Hammering, paint fumes and laughs are all around us. "These are my sisters, Katie and Ally," Jesse says. "They are the designated babysitters of the club." She points to the two kids playing in the living room. "You've met Billie Rose. The ornery little boy with her is Jackson. He's our nephew. Raffe and Rachel are his parents. You met Raffe the other day."

"The pretty guy?" I ask.

"Yep. Rachel is Dirk's sister."

"And Dan is Dirk's cousin?" I ask slowly, trying to figure out who is who.

She nods and continues through the house, introducing me to so many people. I'll never remember all their names. In the kitchen we find the two women who saw me naked this morning. "This is my stepmom, Candice, everyone calls her Mama Bear." Mama Bear pulls me in for a quick hug.

"And this is Raffe's wife, Rachel," Jesse finishes.

"It's nice to meet you both." I shake Rachel's hand. "Sorry about this morning." I give them both an apologetic smile.

"Oh, girl, I should be apologizing to you for the way my husband acted. He's enjoying teasing Dan," Candice says, going back to the big pot she's stirring on my stove.

I chuckle nervously. "Yeah, seems like Dan and I have been giving him plenty of opportunity for that."

"We should have known Dad was up to something when he started laughing the minute he saw Dan's bike in the driveway," Jesse adds.

Deciding to veer the conversation, I turn to Candice. "Whatever you're making smells wonderful," I tell her.

"Rachel and I are in charge of lunch today. When we put the men to work, we like to feed them good."

113

"This is just like a barn raising in the pioneer days," I say, a bit in awe that these people are so willing to help someone they don't know.

"Kind of. You can get a lot done if everyone pitches in. It's one of the best things about being a part of the club," Rachel says, wrapping her arm around me. "And since Dan informed us that you are his girl, I guess that makes you one of us too. Welcome to the family."

Another part of my heart thaws at her words. Tears form in the corner of my eyes. She notices and hugs me a little tighter. "It's a lot to take in but you'll get used to it." She studies me as I rub my neck. "Jesse told me you had a bad fall. I'm a physical therapist, maybe I can help you work out your kinks."

I drop my hand and wipe my eyes. "I'm feeling better, I'm just a little bruised."

"Well, let me know. My hands are like magic." She wiggles her fingers in front of me. Just then, a loud crash comes from the living room, drawing her attention away from me. "Jackson," she yells. "What did you break now?"

Jesse rushes out and scoops Billie Rose up in her arms before she cuts herself on the glass that is all over the floor.

Jackson looks up at Rachel with tears in his eyes. "I'm sorry, mama."

"What did I tell you about playing ball in the house? Tell Lily you're sorry for breaking her pretty painting."

"I'm sorry," Jackson says, looking at the floor.

I bend down so I can get him to look me in the eye. "It's okay, it's only a painting."

114

"I'm so sorry." Rachel grabs a broom, quickly trying to sweep up all the glass.

My eyes stay locked on Jackson's. "Do you know how many windows there are in the world?" I ask him.

He shakes his head no, wiping a finger under his nose.

"There are billions and billions," I tell him, throwing my hands out for effect. "How many of you are there in the world?"

He tips up one side of his mouth and holds up a finger.

"One. You're right. I can always get more windows, but I'll never get another friend like you." I poke him in the tummy, and he laughs. His brown eyes sparkle brightly with unshed tears. "Do you want to help me paint another one?"

He nods excitedly.

I stand, turning toward Rachel. "Is it okay if Jackson and I go outside and paint another window? There are more out back, in the shed."

She nods at me, tears in her eyes. I grab her hand. "It's okay, Rachel. It's just a window."

"It's not that, it's just… Jackson has ADHD and…"

"It's hard," I finish for her.

She nods, fighting back tears. Rachel bends down in front of Jackson. "You be good for Lily, okay?"

He shakes his head as he tugs at my hand, pulling me outside. "If anyone wants to join us, we'll be out back," I yell over my shoulder as the little guy pulls me out the door.

Jackson and I drag a few windows out and I crack open my paints. "What is one of your favorite things?" I ask as he hops around me.

"Bugs. I like bugs. Black ones, yellow ones, red ones..." he stops to watch a bird swoop down in a tree. "Did you see that?" he asks, but before I can respond, he is sticking his finger in bright red paint.

I laugh, pulling him down gently onto the ground with me. "Since you already got paint on your fingers, I'm going to show you something cool." I take his finger and press it to the glass.

"It's just a red dot," he grumbles.

"Just wait." I take some black paint and turn his fingerprint into a ladybug.

His eyes go wide. "More," he says, pressing his finger against the glass again.

"Okay, we've got the ladybugs." I wipe his finger off on a paper towel. "How about caterpillars? Do you like them?"

"I like all bugs."

We spend the next hour creating bees, butterflies, lightening bugs, dragonflies, and flowers all out of his fingerprints. I add some grass and a bright sun in the corner of the pane.

When his painting is done, I prop it up for him. He scrunches his nose. "My mom won't like the bugs, but she will sure like the flowers," he says, tipping his head back and forth as I hold the window up for his inspection.

"After it dries, you can take it home," I tell him. "It's a really cool painting."

"You can hang it in your house since I broke yours." He drops his eyes to the ground, his cheeks turning pink.

"I would love to hang your painting in my house."

He peeks at me through the hair that's fallen over his eyes. "Really?

"Absolutely. I'm going to hang it right where my old one was. This one is even better."

He smiles brightly at this.

"Do you have a bug catcher at home?" I ask.

"What's a bug catcher?"

"Oh, every bug lover needs one. Let's go in and get my tools and I bet we can build one."

He jumps around, following me inside. We grab everything we need, stopping to borrow some leftover scraps from the new wood flooring.

Once outside, we get to work. He adorably sticks his tongue out in concentration when he nails two pieces of wood together.

We find some old screen in the shed, to keep the bugs safely inside our new bug catcher and then I let him paint it. Now, he knows what to do and gets right to work, dipping his fingers in paint to create all the different bugs.

When he's done, he smiles proudly. "Now I just need to find some real bugs!" he exclaims.

"Lunch time!" Candice yells out the back door.

I look at Jackson and poke him in the tummy. "After lunch, we'll go on a great bug expedition. Maybe we can bring Billie Rose with us."

"Okay," he says, grabbing my hand while clutching his bug catcher in the other.

"I like you," he says quietly as we walk up to the house.

A pain clenches in my chest as I think about how I almost missed all this. Jenny would be so proud of me. "I like you too, Jackson." I squeeze his hand in mine.

Jenny's baby would have been the same age as Jackson. Somehow, she talked my dad into letting her have it. He was even going to allow her to be part of the adoption process. I remember the day they came home from the agency; she told me she had found the perfect couple. It was a chapter wrote by the fates themselves she had said.

I'd never seen her happier. Her unexpected pregnancy delayed our escape plan but we both promised each other that as soon as the baby was safe in his or her new home we would run.

We had already been putting it off until I graduated college, but we knew it was risky. My dad was tiring of her. She and I both realized it. Once the baby came, we knew we would have to leave straight away.

But then she had her accident, right before the baby was born.

"Oh look, a dragonfly." Jackson points to the sky above us.

I shade my eyes against the sun, squinting into the bright light.

"Dragonflies are my favorite," he tells me. "There are lots and lots of them at the lake."

I smile down at him. "You know Jackson, I think you and I are meant to be best friends because dragonflies are my favorite too."

He and I smile at each other.

These people and this little boy are slowly bringing blood back to my empty heart.

Chapter Sixteen

Dan

No one says a fucking word to me about Lily while we pick up the used furniture she bought. I'm going to have to help her restore some of this shit. Dirk mentioned that she had told him she had a privileged life before coming here. Evidently, she doesn't have the privilege now.

When we get back with the furniture, the women are all gathered in the kitchen. All the women except mine. "Where is she?" I ask gruffly.

"Hello to you too, big guy," Jesse smarts off.

I grab her and pull her into my arms, tickling her. "Okay, okay, Jesus, she's outside with Jackson."

Rachel wraps her arm around Raffe's waist. "Jackson broke her window painting." Raffe grimaces as Rachel continues her story. "Lily handled it so well. Jackson responds to her in a way I've never seen before."

Raffe and I both move to the window. My blue-haired girl is sitting in the grass with Jackson. He's focused on what they are working on. "What are they doing?"

"They painted another window but now they are making a bug catcher," Rachel tells us. "When they came in to grab the tools, he was talking a mile a minute. He was pretty excited."

"Well, she was a kindergarten teacher," I tell them.

"I bet she was a good one. She should look around here for a teaching job," Raffe says.

"She told me she's looking for something different," Jesse chimes in. Her and Dirk are leaning on each other, watching them out the back door.

"Damn, I'm hungry, Mama Bear, is it lunch time yet?" Raffe asks, kissing Candice on the cheek. She swats him on the ass before shooing everyone out of the kitchen.

"How do you not weigh three hundred pounds? You're always hungry," she mutters. She opens the back door. "Lunch time!" she yells to Lily and Jackson. They both look up, smiling and nodding at the same time.

I watch as she talks to Jackson. He grabs her hand, and they start walking toward the house. Both pause to squint at the sky. God, she's fucking beautiful. Seeing her holding Jackson's hand makes me ache to see her with my child… our child. Fuck, fuck, fuck. Maybe it's just my biological clock ticking.

I wait for them by the back door. Candice studies me as she dumps salad in several large bowls. "You know Bill and I are going to watch out for her at the bar."

121

Grunting, I don't take my eyes off Lily.

"She really has caught your eye, huh?" she asks.

"She's more than caught my eye, she stole my heart," I admit.

Candice walks over and puts her hand on my shoulder. "I've seen the way the women in the club treat you. You deserve more than that." She looks out the window as Lily and Jackson approach. "Lily isn't one of them, remember that."

I nod in understanding as the door swings opens.

"Uncle Dan." Jackson barrels into me, climbing up my legs like a goddamn spider monkey. "Look what I made." He shoves a wooden box with a screen covering it in my face. "Do you know what it is?"

"Hm, a cage for trolls that like to come out at night and nibble on your toes." I grab his feet, flipping him upside down, pretending to eat his toes.

He giggles, struggling to catch his breath. "No, Uncle Dan, stop," he gasps.

Lily grabs him under his arms and pulls him upright, so she is holding his torso while I still bite at his feet.

He starts to kick, so I let go.

Lily helps him to stand. "Uncle Dan. It's a bug catcher," he says, exasperated with me.

"Oh, I see it now." I get down on one knee to inspect his creation. "Where are the bugs?"

"Lily and I are going on a bug hunt after lunch. She promised."

I glance up at Lily and she smiles at me. "Do you want to go with us?"

"Yes." I pull myself to my feet and reach out to take her hand but Jackson steps between us, grabbing it first. He pulls her away from me. She grins over her shoulder as they head out the front door.

That little shit.

The food is set up on a long table. Some of the guys are pulling picnic tables out of a few pickup trucks. The club always comes prepared. Jackson breaks away from Lily to show off his new bug catcher. Jackson is a handful but everyone in the club loves him.

Without Jackson by her side, Lily looks a little uncomfortable. I grab her from behind, making her yelp.

"Dan, you scared me," she scolds.

"I thought I better make my move before your little sidekick comes back and steals you away from me."

She laughs up at me. "He's a great kid. I had fun with him this morning."

"Hungry?" I ask, wrapping my arms around her waist and walking us to the food table.

"Yes, everything smells divine."

I chuckle at her choice of words. She's definitely grown up in a different culture than the rest of us but it's refreshing. We load up our plates, then find an empty spot at the end of one of the tables. I sit down and swing my knee out, patting it for her to sit down.

She glances around nervously. Her face is an open book. She's worried about how this will look but when she sees Candice sitting between Bill's legs on the steps, she visibly relaxes and carefully perches herself on my knee.

"So, I was thinking, why don't you let me buy you some nicer things for your place. Some of that furniture looked rough."

Lily pops a chip in her mouth, shaking her head. "No, thank you. I like the stuff I picked out. I'm going to fix it up."

Jeremy and JD are sitting across from us. They both fidget nervously. No one has ever had the balls to tell me no.

"Lily, the dresser is missing knobs, and one drawer is about to completely fall apart."

She narrows her eyes at me. "I'm going to fix it."

JD who is usually as quiet as a damn church mouse, speaks up. "Do you like old things?"

She sets her sandwich down and faces him. "I like the idea of taking something that people have no use for and resurrecting it. I've always had new things." She scrunches her cute little nose up. "New things are boring."

Jeremey chuckles and pats JD on the back. "Well, Lily, JD is going to be your new best friend. He owns a junkyard, hence the name JD, Junkyard Dog." JD shifts anxiously. The reason JD owns a junk yard is because he prefers things over people.

Lily claps her hands together like a kid at Christmas. "Oh, can I look around your yard? Maybe I can find some things for the house."

He rubs his hand over the back of his neck. "Yeah, sure. I'm not sure my junk is what you're looking for though."

She hands him her phone. "Give me your number and I'll call you sometime this week."

He looks at the phone in her hand as if it's going to bite, but he takes it from her and enters his number in before handing it back.

I don't even have her damn number. Fucker. But I can't be mad. None of the ladies give him the time of day. Owning a junk yard isn't most girl's jam. They usually get turned off the minute someone mentions it. But Lily is different. She speaks to him just like she does everyone else, and I like that.

"I'm actually looking for a tailgate."

This perks him up. "Oh, shit, girl, I got a ton of tailgates. Chevy, Ford, you name it, I got it." He smiles at her. Come to think of it, this may be the first time I've seen the man smile.

"Cool, I'm excited to see what you have." JD blushes. Lily turns her attention to Jeremy "What do you do?"

He leans back and stretches. "Well mostly women." He chuckles and winks at her. "Just kidding. I'm a mechanic. I work in the shop at the warehouse. My passion is custom paint jobs."

"Oh, that sounds interesting." She leans forward. "Jesse told me I had to name my car. I've never heard of that. Is that a club thing?"

We all laugh. Jeremy answers, "Don't tell Jesse but none of the rest of us have a name for our rides."

"Oh." Lily frowns. "I thought it was a great idea."

He chucks her under the chin, almost earning him my fist in his face but he removes it quickly. "What do you drive, sweetheart?"

"A 1964 Volkswagen Beetle," she says proudly.

He looks around the driveway for it.

"Oh, it's not here," she tells him. "I left it at the bar last night." Lily glances at me shyly.

Jeremy raises his eyebrows toward us, but he is a good guy, and he sees she's embarrassed, so he doesn't question it. "If you're coming to the barbeque next week maybe I can take a peek under the hood, give her a tune-up if need be."

"She?" Lily teases.

"Cars are basically female," he deadpans.

"So, it's okay for cars to be referred to as female but not okay to name them?" She arches an eyebrow in challenge and damn if it doesn't make my dick hard.

He smacks his hand on the table, laughing and looks over his shoulder at Jesse. "Where did you find this girl?"

"She found me," Jesse yells back, winking at Lily.

"Lily. Lily. Lily." Jackson tugs on her arm. "Let's go find bugs."

126

She laughs, popping the last bite of her sandwich in her mouth.

He drums his little fingers impatiently on the table.

"Did you eat your lunch?" I ask him.

He nods, not taking his eyes off her.

"What all did you have?"

He sighs and turns to look at me. "One pickle and two carrot sticks."

Lily giggles and Jackson's gaze slides back to her. His ornery eyes twinkle mischievously. He has big brown eyes and a floppy head of hair that is usually hanging over one if not both of his eyes.

"How about you have a piece of fried chicken or a sandwich and then we can go look for bugs."

He sticks his tongue out at me, then runs away, looking over his shoulder to see if I'll chase him. Grumpily, he grabs a plate and tosses a sandwich on it. He walks back over to us and settles by my side. He rubs his face over my arm as an apology for sticking his tongue out. I ruffle his hair. "Where's your mom and dad?"

He shrugs while shoving half of the sandwich in his mouth.

Lily grabs our empty plates. "I'm going to go help clean up and then we can go on our bug hunt."

He shoves another large bite in his mouth. "Okay," he says, crumbs falling all over his shirt.

This kid.

After Lily finishes helping clean up, she says a quick good-bye to everyone who helped work on her place this morning. Dirk and Raffe are moving the last of the furniture in. I'd help but we have to go find some damn bugs.

Jackson bounces ahead of us as we walk, Billie Rose on my shoulders. It's peaceful in the woods behind her house. "So, what did you think about the club?"

Lily smiles up at me. "Everyone is so unique. I loved having them all here."

"Well, this was just a handful. Next weekend, several chapters are coming down for a fundraising run. I'd love it if you'd ride with me."

"It sounds fun. What are you raising money for?"

"Victims of sexual assault. We do a couple of runs every year. We have a few survivors in the club, it's important to us."

Lily focuses on the ground.

"So, will you go with me?" I ask, slowing my steps.

She gnaws on her bottom lip but shakes her head yes.

I stop, grabbing her arm and pulling her to face me. Billie Rose pats my head wanting down. I set her gently on her feet. "Jackson, why don't you stop and look for bugs around here." Jackson drops to the ground, scrounging through the fallen leaves. Billie Rose runs over to help him search.

"What's going on up here?" I tap Lily's temple.

She stares into my eyes for several minutes. An unseen force pushes me to hold my hand out to her. She takes it and squeezes as if she's afraid I will slip away. Her lips part and she gasps for air as if she had just been underwater.

Chapter Seventeen

Lily

I thought my anxiety had left me, turns out I had been so busy with my new surroundings, it just hadn't had an opportunity to pounce. What am I doing here? These people are helpers. I've never been a helper in my entire life. I've never been anything other than a damn doormat or worse, an enabler.

Dan says something to me, but it sounds muffled like I'm underwater. My eyes clamber around his frame until I find his amber ones. They pull me back to the surface, back to reality.

"I'm… I'm sorry, what did you say?" I don't look away; afraid I'll slip back under.

He places his warm palm against the side of my neck, letting his fingers naturally curl behind. "Are you feeling okay?" he asks.

"Yeah." I shake my head, finally able to remove my gaze from his. "It's been a long day. I think I'm just a little sleepy."

"Lily," he warns.

"Dan." I wrap my arms around his waist and stare into his handsome face. "You did keep me up most of the night."

The lines around his eyes soften. "Or was it the other way around?" He wiggles his eyebrows at me.

I lay my head on his chest and watch the kids sift through leaves on the ground. "I love it here," I whisper.

Jackson bops his head up. "I found something," he yells.

Billie Rose sticks her nose down where he is pointing, giggling. Whatever it is, she must not be scared of it. I'm sure she's as strong as her mother. Dan and I walk toward them hand in hand and crouch down to see what they found.

It's a furry little caterpillar. "Good find, Jackson," I praise. "Let's get him in the bug catcher."

We pick up the leaf he is perched on and carefully place it inside. We add part of a branch and some other foliage to make him feel more at home.

Jackson is patient as Billie Rose helps add some of the items. "Good job, Rosie," he tells her.

Dan grins down at them. The fondness he feels for the two of them is clearly evident on his face. "We should get back. Your mom and dad will want to be getting home."

"I can't wait to show them," Jackson says excitedly.

Dan scoops Billie Rose up. She tucks her face under his chin and my heart literally starts to melt. Drip, drip, drip. Seeing such a big brute of a man with a tiny child in his arms, is too much for my ovaries to take.

I take Jackson's hand and we walk back to the house together. A great end to a great day. If this is what family feels like, then I want in. I'm not sure if there's a place for me but if there is, I want it more than I've ever wanted anything.

Back at the house, Jesse, Dirk, Raffe and Rachel are relaxing on the porch, waiting for us. Jackson lets go of my hand and runs ahead to show them his caterpillar. Dan sets Billie Rose down and she rushes to join him.

"The mission was a success," I tell them.

Raffe ruffles his son's hair and comes to stand by me. "Thank you for hanging out with Jackson today. He really seems to like you. I'm sorry about the painting he broke."

"Oh, no worries. It was just an old window. I had fun with Jackson today. He's a great kid."

Raffe's eyes drift over my face, he's studying me carefully. "Jesse said you used to be a teacher?"

"Yeah, I'm used to being around kids Jackson's age."

"Maybe you could spend some time with him each week. You seem to be able to keep him interested in things. Rachel and I struggle with that. He's always bored and getting into trouble." He runs his hand through his blond hair. "I mean, we would pay you."

"Awe, you don't have to pay me. I would love to spend time with him. Besides, you all have done so much for me."

132

"We fixed the floors and did a little painting on a house we own." He pulls his cigarettes out and lights one up. "Come on, let us pay you."

"No. Absolutely not. You guys have all been so nice and that alone is enough for me."

"Rachel and I will talk about it and maybe we can meet up next weekend and come up with a time that would work for all of us."

"That would be wonderful."

Jackson runs up and wraps his arms around my legs. "Thank you, Lily."

Crouching down, I tip his chin with my finger. "Thank *you*, for my painting. I'm going to hang it up tonight so the next time you come over, you can see it."

He jumps excitedly.

"Now, you take good care of your caterpillar. Maybe put some fresh grass in his cage in a few days. Okay?

He nods and pulls the cage up between us. We both look at the furry little caterpillar before locking eyes with each other through the screen. He smiles and so do I.

When I stand up, Raffe's eyes catch on my necklace. He frowns. "We'll see you next weekend, Lily," he says, his eyes darting back to the dragonfly around my neck.

"Yeah, thank you for helping me today." I wrap my hand around the pendant.

"Come on, Jackson, we better get home."

Jackson waves as they climb in their truck. Rachel pauses by me. "It was so nice meeting you, Lily. I look forward to next time."

"Me too." I hug myself as they back out and head down the road.

Dirk and Jesse tell us they are leaving too.

"Next weekend." Jesse points to me.

"She'll be there," Dan answers for me.

Jesse smiles at him. "Didn't think I'd ever see the day Dan let a chick ride on the back of his bike."

"I let you ride with me." He crosses his arms across his chest.

"Not the same thing," Jesse sing songs as she sits Billie Rose in her car seat.

Dirk knocks on the side of his truck before giving us a one finger salute. "See you motherfuckers next weekend."

I burst out laughing. The way these people interact is befuddling, yet the most endearing thing I've ever witnessed.

Dan and I watch them drive away and then it's just the two of us. The only sound is the wind whistling through the trees and the soulful song of the crickets.

Dan is the first to speak. "I suppose I should take you back into town to get your car."

"Yeah, I suppose," I say quietly.

We walk back into the house, and I slowly spin in a circle. "I can't believe how hard everyone worked today. Everything looks beautiful and now that I have some furniture, the place feels even cozier than it did the first time I walked in."

Dan glances around the room. "Do you need me to help organize any of this stuff?"

"No, I'm not sure where I want everything. I'm sure it will come to me. But thank you for the offer."

His eyes stop on the place where my painting was hanging. "Sorry about that." He points to the wall.

"Don't be. When Jackson shattered the glass, it enlightened me."

Dan plops down on my couch. Which by the way looks comfy as all get out. The furniture in my parent's home was definitely not comfortable, but it was showroom beautiful.

"How did it enlighten you?" Dan asks as he stretches his muscular tattooed arms along the back of the couch.

I sit down, turning to face him. "I've spent my whole life looking out a window, watching everyone else live. When Jackson broke that window, it made me think maybe I'd finally found something that was on the same side of the glass as me." My heart pounds at my admission.

His amber eyes bore into mine. "I'm right here. We are on the same side of the glass. Don't ever feel that we are not." His hand wraps gently around my throat as he pulls me close to him. His beard tickles the side of my face as he leans in. "You'll never be alone on one side. Do you know how I'm sure of this?" he growls lightly in my ear.

I shake my head no.

His grip tightens around my throat. "Because I will hurt anyone who puts you there and then I'll shatter the glass. I'll never let you feel that way again."

I close my eyes. Falling. Falling. Falling.

Dan's lips graze my neck. His tongue sneaks out to taste me as he makes his way down. He places a gentle kiss at the juncture of my neck and shoulder. When he pulls away, his eyes are a blaze of amber.

"What is happening?" I whisper across his face.

"I think you know," he says before he pulls me to my feet. "Let's go get your car."

I nod numbly as I ponder his words. Do I know what's happening? No. No, I don't. All I know is that it's easy to talk to Dan. It's as if I've known him my whole life. I also know that I hate the thought of being away from him. It's frightening. It can't be real. I pinch myself just to make sure this isn't a dream. Men don't say things like Dan just said to me.

Dan chuckles as he shuts the light off and locks the door.

When he throws his leg over his bike, I finally regain my voice. "So, you feel it too?" I ask. Whatever this is, I need to know it's not just one sided.

"I think you know the answer to that question too. But if you need to hear it then yes, I feel it."

"I'm a little scared," I say, giggling nervously.

He pushes a helmet into my chest. "You should be." He grins at me wickedly.

I shove the helmet over my head and climb on behind him. My heart beats happily even though I know I don't deserve any of this.

The bar is hopping tonight, the entire parking lot is full. Dan shuts the engine off and helps me off his bike. We stand silently, our arms wrapped around each other. The beat of the jukebox filters outside every time someone opens the door.

"I feel like a fucking teenager again," he mumbles. "I don't want to say goodbye."

A smile breaks out across my face. "Are we still going on that date you were talking about?"

"Of course. I'll pick you up at nine tomorrow morning. Pack an overnight bag."

Raising my eyebrows, I tease him, "Oh, I don't know. I'm not the kind of girl that sleeps with a guy on the second date."

He throws his head back and laughs heartily. I place it all to memory. Every laugh line, the tooth that is slightly crooked, the way his beard is greying in the middle, the hair that brushes across his brow in such a sexy way, the...

Dan interrupts my thoughts. "Tomorrow, nine, pack that bag and dress comfortably. We'll be on the bike for a few hours."

I suck my bottom lip between my teeth and nod shyly. "I can't wait."

He shakes me in his arms. "Damn, why is this so hard?" He leans down and kisses me. The old saying, *he made my knees weak*, yeah, I thought that was a myth too. Turns out it's possible. Holy moly.

When he pulls away, he opens my door. "Go on. Get out of here before I keep you up all night again."

I get in the driver's seat and smile up at him. "I didn't mind."

He bites his knuckles before shutting my door. He kisses the tips of his fingers and presses them to my window before waving me away.

What an amazing day. The only thing that would have made it better would have been if Jenny had been here.

Chapter Eighteen

Jenny ~ Nine Years Earlier

Sometimes, in life, we live for other people. That's what I did. I lived solely to keep my friend safe. Day in and day out I lived. But on the inside, I was dead. My body went through the motions while my mind lingered in the past. Back to when I was safe and sound. Back to when the world still looked innocent in my eyes.

I walked around freely, nobody realizing who I was. It was almost as if I was invisible. Sometimes, I wondered if I was already dead. How could person after person walk by me on the street and not see me. I guess it was for the best because if they had, my friend would be dead.

But then the Senator moved me into his home, and my faux freedom vanished.

For six days he didn't leave my side. When he finally did, he said he would be back in a few days. My freedom was temporarily returned to me, as long as I abided by his rules.

I walked out the front door as soon as his car pulled out of the driveway and I kept walking until I found myself here, looking out across the bay. It's so beautiful. So different from Los Angeles.

My fingers wrap around my necklace, fond memories rising to the surface of my mind. I quickly climb over the railing as a faint mist rolls in across the water. I can end the pain. Soon, it will all be over.

"I like your necklace," a quiet voice says above me.

I glance up to see Lily leaning over the railing. Her father introduced us a few days ago. It's the first time she's spoken to me. She must have followed me out of the house. "Thank you," I reply, my teeth chattering as the mist seeps into my bones.

Slowly, she lowers her hand down to me. "Did someone give it to you?" she asks calmly.

I nod. "A friend of mine gave it to me. He told me dragonflies have two sets of wings so they can carry angels on their backs." I'm shaking all over as fear filled adrenaline surges through my veins.

Lily lowers her other hand, wiggling her fingers in the air. "Maybe we could be each other's angel."

"Why do you need an angel?" I gasp as the cold wind whips my hair in my face. She looks like a princess. Then again, every princess has a villain in their story.

"Because I'm dead inside," she answers.

Same as me.

Lily's big brown eyes stare down at me.

She sees me.

And I see her.

I reach out and let her help me back over the railing.

We stare at each other for a long time, both of us struggling to catch our breath.

"We run," I say, holding my hand out to her.

She wraps her dainty fingers around mine. "We run."

Chapter Nineteen

Lily

Being with Dan almost makes me forget everything that happened back home. Almost. I hug him around the waist, reveling in the way his hard body feels pressed against mine. The rumble of the bike, the wind, the open road, and him. Him. Him. I take a deep breath, catching his masculine scent on the breeze.

We drive for a few hours, stopping once to use the restroom and to give me time to stretch my legs. When we get to our destination, my heart stops. It's a farm. Sunflower fields surround us.

"The Fall Festival has been going on here since I was a little kid," he tells me.

"I've never seen anything like this." My gaze roams over the parking lot. Families are pulling strollers out of the back of their cars, children dancing around excitedly. It's contagious.

Dan takes my hand and pulls me inside the gate. "Two please," he tells the woman in the ticket booth.

When I notice a big barn and what's outside, I squeal, "Baby goats!"

He laughs. "I guess we'll go see the goats first."

We walk hand in hand through the festival, stopping to pet all the animals. As the day winds down, we buy some kettle corn and find a quiet bench to sit and rest for a while.

"Thank you for bringing me here. I love it." My eyes dance over the fields as the sun drops low in the sky.

"You're very welcome," he says, leaning over to kiss me on my temple. He wraps his arm around me, pulling me close.

"Did you come here a lot as a kid?" I ask, shoving a handful of popcorn in my mouth.

"Every year."

"Do you have any siblings?"

"Nope but Dirk and Rachel are like siblings to me. Where was your favorite place to go as a child?" he asks, digging in the box for a handful of popcorn.

My eyes scan the horizon as I try to think of something, anything to tell him. "I liked to go to the bay."

"San Francisco Bay?"

"Yeah, my aunt and I used to hang out at the bridge."

"I've never been there. Maybe we should make a date of it." He squeezes my shoulder lightly.

"Oh, I don't know. I don't think I'll ever go back there," I tell him sadly. I decide to change the subject before I spoil the day. "What's your favorite color?"

He laughs. "Black."

I wrinkle my nose up.

"What's yours?" he asks.

"All of them."

"Why does that not surprise me?" He chuckles. "I thought you would say blue."

My hand pulls at a stray hair, I curl it around my finger. "What is your favorite food?"

"Easy. Steak. You?"

"I don't have a favorite. I'm still looking." I grin at him as the sun dips lower, making his eyes glow so much it warms me up.

"Interesting," he says, staring out at the fields. "It's good to be back here. I've missed it. My mom used to take me here every year. She would have loved you."

"I'm sorry." I lay my hand on his leg.

"She's not gone. Well, she is, and she isn't. She has early onset dementia." He stares out at the fields, the sun kissing the flowers with pink and purple highlights. "The last time I was here, she sat with me on this very bench and told me about her condition. I was so upset, so lost."

He pauses, clasping his hands in front of him. "Anyhow, she told me a story about sunflowers and how they always face the sun. I asked what happened when it was cloudy. She didn't hesitate. She said they face each other, becoming one another's sun."

"Oh, that's lovely." I place my hand over my heart.

He stares straight ahead. "You are my sunflower, Lily. When you walked into my shop, you turned my cloudy day into a bright, sunny, beautiful one."

My heartbeat slows as I stare at the side of his face. When his amber eyes turn my way, I hold my breath. The amber color reminds me so much of the sun that pulled me from the murky depths of the bay. "Dan," I whisper.

He runs his fingers through his beard and then looks at his hands. "You must think I'm a goddamn lunatic."

"No." I place my hand on the side of his face, pulling it toward me. "I don't think you're a lunatic at all."

"Are you sure? Because I feel like one. Goddammit, Lily, I'm so fucking high on you right now."

My hand falls away from his face.

"I'm sorry, shit, I shouldn't have said that." He stands, ready to walk away.

"Well, if you're a lunatic then so am I. Last night after we said goodbye, I missed you terribly. But there's a lot you don't know about me." I bite my lip and turn away from him.

He sits back down, pulling me onto his lap, not giving a care who might see us. "I want to know everything about you."

"I don't know, Dan. I want to forget everything before coming here."

"That can't be true. You wouldn't want to forget about your aunt, would you?"

I snuggle into him, reveling in the warmth he provides. "No, I suppose not. She was my bright spot."

"It's been two years since I've been home. Meeting you made me want to come back. I don't know why, like I said, you are my sunflower on a cloudy day. I felt like I could do it with you by my side."

"Is that where we are going after this? To your parent's house?" I wrap my arms around his neck, placing my forehead to his.

"If you'll go with me?" he asks hopefully.

"Yes, I'll go with you. Your mother sounds lovely."

"She won't recognize me," he says, pain etched into the space between his brows. I lean in and kiss him there, wanting to erase his hurt. My kisses become frantic as I place them all over his face. He grabs the hair at the base of my neck to stop me. He stares deep into my eyes. "Do you think you can kiss me better?"

A grin spreads across my face. "Is it working?"

The corner of his mouth turns up. "It's working too well." He grabs my hand and moves it over his growing erection.

"Oh, oh shit. I'm sorry," I yelp, pulling my hand away. "I didn't mean…"

He kisses me soundly on the mouth to shut me up.

Breathless, he leaves me breathless.

We finish the day with a hayrack ride out to the pumpkin patch. We purchase a few smaller ones, hoping we can fit them in his saddlebags.

When we get to his childhood home, I shake my hands out. I'm so nervous. Before we even get to the door, it swings open. A big guy as huge as Dan bursts through. He wraps his son up in his arms, picking him off the ground.

"Goddamn, boy, it's good to see you." He puts Dan on his feet and then turns to me. I brace myself for what's coming. Yep, soon I'm wrapped up in strong arms, my feet dangling in the air. Ouch, that really hurt my aching ribs, but I'm glad for it. It reminds me I'm alive.

"Oh, she's a tiny thing like your mother," he tells Dan, setting me back on my feet.

"Dad, this is Lily. Lily, this brute is my dad, Ray." Dan's eyes shine proudly over his father. A pang of jealousy sticks me in my heart.

"It's nice to meet you," I say softly.

Ray let's his eyes roam over my body, taking me in. When he's finished with his assessment, his gaze travels back to his son.

"How's mom?" Dan asks nervously.

"She's good, her health anyway. Mentally, well, it depends on the day." He motions for us to come inside. "Come on, let's go in and have supper. Your mom made all your favorites."

"She remembered?"

His dad pauses. "I may have nudged her in the right direction." He places his arm around Dan's shoulders when he notices the disappointment on his son's face. "She did remember how to make it. That's something to hold onto, kid."

"Yeah," Dan says sadly.

The house is cozy. There is a lot of biker memorabilia hanging on the walls. I pause to look at a photo of a small boy on a Harley, a young couple standing beside him with big grins on their faces. Awe, Dan was such a cutie.

"Don't be asking to see any butt naked pictures of me because there aren't any," Dan says over my shoulder, laughing.

"You were so cute," I tease.

The house is warm and smells like cinnamon. I close my eyes and try to imagine what growing up here would be like.

He grabs my hand and walks us into the kitchen. A petite woman with the most beautiful, white, flowing hair turns to look at us as she sets the table. Dan's father walks up behind her and wraps his arms around her waist. He whispers something in her ear. She smiles and dips her head.

Dan seems frozen in his spot, he gulps loudly. I squeeze his hand and we turn to face each other. Slowly, a smile grows on his handsome face. "Thank you, sunflower," he whispers. I nod and step forward.

148

"Everything smells so wonderful," I say to his mother.

She pulls herself away from her husband to move closer to me. Her eyes are the same color as Dan's and they bounce over my face, pausing on my hair. She reaches out and runs a stray piece through her fingers. "Your hair is beautiful," she says, not taking her eyes away from it.

"I think yours is beautiful too."

Her eyes dart to mine and she drops my hair to pat at her own. "I've thought about dying it, but he likes it this way." She glances over her shoulder shyly to look at her husband.

"I think he's right. It's beautiful just the way it is."

She suddenly notices Dan. "Who is your friend?" she asks me.

My heart breaks into a million shards when I realize she doesn't know her own son. I quickly recover, reaching back to grab Dan's hand and pull him forward.

"This is my boyfriend, Dan. Isn't he handsome?"

She studies him for a moment. "He's very handsome." She raises her eyebrows to me, smiling. "Nice to meet you, Dan." She holds her small hand out to him.

He takes it in his. "Lily is right, supper smells wonderful."

"I hope you like steak and potatoes." She pats his arm.

"Yes, ma'am, I sure do."

The meal is wonderful, and the conversation light. Dan's mom strays away from the conversation often, staring blankly at the wall opposite her. But then it's like someone flips a switch and she will comment on whatever we are talking about.

"Dan and I spent a wonderful day at the Harvest Festival," I tell her.

She blinks a few times. "The Harvest Festival?" she asks.

"Yes, it was gorgeous with all the sunflower fields. My favorite thing was the baby goats." I feel Dan's eyes on me, making me nervous. I hope I don't upset her in some way.

"Did you go for a hayrack ride?" she asks.

I notice Dan set his fork on his plate, sitting up taller in his chair.

"We did. Dan told me it was a family tradition to finish the day with a hayrack ride out to the pumpkin patch."

Her eyes slide to Dan and it's as if she just noticed him there. "Dan, when did you get home?" she asks, standing up and rushing to his side. Tears form in the corners of his eyes as he stands slowly.

He wraps her up in his arms. "Hi, mom, Lily and I just got here," he says softly.

My eyes meet Ray's across the table. He is watching his wife and son embrace. He turns to me, nodding his head in thanks. It wasn't me. I didn't do anything.

Dan's mom turns back to me. "Oh, honey, I don't think anyone properly introduced us. I'm Angela, it's so nice to meet you." She removes herself from Dan to shake my hand. "You're such a pretty little thing. Dan's never brought a girl home before. You must be special."

She reaches up and pinches his cheek. He blushes. Full out.

Angela pushes him back down in his seat. "I think I have chocolate cake for dessert. Eat, eat." She motions for him to keep eating. Rushing around the kitchen, she comes back with the cake, setting it down beside him. "It's your favorite," she coos, patting him on the head.

She sits back down and picks up her fork to finish her meal. Her eyes keep going back to him though, like she can't get enough of him.

The look of happiness on Dan's face brings me so much satisfaction. I want to make him happy like this every day.

Angela asks him a million questions. She even asks about Dirk and Rachel. Dan answers her excitedly like he's a kid home from college. Not that I know what that would be like, but that's how families act on tv. I guess he's had two years of stuff he's been dying to share with her.

My hand rubs over my chest, drawing her attention back to me. "Do you like the cake, sweetie?"

"Oh, it's wonderful. Would you mind sharing the recipe with me? I know I'll never be able to make it as good as yours, but I would love to try."

She hops up and grabs a pen and paper. Quickly, her hand glides over the paper as she tells me exactly how to do it. "The trick is to pull it out a few minutes before you think it's done."

When she slides it over to me, she glances from Dan back to me. "When is the wedding?" she asks, a serious look on her face.

151

I choke on my tea. Dan stutters, "Mom, we just met a week ago."

His dad laughs and leans over to give his wife a kiss. "How long did it take for you to marry my ass?" he asks her.

She giggles like a schoolgirl. "Two days," she says, staring longingly at her husband.

"Wow. You must have known right away." I lean back in my chair, my eyes darting to Dan who looks embarrassed by his mom's comment.

They stare at each other. "We did. The minute I saw this woman, I knew I wanted to spend the rest of my days with her. I didn't know what family was until I met her."

A lump forms in my throat as I watch them.

Dan holds my hand under the table. When I feel like I can keep the tears at bay, I glance at him. He smiles warmly before nodding his head toward them. "They used to embarrass me with all their public displays of affection, but I think I get it now."

Ray laughs and his mom blushes prettily at Dan's admission. "Were we that bad?" she asks.

"Yes. Yes, you were but it's fine. I grew up knowing what love looks like."

Where did this man come from? He says the most thought provoking, deep things. It's not normal. I've never met a man like him.

"I think a winter wedding would be wonderful," his mom teases.

"Mom," he scolds. "You're going to scare her off."

152

I laugh at this. "If I was going to get scared off, I think it would have happened when you threatened to rip body parts off of anyone who looked at me."

His dad roars with laughter.

Angela tsks, "So, much like your father." But she smiles at him with so much love that even I can feel it.

"In my defense, men were ogling her like a bunch of vultures. I was only trying to protect her.

His mom's eyes soften at the corners. "I know you'll protect her, you're a good boy, Dan."

We finish the evening off by carving pumpkins. While Dan and his mom are out lighting them on the porch, his dad pours us a glass of wine. "I'm glad Dan finally found his way home."

I shift nervously on the couch. He hands me a glass.

"I know it's hard on him when she doesn't remember." He takes a drink and sighs. "She may not notice his absence but boy, I sure do."

"Maybe he's finally coming to terms with her condition," I offer, not sure what to say.

"Maybe it's you." He taps his glass on his knee.

"Oh, I can't take the credit. He asked me to come with him. I didn't suggest it."

His gaze slides over my face. "You haven't mentioned your family."

Wringing my hands nervously in my lap, I think of how to respond. "I don't really have a family."

He nods his head slowly. "Does Dan feel like family?" he asks me seriously.

Tears escape my eyes without permission. "He feels like home."

"And home is family," he says quietly. The screen door creaks open. Dan and his mom's laughter wafts down the hallway. "You know, even on the days she doesn't remember me, she never seems frightened. Her mind might not remember me, but her soul sure does."

Okay, now I see where Dan gets it. I wipe my eyes as they join us. Not only does my heart want Dan, but it also wants his friends, his family... I want it all.

After we each finish our wine, I notice Angela starting to stare off again. "You ready for bed, sweetheart?" Ray asks her.

"Do I sleep here?" she asks him, confused.

Dan tenses next to me.

Ray kneels in front of her, taking her hands in his. "You do. I'm a lucky guy because you and I are roommates."

Her head drops and she hides behind her silver hair, giggling. "I don't even know you," she says shyly.

"But you want to, don't you?" he asks, full out flirting with his wife.

She nods, holding her hand out to him. He pulls her out of the chair and twirls her around the living room a few times, leading her in a silent dance. Her eyes lock on him and I see what he means. She may not remember she is married to this man, but she loves him none the less.

Ray hollers over his shoulder, "See you two in the morning."

"Goodnight," I answer as they disappear into their bedroom.

Dan doesn't say anything, he doesn't even move. After several minutes of silence, I slide onto his lap, straddling him. I wrap my arms around his neck and hug him tight. His body trembles as he tries to keep his emotions from spilling out. "I've got you," I whisper in his ear. "I won't let you fall."

He tightens his grip around me. We stay like this for a long, long time. Eventually, he pushes me off his lap gently. We quietly make our way into his room. He closes the door behind us. It's dark as we undress each other. Both of us need to feel the other, skin to skin, soul to soul.

We slide into his bed and cling to each other. Whatever is happening between the two of us is strange, it's powerful, it's wonderful. I left home, hoping to forget the past, to find a new home, maybe discover who I was… I never expected this. *Please, please don't take it away from me.*

Chapter Twenty

Dan

Sometimes, you go through life on autopilot. That was what I did until I met Jesse. She opened my heart a tiny bit. Just enough for Lily to slip through. Now it's been blown clean open. I'm fucking terrified.

If I hadn't met Jesse first, I don't know that I would have paid Lily much attention. I had a one-track mind. Work, work, work. Then Jesse reminded me how much I needed people in my life. Friends and family.

It was not quite a year ago that I sat on the dock, watching dragonflies dart over the lake. I pulled out my sketch book and went to work, thinking about the dragonfly story Raffe had once told me. I wished and prayed I would meet someone. Maybe someone as sweet as my mother.

Then Lily showed up wanting a dragonfly tattoo. If that's not fate, then I don't know what the fuck is. Lily has a kind soul. She has a way with people. Especially, people who are different. Jackson, JD… my mom. God, seeing how she interacted with my mother made my chest ache.

I need to learn everything there is to know about her. Bits and pieces are all I get. I want more.

My crazy ass wants to storm the walls around her heart and then stick my flag in it, effectively claiming it for myself.

When we woke up this morning, she insisted I go to breakfast with my dad. She stayed at the house with my mom, and they baked cinnamon rolls. My dad was ecstatic to spend the morning with me. I guess I hadn't really thought about how all this affected him.

I found Lily and my mom going through scrapbooks when we returned. They were both laughing and drinking coffee at the table. I thought maybe my mom would remember me, but she didn't. That's not entirely true, she remembered, but she thought I was ten. She kept asking my dad if it was time to pick me up from school.

When we left, I promised my dad I would come home more often. He said he would like to come visit me too but wasn't sure how mom would react away from her familiar surroundings.

If it weren't for Lily, I don't know if I would have gone home. With her by my side, I felt like I could do it. I can't explain it. I just know that she brings peace to my heart.

"You sure you're okay?" she asks as I drop her off at her house.

"Yeah, thanks for going with me."

"It was so much fun, and I loved meeting your family." Her smile drops, she turns away from me, hoping I don't notice but I do. I notice everything about her.

"Hey, what's wrong?"

"I wish I had a family for you to meet." Her big brown eyes swim in sadness. It breaks my big fucking heart.

"Maybe someday you'll feel strong enough to go back home. It took me two years to visit my parents."

She shakes her head feverishly back and forth. "No. No, I'm never going back there. I'm sorry you'll never meet them. I'll never share you with them. They don't deserve to know someone like you."

The night we spent at the bar she told me a little about them. How they were never home. There seems to be more going on than absent parents. Something that scares her. I don't like it.

"I'm perfectly okay with you keeping me all to yourself," I tease, grabbing her around the waist and pulling her close to me. "Can I come over tonight?" I whisper in her ear.

She giggles. Thoughts of her family long gone. "Yes, but I have to work till nine."

I growl, biting her neck. She leans her head to the side to give me more access. Her hands fist my shirt, and she makes the cutest little mewling sound. "I hate that you're working at the bar," I tell her honestly once I remove my teeth from her flawless skin.

"Dan, I need something to do for a while. I can't sit here all day doing nothing." She puts her hand on her hip, stomping her little foot.

"Okay, but if I don't think it's safe, then that's it, you're done."

Her eyes narrow. "Why wouldn't it be safe?"

I laugh and back away from her. "It's a bar, sweetheart, they'll be all kinds of jokers in there."

She chews on her nail, thinking about it. "I love that you are worried about me, but I want to do this. At least until I find my passion."

"How about I come at closing, just to make sure you get home safe?" I dip my head to catch her eyes.

She smiles and holds out her hand. "Deal." I take her hand but instead of shaking on it, I jerk her close and lean down to kiss her, putting as much as I have into it. God, she tastes like heaven.

When I pull away, her fingers dance across her lips. "Jesus, Dan," she says breathlessly. "What were we talking about?"

I swat her on the ass. "See you tonight."

She leans against the door frame, waving as I pull out of the driveway.

When I get to the shop, Raffe and Jesse both look up.

Pointing to Raffe, I drop my leather jacket on the hook by the door. "Soon, you're going to run out of room just like Dirk has."

He shrugs. "I needed some relief."

Jesse gives me a look as I lean over to see what they're doing.

"What's going on?" I ask him.

"I don't know, man." He lays his head back on the chair, watching Jesse trail her needle over the empty space above his knee. "I've been thinking about the past a lot lately."

159

I sit down, concern creeping up my spine. Raffe has an ugly past. He's one of the reasons we do our run a couple of times a year. He was a victim of trafficking.

"Anything I can help with?"

"Naw, I'm sure I'll pull myself out of the funk. Being here is already helping." He closes his eyes, so I leave him to his thoughts and busy myself drawing up a design for a customer I have coming in later today.

Jesse smacks her gum between her teeth. "How was your date?"

Raffe's eyes open, suddenly interested in our conversation again.

"Good."

"Where did you take her?" she asks while focusing on Raffe's leg.

"Home."

She stops her gun and both she and Raffe stare at me with their mouths hanging open.

"What?"

"You took her home? Like to your parent's house?" Raffe asks, rubbing his hand across the stubble on his jaw.

I nod, concentrating on my work. I'm slightly embarrassed, I don't know why.

"Dan, that's great. How's your mom?" Jesse asks, scooting her stool over to me. She pulls her gloves off and places her hand over one of mine, effectively forcing me to stop what I'm doing.

Reluctantly, I face her. "She's okay." I try to go back to my work, but she isn't having it. She keeps her eyes locked on me, waiting for more.

"She's doing as good as can be expected. My dad was happy to see me."

Jesse senses my guilt. "We all have to go at our own speed, Dan."

I nod. "Lily told them how we had spent the day at the Harvest Festival, and it sparked something in Mom. She remembered me."

Jesse puts her hand over her heart, glancing back at Raffe. He blinks, swallowing hard.

"Dan, how wonderful for you," Jesse says in awe.

"It was amazing. I talked her leg off. I gave her a condensed version of the past two years." I smile, thinking about how good it felt to have my mom listen to me again.

"Jesus, Dan, I'm so happy for you," Raffe says quietly.

"Anyhow, I'm going to try to go home more often. We even talked about them coming to visit here."

Jesse smiles. "That would be fucking awesome."

"Get back to work," I grumble, done talking about this.

She laughs but obeys, going back to work on Raffe. The rest of the afternoon drags on. I find myself watching the clock. Minutes never moved so fucking slow.

But as soon as I pull into the parking lot at the bar, time seems to go back to its normal speed.

When I step inside, Lily immediately turns her head my way while still talking to the customer in front of her. A beautiful smile breaks out over her face.

I walk over and take a seat at the end of the bar, nodding at the patrons I'm familiar with. Lily finishes with the customer she was helping, then makes her way down to me. "Hey, stranger. What can I get for you?" She winks at me, sending blood pumping straight to my cock.

I growl, leaning over the bar, inhaling her sugary scent. "I'll take one of these." I place my lips to hers, not giving a fuck who's watching.

She smiles against my lips. So fucking sweet.

When I pull away and settle back on my stool, she swipes a bar towel over the counter, giving me the most tantalizing view of her tits. That's great and all but everyone else is getting the same view. "That will be twenty dollars." She smirks, narrowing her eyes at me. Her tongue sneaks out to run over her top lip.

Laughing, I look down the bar toward Bill. He shakes a finger at me in warning. I ignore him and turn back to Lily. "What time do you get off, sweetheart?"

She looks at her imaginary watch. "In five," she says, tossing the bar towel over her shoulder. She grabs a beer out of the cooler, pops the cap, and slides it in front of me.

Lily braces her arms on the counter, watching as I bring the bottle up to my lips. She blinks slowly, her lashes brushing seductively over her soft skin.

162

"How bout I give you a ride home?" I run the pad of my thumb over my bottom lip. Her eyes trace the movement, her breath slowing.

"I don't usually let strangers take me home."

"No?" I tip my head, carefully studying her reactions. She likes this. The role playing is turning her the fuck on.

"What if I fuck you in the parking lot, then we won't be strangers anymore?"

Her eyes widen, clearly unused to such crass talk. She recovers quickly. She walks away from me, but I can tell she's still playing the game as her hips swing from side to side. Lily glances at me over her shoulder, offering me an innocent smile. It fucking makes my balls ache. Jesus.

Lily takes her apron off as she speaks to Bill. He nods, smiling. He hands her a timecard, and she writes on it, pausing to give me a quick once over before she goes back to it. She hands it to Bill. He gives her a quick hug, looking at me over her shoulder. I see him whisper in her ear. When he releases her, her cheeks are rosy red. Fucking Bill.

She grabs her keys off the back counter and heads out the door, not saying a fucking word to me. Bill shrugs before roaring with laughter. Glad we've been a source of entertainment for the fucker.

I place a twenty on the bar and follow her outside. She's fumbling with the keys of her car. Is she trying to run from me? But then I see the corner of her mouth tip up. She's fucking playing with me.

We'll see how far she wants to take this. I sneak up and grab her from behind, wrapping my hand over her mouth to stifle her scream. My arm sneaks around her middle like a vice, pinning her to my hard body.

I lean down whispering into her ear, "This is why they teach little girls like you not to talk to strangers."

Lily breathes heavily through her nose. Her pulse jumping visibly in her neck.

She shifts her feet, gravel crunching beneath her sneakers. My cock strains painfully against her ass. I close my eyes, savoring the feel of her helpless in my arms. "If I uncover your mouth, are you going to scream, sweetheart?"

She shakes her head no.

I slide my hand from her mouth, dropping it lightly across her throat. Thump. Thump. Thump. Her pulse beats fast beneath my palm.

"I'm going to fuck you, just like I promised, then I'm going to take you home and fuck you some more." I feel her swallow and my cock jerks in response. Sweet little Lily is perfect. Fucking perfect.

Chapter Twenty-One

Lily

Fuck this is hot. The fact that this turns me on is somewhat humiliating. Especially, since… fuck don't think about that now. Dan growls in my ear as he drags me to the back of my car. He grabs my hands, pulling them to the top of my vehicle.

"Don't you dare fucking move them," he tells me.

My pussy clenches at his demand. He kicks my feet, forcing me to spread my legs wide for him. His big hands slide up my thighs, pushing my jean skirt over my hips. I glance around, suddenly worried someone might see us.

He tsks in my ear as he unbuckles his belt. "Eyes closed," he demands, pushing my panties aside with a finger. His beard brushes across my cheek. "Mmm," he moans. "So fucking wet for me."

My legs shake, his praise sending an abundance of endorphins through my system. I wonder if anyone is watching but my eyes are closed, so I don't know. Fuck if that doesn't excite me.

I'm living. I feel so fucking alive. I moan, rolling my forehead over the back window as he slides into me from behind. He thrusts hard and fast, rolling my clit between his finger and thumb. It feels so fucking good.

He grips my hip almost painfully as he comes inside of me. I come right along with him, groaning my release against the window, my breath steaming over the glass.

"Fuck, Lily." He rests his forehead between my shoulder blades, bracing his arms on either side of my head.

When I glance around to see if anyone saw us, he raises his head from my back. "I wouldn't have let anyone see you," he says, turning my face toward him.

"I know," I whisper, turning in his arms. I wrap my fist in his t-shirt and tug on it. "I guess we're not strangers anymore." He laughs and swats me on the ass.

"Go on." He steps away from me, tucking himself back in his pants. He waves his hand toward my beetle as I yank my skirt back into place. "I'll follow you." He waits until I get inside my car before tossing his leg over his bike.

Dan kept his word, fucking me all night long. When he finally lets me rest, I fall into a deep sleep.

I stretch happily in my bed and then I hear one of them. Oh no. I get up, tiptoeing across the house to the other wing. The crying gets louder the closer I get to the locked door. It's always locked, but I still check every time on the off chance it will open.

Of course, it's locked. My heart beats loudly as I stand in my princess jammies, listening to the girl whimper on the other side of the door. I want to help her. I'd go wake daddy to help but he's never in his room and the servants just shoo me back to my bed, telling me I'm hearing things.

Maybe I'm dreaming. It's just the same dream, that's all. I turn to run back to my room when I hear him.

He's in there with the girl? I drop to my knees on the plush carpet, trying to peek underneath the door. I can't see anything.

"Shh, stop crying, sweetie," my daddy says. He makes a weird sound.

I don't like it.

I don't like it.

Jumping to my feet, I cover my hand over my mouth, trying to stop the vomit that seeps through my fingers.

The door swings open. Daddy only has a pair of pants on, unbuttoned and hanging loose. He closes the door quickly, not giving me a chance to see who's crying. "What are you doing up, Lily?" he scolds. He's angry.

"I... I don't feel so good." I pretend I didn't hear anything.

He sighs, turning me toward the bathroom. He busies himself, turning on the shower as I wash my hands in the sink. "Get in the shower and rinse yourself off." He walks out of the bathroom not looking at me.

When I finish, I see he has placed a clean set of pajamas on the counter for me. I dress quickly. When I open the door, he is leaning against the wall, running his hands through his hair. It makes him look scary. I've never seen him with a hair out of place.

"Feeling better?" he asks.

I nod, dropping my eyes to the floor. My ears strain for any sign of the crying girl but it's quiet now.

"Let's get you back to bed."

I startle awake, running to the bathroom. Leaning over the toilet, I cover my ears trying to silence the crying. It never goes away. It's become a white noise in the background of my life. Sometimes, it's quiet but it's never gone. Rocking back and forth, I try not to get sick. "Stop crying, stop crying, stop crying," I whisper my chant to the porcelain bowl.

A warm hand touches my back, making me jump. "It's just me, Lily," Dan says quietly, removing his hand from my back.

Shit, I forgot he was here. My eyes drop back to the toilet, praying for this to be part of my nightmare. But it's not. His warm hand lands on my back again. He rubs circles over it until my heartbeat slows, the nausea retreats and the crying crawls back to the corner of my mind.

I sit back on my haunches and take his hand, allowing him to pull me upright. I scoot over to the sink and splash some cold water on my face. When I stand to pat my face dry, my eyes connect with his in the mirror.

He frowns. "Do you want to talk about it?"

I shake my head no. "It was nothing, just a nightmare," I tell him, tucking the towel back onto the rack I pulled it from.

When we climb back into bed, he pulls me into a spooning position. His hot breath rushes over my ear as he leans in. "Lily, I want to know everything about you. Not to punish you but so I can understand how to love you." He squeezes me, his lips brushing the shell of my ear. "I want to love you. Please let me love you."

I choke on a sob, letting him comfort me in his arms. "I want to tell you everything. I just don't know how," I murmur softly into my pillow.

"That's okay," he says quietly. "As long as you don't shut me out."

"I'm afraid you'll hate me." Another sob escapes me.

He presses his mouth to my temple, speaking against it. "I could never hate you."

I try to shake my head and pull away from him, but he doesn't release me. Instead, he growls and wraps one of his big legs across me. "I. Will. Never. Hate. You," he says almost angrily, seemingly insulted that I could even think such a thing.

He relaxes when I cease my struggle. "Tell me what your nightmare was about?" he suggests softly.

I close my eyes and fall. "When I was young, I heard girls," I pause, thinking about it, "sometimes, women, crying."

"Why were they crying?" he asks, holding me tight.

"I think my dad was hurting them." He stiffens behind me, but he doesn't move away.

"Lily, why do you think that?" His finger brushes over my stomach in a relaxing motion. He's trying to keep me calm and talking.

"He was the only one in there with them." I bite the inside of my cheek.

"Did he hurt you?" he asks gently.

I shake my head no.

"You're wrong," he whispers, turning me over so he can stare down at me. "He did hurt you. By hurting them, he hurt you." He closes his eyes and when he opens them, I see how much he hurts for me. So much pain… will it ever end?

Chapter Twenty-Two

Lily

J D seemed surprised that I called. I need something to take my mind off things. "So, this is my tailgate section." He points to a piece of land lined with tailgate after tailgate. All types, colors, and condition.

"Wow." I glance around the junkyard. Everything is so organized. Not what I expected a junkyard to be.

"See anything you like?"

I step between them, looking for the perfect one. When I find a gold Ford tailgate, I point to it, jumping up and down. "This is it!" I exclaim.

He laughs and helps me carry it up to the front. As we're walking, I notice some cool gear looking thingies. We set the tailgate down and I ask him, "What are those?" I point to the box filled with them.

"Sprockets. They go on motorcycles." He walks over and picks one up. "They turn the chain."

"I love them," I say, running my finger over the cold metal.

He laughs. "You're a strange girl."

I smile up at him.

"I mean that in a good way," he adds quickly.

As I stare at the sprockets, an idea comes to mind. "Hey, Dan told me there is an auction this weekend after the run. He asked me to paint a picture and donate it, but I think I have a better idea. Do you know anything about electricity?" I ask, raising my eyebrows.

"Enough to not get myself zapped. Let's hear this idea."

I tell him and we set to work. "These are so fucking cool, Lily. I might even bid on them myself."

"Why? We can always make more," I tell him, wiping my brow with the back of my hand.

He stops what he's doing to stare at me. "Yeah, we could, couldn't we?" J.D. smiles shyly, turning his ballcap backwards. He dips his head and gets back to work. He glances at me from time to time, like he can't believe I'm really working beside him.

The rest of the week flies by. The excitement of the run not only pulsed through my veins but through the entire club. I've gotten to know a few of them as they come into the bar for a drink or to grab a burger. I tell you; Mama Bear makes the best burgers I've ever had.

I bet I've gained fifteen pounds since coming here. Dan seems to appreciate it. He comes every night to make sure I get home safely.

Sometimes, he stays with me, other times, he walks me to the door and kisses me goodnight.

We both struggle on those nights. I hate being away from him and I know he feels the same. It's only been a few weeks, but I feel like I've lived here my entire life. I never want to leave and if I had it my way, Dan would be in my bed every single night.

Jesse knocks on my door the morning of the run. "Hey, Jesse, what are you doing here?" I wave to Dirk who is sitting on his bike smoking a cigarette.

"I wanted to bring this by." She drops a leather jacket in my hands.

My fingers curl around the soft leather. "Jesse," I whisper. I don't know much about the biker culture but I'm sure this must be a great honor.

"JD brought over the sprocket lamps you guys made. He was gushing, Lily. JD doesn't gush."

I laugh lightly. "He was pretty proud of them."

"They are perfect. I'm sure they'll bring a pretty penny. Bikers love that kind of shit," she says, looking over her shoulder at Dirk before turning her eyes back to me. "Anyhow, you're part of this club and you deserve it."

"Oh, Jesse. I don't even know where I would fit into the club. I'm honored but…" she cuts me off.

"You don't have to be like us to be one of us." She shrugs. "You're the color, Lily." She turns, taking a step off the porch. "See you on the road."

I watch as she shoves a helmet over her long, silky, black hair. Dirk salutes me and they are off.

My eyes drop to the jacket in my hand. I hold it up, smiling at the patches on the back. There are two. One says Property of Big Dan, the other is the Rebel Skull logo. Dan pulls in as I'm standing there, squeezing the life out of it like an idiot. How embarrassing.

He laughs as he shuts the bike off. "You know, I was supposed to give you that." He points to my new prized possession. "Jesse said she found you, so it was her right."

"You don't agree?"

Climbing the steps slowly, he smiles at me. "This is a big deal in our club. It's equivalent to a marriage."

I swallow, staring at him. "But..."

He holds up his hand. "I don't care about your past. We'll get through all that, eventually. Nothing you tell me will change anything."

"Aren't you supposed to get down on one knee or something?" I tease shyly, pulling the jacket up to cover my mouth.

He takes the last step and drops to one knee. Dan hugs me around the waist, pressing his face into my stomach. "Will you please wear my patch?" he mumbles into my t-shirt.

Sliding my arms through the sleeves of the jacket, I answer him. He gazes up at me, happiness swimming in the amber liquid of his eyes.

As I'm riding on the back of Dan's bike, I allow my mind to run through my life these past few weeks. I'm changing. I feel the shift. I'm on the other side of the glass, living, breathing, loving. I cut the last tie to my father yesterday.

I drove to a bank in a neighboring town and transferred every last penny into Jesse's charity account. I didn't want anyone to know it was from me. JD asked Jesse for the account information, promising me he wouldn't tell anyone who made the anonymous donation. I didn't tell him how much I was donating. I told him I had a little money left over from my previous life and I really wanted to help. I downplayed it as best I could. He seemed to accept that I didn't want the attention and that is true, so it wasn't really a deception. At least that's what I'm telling myself.

Being on the back of Dan's bike is freeing. I let go of Dan for a second, spreading my arms out wide. I'm free yet secure in the fact I have Dan and his entire club at my back. I pull my arms in and grab him around the waist tightly. Insecurity is taking over my thoughts.

Do I really have them? Is it an illusion? What if they knew who I was? What if they learned my secrets?

Chapter Twenty-Three

Lily

The charity run ends at the warehouse. I've never seen this many bikes in one place before. Dan drapes his arm around my shoulder as we walk through the items that are up for auction. The whole day has been about having fun and raising as much money for Jesse's charity as we can.

Dirk stands up on the back of a flatbed trailer. Before he starts the auction, he invites any survivors of sexual assault up onto the stage. I blink back tears as people start forward, Dirk reaches down to help pull them up beside him. Raffe and Jesse go up right away. Then Jesse's little sister, Katie, joins them.

Dan's gaze rests heavily upon my face. I don't dare turn toward him. My feet are frozen in place, my heart about to burst out of my chest. Dirk's eyes graze the crowd, stopping on me. I lower my head. I know what he thinks, what Dan thinks, but no one hurt me.

I wait until the bidding starts before I excuse myself to use the restroom. Dan walks me up to the warehouse. It's beautiful inside. "Is this where you live?" I ask him.

"Yep. Some of us live here. A few come and go. Dirk is the president, so he and Jesse are here most of the time.

I follow him upstairs. He opens the door to what I am assuming is his room. "The bathroom is right there." He points to a door on the right.

Dan is so organized. Everything has a place. I stifle a giggle as I take in the skull toothbrush holder. When I walk out, he is sitting on his bed, waiting for me. "Ready to go back down?" he asks, tipping his head. My gaze travels over the ink on the side of his neck. I want to lick him there.

He smirks as if he can read my mind. "You want to stay here with me tonight, honey?" He pats his bed.

My heart rejoices at the thought of staying here with him. I nod, smiling shyly.

He stands, taking a step toward me. He grabs my hand and squeezes it. "We better get back down there. I want to be first in line for the food."

JD runs up to us as soon as we walk out onto the patio. "Lily, our lamps brought a hundred dollars each!" he exclaims.

"Awe, that's great," I tell him as he picks me up off my feet, hugging me tight. When he sets me down, everyone is staring at us, but he doesn't even notice he's so excited.

"Hey, I'm going to go grab a bite, but I'll see you tomorrow morning and we can work on your porch swing."

"That sounds great. See you then." I watch as he grabs a hot dog off a tray before darting inside.

Dan rubs his jaw. "You sure have him fired up. I've never seen him so excited about anything."

"He and I see the world the same. Where some see junk, we see beauty." I sit down in one of the lounge chairs, looking out toward the lake. It's so beautiful here.

Dirk comes out of the warehouse, his eyes homed in on Dan. He waves him over. "You okay here for a minute? Looks like Dirk is calling a meeting. Shouldn't be long."

"Yeah, I'm perfect," I tell him, kicking my feet up on the rail surrounding the patio. Rachel walks over and hands me a glass of wine.

Dan shakes his finger. "Don't get her drunk," he warns, winking at her.

"Boo." She flips him the bird before taking her boots off and tucking her feet under her.

Dan kisses me on the forehead and then disappears inside the warehouse.

"Did you have fun today?" Rachel asks, taking a sip of her wine, smacking her lips together.

"I had the best time," I say dreamily.

Jackson runs up to us, holding his bug catcher. He thrusts it in my face, tears running down his chubby little cheeks. "It's gone," he cries.

My feet drop to the patio. I sit forward, peering into the catcher. "Oh, Jackson, he's not gone. He's just in a chrysalis."

Jackson sets it on the table between his mom and me. He chokes on a sob, wiping snot all over the sleeve of his shirt. "What's that?" he asks, hiccupping.

"See right there, hanging on the branch?"

He nods, lowering himself onto his knees to peer inside.

"The caterpillar is in there. It protects him while he grows."

He looks at his mom and she nods in agreement.

"How long is he going to be in there?" he asks, his interest piqued.

"At least ten days, maybe a little longer." I smile at him. "You must have taken good care of him."

He nods proudly, his brown hair flopping over his eyes. My fingers brush it away. "He isn't going to look the same when he comes out though. He's growing into a butterfly."

Jackson's eyes go wide. "That sounds like magic," he says in awe.

"Not magic. It's science," I correct but then I add, "It is pretty amazing though, isn't it?"

He nods. "I'm going to go show daddy." He hops up, grabs the catcher and zips inside.

Rachel watches him before turning her eyes back to me. "He talked about you non-stop for the first two hours we were home the other night. Lily this, Lily that." She laughs lightly before bringing her glass to her lips.

"I'm sorry."

"No, don't be sorry. We haven't seen Jackson stay on one thing for more than two seconds. One afternoon with you and he's been carrying that bug catcher with him everywhere."

Raffe joins us, laughing. "Your son needs his mom," he says, plopping his butt down in the chair on the other side of me.

Rachel drops her feet to the ground, shoving them back into her boots. She sticks her tongue out at him.

"Hey, it's your turn." Raffe rubs his hands together like he won the lottery.

Rachel starts to walk away but stops. "What am I getting myself into?"

"It's better if it's a surprise," Raffe answers, blowing her a kiss.

She huffs and walks off.

He raises his eyebrows and leans over, whispering, "Jackson opened a new box of cereal, and that shit went every-fucking-where."

I laugh, covering my mouth.

He continues, "We take turns cleaning up after him. It's pretty much a twenty-four-seven job."

I hear Rachel yell from inside, "Jackson!"

He comes running out, hiding under the table, shoving a handful of dry cereal into his mouth.

Chuckling, I turn back to Raffe. He's staring at my necklace again. He glances away quickly. "Hey, Rachel and I were talking, would Wednesday evenings work for you to hang out with Jackson? We could meet here or bring him over to your place."

My fingers trail over the silver dragonfly. "Yeah, that would work fine for me. I'm excited. I have some ideas of things we can work on together."

He watches my fingers. "Great. We'll plan on it." He leans forward to get a better look at my necklace.

I shift uncomfortably in my chair.

"I'm sorry. My friend had one just like it. I've never seen another." He rubs his hand over his chest, his face dropping.

My heart stutters as I study him. No. Nope. Couldn't be. I shake my head to clear my thoughts.

"Maybe it's just because I've been thinking about her a lot today with the charity run and all. She and I were trafficked. I haven't seen her since the day they separated us," he says sadly.

I swallow hard as I listen to his story. He is heartbreakingly beautiful. Blond hair, blue eyes, straight nose, high cheek bones. Doesn't mean anything though. No. Nope. Can't be.

"I gave her the necklace on her fourteenth birthday. She had it on when…" his words trail as he watches Katie and Bill head down to the dock with fishing poles in their hands. "Anyhow, she was such a free spirit. I've looked for her, but I've hit a dead end every time."

I'm blinking back tears, hoping he doesn't notice. This can't be happening. There is no way. No way. There are over three hundred twenty-eight million people in the United States. For me to end up here…

I run my finger over my little flip phone.

I could show him.

Then he would tell me it's not her.

It can't be her.

He leans forward again. "May I?" he asks.

I nod slowly, dropping my hand from the pendant. Raffe reaches out and traces his finger over it. "Damn, I miss her," he whispers. He's caught up in his own emotions, not noticing the turmoil running through my veins. "Jenny, where the fuck are you?" he asks the little dragonfly. He rubs his hand over his eyes, sliding back into his seat.

No.

No.

My heart beats wildly in my chest.

Jackson runs up. "Lily. Lily. Lily. Let's go see the dragonflies," he begs.

Raffe opens his eyes, locking on my tear-filled ones.

Hastily, I rise from my chair, stumbling. Jackson grabs my hand and pulls me down the hill toward the lake. I glance back at Raffe. He stands slowly as his gaze trails us.

"There are so many, Lily. You will see," little Jackson rambles on.

We walk past Bill and Katie. They smile at us.

"I'm showing her the dragonflies," Jackson tells them, proudly puffing up his chest.

He jumps up and down, pointing over the water when we reach the end of the dock. "See! I told you," he squeals excitedly.

My heart squeezes painfully as my eyes drop to the little boy beside me. Oh god. I choke on a sob, anxiety flooding my system.

The dragonflies dart over the dark water of the lake. I close my eyes, trying to stop my racing thoughts but it's too much. I open my eyes, seeing a different time, a different day.

The water looks so peaceful. Wouldn't it be easier?

I barely notice Jackson tugging on my hand.

That's why she left. It was easier. Maybe I should join her. I thought I could hide but where do you hide from memories?

"Uncle Bill, somethings wrong with Lily," Jackson yells, it's muffled… he sounds so far away.

Far away.

Far away.

I lean forward, wanting to reach out and run my hands through the ripples in the water when someone wraps an arm around me.

"Katie, take Jackson back up to the house and get Dan," Bill rasps.

I struggle to free myself so I can fall. All I need to do is fall. Please, just let me fall. Maybe this time it won't hurt.

"Lily, honey, look at me," Bill says, trying to turn me away from the water.

My body feels heavy, my mind foggy, my heart broken, my soul lost.

"I wasn't jumping," I whisper to the dragonflies. "I was falling, falling, falling," I repeat.

Someone grabs my face, turning it toward the sun.

My sun.

Amber eyes draw me closer and closer until I come up for air, gasping.

Dan pulls me into his chest, allowing me to collapse in his arms. "What is going on?" he breathes into my hair.

I roll my head back and forth over his solid chest.

Jesse runs her hand over my hair, standing behind me. "Lily, talk to us, girl."

"I… I'm not feeling very well. Can you take me home, please?" I sob into Dan's shirt.

"No," Dirk says from somewhere to the side of us. "She stays."

Oh god. They are going to hate me.

"I agree," Raffe says quietly in the background.

I cry harder.

Dan squeezes me. "Let's go up to my room, baby."

184

"No, I just need to go home," I hiccup.

"Not happening, sweetheart." Dan scoops me up in one swift motion and carries me inside. It's alarming that he can carry me like I weigh nothing more than a feather. I hide my face in his neck so that I don't have to see their faces. They must think I'm crazy.

I am. I am crazy. I cry and cry and cry until he dumps me on his bed.

Scurrying to the headboard, I curl myself up in a little ball.

I tap on the wood of his headboard with my finger as I listen to the voices murmuring in the hallway. None of what they say makes it clear to my ears.

If I can get Dan to take me home, then I can pack and be on the road by dark.

Why would she have led me here? Why?

The door clicks shut quietly. The bed dips with his weight. He doesn't say anything.

I wipe furiously at my eyes, angry that I let myself fall apart in front of everyone. Every fucking one.

"I'll always be your sun, Lily," Dan says, breaking the silence.

"Please take me home, Dan," I plead.

"Is this about your dad?"

My head falls against the headboard. "Dan, please."

"Did he hurt you?" he asks, deadly calm.

"He didn't hurt me!" I yell, jumping from the bed. "Don't you see? He hurt them. He hurt them and I didn't' do anything to help."

I grip my hair tightly. Wanting it to hurt. Needing it to hurt.

"He hurt *her*," I scream, falling to the floor. The pain is too much. Too much.

Dan sits down on the floor, leaning his back against the bed. He pulls me onto his lap. I try to push away but his tree trunk sized arms lock me down tight, my back pressed against his chest. He speaks gently into my ear, "I'm not going anywhere, Lily. We are going to get through whatever this is, together."

"He hurt her." I moan. There is nowhere to run. Nowhere to hide. Dan is forcing me to succumb to the pain. It's almost unbearable.

A knock on the door makes my heart stop. It's him. I know it's him.

"It's not locked," Dan hollers over his shoulder.

The door creaks open and soft footsteps come to a stop beside us. Raffe lowers himself to the floor in front of me. He doesn't say anything right away, he just looks at me as I try to reign in my emotions.

"Do you know Jenny?" he asks after I've settled down.

I don't answer. My heart is being torn to shreds as I think about losing these people, this place. But I can't lie. I'm a terrible liar. Jenny always said so.

Before I can speak, Dan answers Raffe's question. "Jenny is her aunt."

Raffe glances from Dan back to me. His brows furrow in confusion. His pain is raw and visible as he reconciles with the fact that his Jenny and mine are not the same person.

But they are.

Oh god, they are.

Chapter Twenty-Four

Jenny ~ 9 years earlier

"Will you tell me what he does to you?" Lily asks me.

"Never," I answer simply, drawing the brush over the nail on her ring finger. I cap the bottle, then reach for the next color.

"Maybe I could go to the police." She watches me shake the bottle before I reach for her hand again.

She lays her dainty hand in my palm. I glide the bright purple color over the next fingernail in line. "He told me has the police in his pocket." I glance up briefly, searching her eyes for confirmation of his threat.

Lily bites her lip and nods.

"We're sticking to the plan. It's a good one. We can keep padding our account with his money until you finish college and then we will run."

"Why wait so long? I don't need to go to college."

"One of us needs an education and I haven't been to school since eighth grade." I blow on her nails, trying to decide on what color to use next.

"For not going to school you give the best advice," she says kindly.

Lily has such a soft heart.

"You are more of a mother figure to me than my own," she continues, smiling at the color on her nails. "I should call you Mama Jenny." She laughs.

I dig through the bag of nail polish. "Ugh, don't call me that. How about Aunt Jenny. I could be like a long-lost cool aunt or something."

She thinks about it, tapping her finger over her mouth. "I like it. It will make it less awkward when my friends ask about you. Not that I have many." Her head drops.

I reach out and tip her chin with my finger. "I'm your friend and now your aunt." We continue to laugh and joke as I finish her nails.

The door swings open and Senator Ramsey steps inside. His eyes look at her rainbow-colored nails in disgust. "Take that off, Lily. Benjamin will be here to pick you up in an hour." He snaps his fingers, making her scurry for the polish remover.

"Yes, sir," she says, her voice quivering.

I narrow my eyes at him as his roam over my bare legs. Asshole.

"I'll allow this for now but if Lily can't keep up with her family obligations, I'll have to separate the two of you." His threat makes her scrub at her nails at warp speed.

"Yes, sir," she says again. In fact, those are the only two words I've ever heard her utter to him.

He snaps his fingers at me like a dog. I follow him out of the room.

As we head to the other wing, he informs me that he likes me as me and her as her. "She isn't free to have your personality," he says, opening the door to my room. I step inside, dropping my head in obedience.

It's never good to fight him behind closed doors. God, I hate him.

I could probably run on my own. He might not know about my friend Raffe. My previous "owners" did, and they threatened to hurt him every time I thought about disobeying.

Senator Ramsey has never threatened my friend. He threatens me with pain or worse.

So, I guess I could run.

He shoves me face down onto the mattress.

I should run but I can't leave Lily behind.

Lily is innocent and beautiful and everything I once thought about myself. If I save her, it would be like saving the me I was before meeting my traffickers.

Several hours pass before the Senator puts himself back together and walks out of my room, telling me he is headed to Washington and will be back in a few weeks.

Just as I'm starting to doze, a sound pulls me from my bed. Someone is crying. I walk the halls slowly, stopping in front of Lily's door. I knock lightly, the sobbing pauses. I push the door open and peek inside. Lily is lying on her bed, facing the windows.

"Lily, are you okay?" I ask, tiptoeing closer to her.

She's shaking so hard I decide to crawl in behind her. When I pull the covers up to slide in, I see a bright red spot on the sheets. My eyes slowly roll up her body. "Oh, Lily," I whisper.

"I told him I wanted to wait but he said it was my duty," she spits out, her tears coming faster now.

My blood boils. Benjamin is the spitting image of her fucking father. And from the looks of it, heading down the exact same path.

Well, fuck this. Lily isn't going down that path with him. Fuck. That.

"Come on, sweetie. Let's get you in the shower and I'll get you some clean sheets."

She stares at me as I set the temperature of the water. "I'm so sorry, Jenny," she cries, tears streaming down her face. "I'm so sorry if my dad hurts you that way."

I pull her into my arms. "You are my bright spot, Lily. Don't ever think you need to apologize for him."

She sniffles before whispering, "I didn't like it."

Tucking a piece of hair behind her ear, I kiss her forehead gently. When I pull back, I look her straight in the eye. "Someday, you will find someone who loves you."

She shakes her head, wanting to disagree with me.

"You will and when you do, please let him heal you, Lily. Let him love you and allow him to show you how good it can be. Promise me." I grip her chin, forcing her to look at me.

She nods.

"Say it," I demand.

"I promise."

"Good. Now get in the shower and I'll change the sheets."

She steps in, closing the door behind her.

My heart breaks for her. I don't think she realizes what really just happened to her. She thinks it was simply her first time. It was more than that. She told him she wanted to wait. He didn't listen. There's one word for that.

As I'm changing the bedding, I think about my first time. I guess I have a hard time with that word myself. Anyhow, I was scared, then that fear turned into anger. My first time was supposed to have been with Raffe. Not that he knew that. In his eyes we were just friends. He didn't know how hard I crushed on him.

It was my fault I never got the chance to tell him.

Some guy had approached me at the mall one day and asked if I had ever thought about becoming a model. He gave me his card and told me if I was ever in the city to look him up.

So, I convinced Raffe to go with me and we hitched our way from the suburbs.

He was beautiful and rebellious.

I was fresh and carefree.

We could have traveled the world, experiencing all the wonderful things. Instead, I led us straight to hell.

Sitting on the bed, waiting for Lily, I wrap my fingers around the dragonfly necklace Raffe gave me. "Please let him be okay," I pray quietly. "And if possible, help me find a way to make it up to him, to make up for all the pain I brought upon him."

I make the sign of the cross, my fingers dragging lightly across my chest. Finishing the prayer, I hope that the big man comes through this time.

Chapter Twenty-Five

Raffe

The charm dangling around Lily's neck has haunted me since the day I noticed it. In my mind, I knew it was too good to be true. Now, I know for certain. Lily knows a Jenny but not *my* Jenny.

Doesn't matter. Lily is hurting and she is one of us. I need to focus on her.

She blinks at me. Big crocodile tears cling to her lashes for dear life.

Dan is holding her arms to her sides, hugging her like he's worried she will fall into a million pieces if he lets go. I reach over to wipe the tears from her face. Her lips part as my hand brushes them from her cheeks.

"She's not my aunt," she whispers.

I wipe my hands on my jeans as I sit back down.

"What do you mean?" Dan asks. He looks at me, confused.

I'm confused too, buddy.

"Jenny isn't my aunt," she says more clearly this time. Lily closes her eyes and when she opens them again, she has a look of determination on her face. "It was a joke between her and I. She wasn't my aunt. She was my friend. She was yours too."

I glance at her, my heart beating out of my chest. She knows Jenny. Fuck. She knows Jenny!

But as I watch her face and process her words my heart begins to crumble.

Was. Was. Was. She *was* your friend.

Oh god, no.

Please, no.

The world closes in around me.

Dan releases Lily from his arms and she crawls over to me. "I'm so sorry," she says quietly.

She reaches up and unclasps the necklace from around her neck. "She left this for me, but I think it should go back to the person who gave it to her." Lily takes my hand, turning it over and tenderly placing the chain in my palm. I close my fingers around it and pull her into my arms.

We hold each other tight. Both grieving our free-spirited friend.

Dan places his hand on my shoulder, squeezing gently before walking out.

Chapter Twenty-Six

Dan

Dirk eyes me the minute I step out of the room. I hold my hand up to him before he has a chance to grill me. "Drink," I simply state. He nods and we head to the bar downstairs. He reaches for the good stuff on the top shelf.

He pours us each two fingers of whiskey before taking the seat across from me. Jesse joins us, taking the seat beside me.

"Rachel took Jackson home and Billie Rose is down for the night." She reaches over and wraps her fingers around my arm. "What can we do?" she asks.

"I don't know. I have no fucking clue what is going on." I shake my head before downing the drink in my hand. Fuck the burn feels good. I slam the glass down, sliding it back to Dirk for a refill.

"You left her alone?" Jesse pushes.

"She's with Raffe." I close my eyes tightly, trying to forget the look of pain on their goddamn faces.

"Do we need to load her up and take her to the cabin?" Dirk asks, flipping that fucking ring in his lip. God help me, I want to rip it out of his face right now.

"No." I slide my glass back to him again.

He smirks but fills it up. "Then what's your fucking plan? Bill barely snagged her from nose diving right into the fucking lake."

That image will never leave my mind. When Katie came to me, frantic, I ran down the hill only to find Bill holding Lily around the waist, fighting to keep her on the dock. She would have plunged herself in if he had not been there.

She was so lost, her eyes unfocused as I turned her to face me. When they eventually snagged on mine, clarity slowly returned to her.

"I don't know if she's mentioned her Aunt Jenny, but I guess she isn't really her aunt." I tap the bottom of the glass on the counter, waiting for the liquor to dull my senses.

"Yeah, she's mentioned her. She gave her the necklace Lily loves so much. It's why she got the tattoo," Jesse says, leaning forward to study my face.

"Well, like I said she's not her aunt. I guess it was an inside joke between the two of them. They were friends."

Dirk stands up slowly. "You've got to be fucking me. Is this Raffe's Jenny?"

I nod, not taking my eyes from the bar. "You ready for the drop kick?" I glance at Dirk and then Jesse. They both nod, stunned.

"I think they met through Lily's dad. She's scared of him if you get what I'm trying to lay down here." I swallow hard, struggling to keep the bile from rising in my throat.

"I'm going in," Dirk says, leaving Jesse and I alone.

Dirk saved Raffe's life. He pulled him out of the trafficking world and gave him a new life, here with us. It was rough for a while. Once Raffe pulled his shit together, we helped him look for his friend, Jenny, but we never found her.

Until now. And fuck... it's too late.

"How?" Jesse mumbles next to me. She grabs the glass out of my hand, filling it for herself.

"I don't know. Coincidence." I shrug.

"That's one hell of a coincidence," she says, coughing. Jesse rarely drinks but I think we can all agree the occasion calls for it.

"Maybe I should go up there. I don't want Dirk scaring her." I look toward the stairs.

Jesse lays her head on my shoulder. "Give them some time. He isn't going to scare her. He's going to reassure her that she's right where she belongs."

I turn and kiss the top of her head.

She raises her face to me and smiles. "You can tell her till you're blue in the face and she won't believe you. She knows she's stolen your heart. If Dirk tells her, it will sink in. Trust me."

I chuckle lightly, feeling a little better. Jesse's right, my family won't let me down. They know how much she means to me.

Chapter Twenty-Seven

Lily

I never knew his name. Jenny was scared someone would overhear us. The people who had her before she came to live with us threatened her family and her friend. He's just as she described except, he isn't a boy, he's a man.

Raffe pinches the bridge of his nose as we both pick ourselves up off the floor. He sits down on Dan's bed, so I take a seat beside him. "Okay, so I'm going to assume by your reaction this is as much a revelation to you as it is to me," he says, leaning over to rest his forearms on his knees."

"I'm sorry I lost my shit. There's just so much…"

Someone knocks on the door and opens it without waiting for a response. Dirk stands in the doorway, his gaze roaming over Raffe, assessing him before turning to me. He takes a deep breath and steps into the room.

"I'm here to mediate," he says, pulling up a chair directly in front of us.

My eyes slide to Raffe. The corner of his eyes soften as he watches Dirk. I hadn't noticed before but now I clearly see how close they are. I hug myself, feeling a bit odd man out.

Dirk notices my attempt to close myself off. He leans forward, pulling my arms away from my body. "I understand there is a lot to talk about but first things first, do you know where Jenny is right now."

I shake my head yes.

"She's gone, Dirk," Raffe answers for me. He takes my hand in his and offers me a small sad smile.

Dirk slides forward and pulls us both into a group hug. "I'm so sorry, man."

This is uncomfortable, awkward, strange, and so wonderful. Tears start to fall down my cheeks again. I've never had anyone to share in my grief over Jenny's death. My father didn't shed one tear for her.

Wait, maybe I can help Jenny get home now. The thought of giving her and her family peace gives me a burst of newfound purpose.

"We need to get her home."

They both look at me.

My fingers tingle and stomach knots as I prepare myself to let the floodgates open. For seventeen years I've wanted to confide in someone. I had thoughts of telling my teachers, and then my professors. My fear of him always won out. I can't say why that fear is so great. He never hurt me. It was just a look, something I saw in his eyes that scared the hell out of me.

I'm not alone anymore. With their help I could do this. My dad would never know.

"You know where she is?" Raffe asks, his eyes bouncing frantically over my face.

I nod, pulling his hands into mine and dragging them to my chest. "We will need her family to help though."

"She's a Jane Doe?" Dirk asks.

My gaze falls to him. He's running his hand over the scruff on his face, his eyebrow pitched high in thought.

"There's so much to explain but yes, she's buried in a public cemetery in San Francisco as Jane Doe."

Raffe grabs my arm, forcing me to face him. "If you know where she is, why haven't you told someone who she was?"

I grimace as his grip tightens on my arm. Dirk reaches out and taps his hand. Raffe drops his gaze, pulling away quickly once he realizes he's hurting me.

"I'm sorry," he says, scooting away from me.

He's getting angry but I understand. It's only going to get worse, unfortunately.

Rubbing the sting he left behind, I explain. "I didn't know who she was. In fact, I still don't know."

"What *do* you know?" Dirk asks, tipping his head slightly.

Sighing, I stand and walk over to the window, staring out over the lake. I can't see the dragonflies from here, but I know they're there. She loved Raffe. I can trust him... them.

"I know she was an amazing soul who had the misfortune of catching my dad's eye. We were going to run away together but we waited too long, there was always a reason to wait, then some things happened." I pause as the memories of those final months crawl their way to the forefront of my mind.

Dirk stands and walks me back to the bed, handing me a bottle of water. "Is this the first time you've talked about this?" he asks.

I nod after taking a small sip.

"What happened to her?" He takes the bottle from my shaking hands and caps it.

That stupid knot climbs up my throat, threatening to close off my oxygen. "She took her own life," I say quietly. "Jenny didn't have any identification. If I had known her last name maybe I could have gone to the police, and they could have contacted her family before my dad found out." I shake my head, the hopelessness I felt floods my system.

Raffe stands abruptly and storms out of the room. I flinch as the door slams shut behind him.

"Don't worry, he's just processing."

My hands shake as I press them over my thighs. I rub over the coarse material of my jeans, back and forth, not realizing I'm rocking myself as I do.

Dirk takes Raffe's spot on the bed. He grips my hands, stopping me. "Do you believe in fate?" he asks.

"I don't know what I believe, Dirk. This is… why? Why would she lead me back here to him? I'm hurting him. I feel like I just stuck a knife in his back."

He wraps his arm around me and tugs me close. He talks over my head, his breath ruffling my hair. "That's not how I see it. Sometimes, you have to hurt people to help them move on. He's been hurting for years, Lily. You just handed him a key, not a knife. Now, he'll be able to get some closure. He just needs to get past the shock, okay?"

Dirk pulls back a tiny bit so he can look into my eyes. When I don't respond, he continues, "Her parents are going to get closure. Do you understand just how important that is?"

"Anyone ever tell you that you would make a heck of a therapist?"

He chuckles darkly.

"Not exactly." He smiles at me. "Why don't we go back down to the party. We can hash this out tomorrow when emotions aren't so high."

"I'm sorry, I didn't mean to ruin the day. You go on, I think I'll have Dan take me home." I give him a smile, hoping he will let it go. I can't go downstairs and face everyone. I just can't.

The door swings open and Dan storms in. He immediately crouches in front of me, his eyes frantically running over my face. "Are you okay?" he asks.

"Yeah, I'm good," I tell him, pulling out of Dirk's embrace.

"Chill, cousin. Raffe just needs a little time to process what your girl laid on him."

"He tore out of here." Dan cradles my face in the palm of his hand before continuing, "I was worried he lost control."

"That's why I'm here, brother." Dirk lays his hand on his shoulder, standing. "Take care of your girl. I'll find Raffe."

He stops at the door, knocking on the jamb. "Tomorrow evening, we hash this thing out." He points to me. "We lay it all on the table."

"Tomorrow," I repeat.

He closes the door quietly behind him.

Dan climbs up on the bed, pulling me into his arms. "I only have one question and then we put everything on the back burner till tomorrow."

I nod once.

"Did you know he was here? Is that why you came?"

"No. She never even told me his name, but she told me so much more. He is kind, funny and sweet. She loved him, Dan."

My eyes trail his thumb as it brushes back and forth over my thigh. I remember the promise I made to her the night Benjamin stole my virginity. It's time to make good on it.

I tuck my face in the crook of his neck, breathing in the scent of pine trees and man. "Will you make love to me, Dan?" I mouth against his skin.

He shivers at my touch, making me sigh, happy that he is still responding to me. I'm sure I don't deserve him, but I want him.

"After you eat," he says in faux gruffness, dumping me on the bed. "Give me ten minutes."

My heart thumps wildly. When he comes back, he has a plate piled high. He sets it on his bedside table, then pulls me back onto his lap. He grabs a grape, biting it in half before bringing it to my lips. *Oh*, he's going to feed me. "Close your eyes," he whispers against the shell of my ear.

I obey and as my eyes fall closed the fruit touches my lips. His finger pushes it into my mouth slowly. He drags it over my bottom lip as he pulls his hand away. *Oh fuck.* The flavor glazes over my tongue, making me moan.

Dan continues to gently push food into my mouth. Sometimes, with one finger, sometimes, two. Part of me wants to be a brat and bite him. The other wants to be his good girl and take everything he offers.

When he's satisfied I've eaten enough, he grabs the bottom of my shirt and pulls it up over my head. It lands softly on the floor. His warm calloused hands run over me lightly. A tremble courses through me, enticing a chuckle out of him.

"Keep your eyes closed," he says as he reaches behind me to flick the clasp on my bra. Dan shifts me so that I'm lying in the middle of the bed. My shoes come off next and then his hands are at the button on my jeans. I swear I can feel them tremble as he releases it.

Soon enough, I'm lying on the bed, completely naked in front of him. I listen as he removes his own clothes. A delicious tingle of anticipation swims happily through my system. I need this, just a moment to forget, for the outside world to melt away.

The bed shifts and that alone makes me moan out loud. He presses his body up against mine, lying beside me. He nudges my head to the side with his nose so that he can have access to my neck. He kisses me there, oh god, his mouth is so warm.

When he places his hand on my stomach, I jerk at the touch. He chuckles low, sending a surge of blood to a place I now need him to touch. I shift my hips off the bed in invitation. His fingers drag lightly in that direction but stop.

My bottom lip pops out in a pout. He captures it between his teeth. Holy shit. He releases it, tapping his finger over my lips. "So impatient, love."

"I need you," I mouth against his finger.

"And you have me."

I open my eyes. He's staring at me, a smile spreads across his handsome face. "Do I?"

"You do. Now shut up and close your eyes."

So, I do. He places a gentle kiss over each of my eyelids and then he gives me everything I asked for and more. He slides a hand under my head and grips my hair tightly, pulling my head back to expose my throat. His mouth descends there, kissing, sucking but it's his other hand that has me mesmerized.

It snakes down my torso, and when he reaches the promise land, I moan loudly. He grips my hair tighter as he kicks a leg over one of mine, effectively holding me right where he wants me. His warm hand covers me and then he presses the base of his palm over my clit firmly.

"Yessss," I hiss as my eyelids flutter. I want to open my eyes and watch so badly, but I also want to please him and do as he asked.

His warm mouth moves lower. When his tongue flicks at my hardened nipple, I begin to writhe in his grip. "Dan," I say breathlessly.

One finger slides into me and I begin to tremble. His palm rocks against me in a slow rhythm. More, oh god I need more. When a second finger joins the first, I try to wiggle against his palm seeking more friction, but his heavy leg keeps me pinned. His mouth works its way back up to my ear.

His breath is hot on my neck. "Are you ready for me, baby?"

I try to nod but I can't. "Please." I almost cry, I want him so bad.

Without releasing my hair, he shifts over the top of me, nudging my legs apart with his knee. When he settles himself and his cock bumps against me, I almost come from that alone.

"Dan, please, I need you," I rasp, raising my hips, groaning as his length glides over me. "Oh, shit, Dan, I'm going to come."

"Open your eyes," he says, his voice rough and demanding.

When my eyes lock on his, I still my hips. There's so much there. He stares back at me. He tugs on my hair, driving his point home. "We come together."

I swallow, his eyes dipping to my neck to watch the movement. He licks his lips. "I'm going to fuck you into tomorrow."

My back arches off the bed as he slides in. He pumps slowly until tears are running out the corners of my eyes. "You're mine, Lily. You can't escape me. No matter how far you run, I will follow." He picks up his pace, shifting his hips slightly.

"Oh, god," I moan.

"Your body is mine, your mind, your secrets…" his thrusts become more demanding. My thighs begin to tremble around his hips. "You will give them all to me, won't you, baby?" he asks.

"I'm yours, I'm yours, I'm yours," I chant mindlessly.

When his eyes snag mine, they are blazing amber. I hold my breath, treading quietly in his rhythmic motions. "Come," his one-word command brutally yanks me to the surface. I gasp, every muscle in my body locks around him. I convulse in his arms as his muscles tighten. The tension pours from our bodies. He drops his head in the crook of my neck, struggling to catch his breath.

Immediately, silent tears fall from my eyes. More years of bottled-up emotions, released once again by this brute of a man. My man. He has me. Dan raises his head and licks the tears away, our bodies still connected. He kisses me in a way that lets me know I'm safe, that we are good, more than good.

After a few minutes, he reluctantly lifts himself off of me and walks into the bathroom, turning the shower on. I try to sit up, but my body is completely drained after the day I've had. He comes back into the room and scoops me up. I don't even have the energy to fight him.

He sets me gently on my feet and begins to wash me from head to toe, then I watch as he washes himself. God, he's beautiful. Dan is built like a

Greek god, chiseled out of stone. He's combing his fingers through his beard when he notices me studying him. He smiles, a brilliant white smile that melts my heart.

"I'm falling," I whisper.

His smile falters and he pulls me against his chest. "Don't be scared, we are falling together," he says softly, running his fingers through my wet hair. He pushes me back so he can look me in the eye. "And we will land, together."

"Promise?" I run my hands over his chest, still uncertain that a man like this could possibly be mine.

"I promise and I don't make promises I can't keep." He taps the end of my nose, making me giggle.

I hug him tight around the waist, believing for the first time in my life that things will be okay.

We fall asleep minutes after our heads hit the pillow, his arm wrapped protectively around me. But like every night, their cries wake me up. I sit up, blinking, trying to get my bearings. The crying starts again. I shove the blankets aside and quickly make my way down the hall. Oh god, please stop crying. Please stop.

A light bleeds out into the hallway from an open door. Quietly, I creep toward it. When I peek inside, I see Jesse pulling Billie Rose from her bed. "It's okay, sweetheart," her voice soothes the crying child.

She walks over to a rocking chair and begins to sing lightly to her daughter. A sob escapes me, the love in Jesse's eyes steals my breath away. Her head bops up. "Lily, you scared me."

I push the door open a little wider. "I'm sorry, you two look so beautiful together."

Jesse smiles, waving me into the room. "She wakes up at least once a night. Some of our friends who have kids tell me I should let her cry herself back to sleep, but I can't do it."

Billie Rose rubs her eyes, trying her hardest to fight sleep, but she isn't winning the battle. Two blinks, one blink and she's out.

I take a seat on the floor by Jesse's feet. "I don't think you should let her cry." My gaze roams over the mural painted on the wall. "Some children don't have anyone to answer their cries."

Jesse stops rocking to stare at me. "You're right. My grandmother always came to me when I was a child. After she died, I lost that. Maybe that's why I'm so adamant about being here for her."

Billie Rose stirs, prompting Jesse to resume rocking. "Did you have someone to answer your cries?" she asks hesitantly.

"I don't remember crying in the night." I glance at her briefly, deciding to open up. "I was the one who was forced to listen to others cry. I tried to get to them, but the door was always locked. My mom was usually gone and my dad... he was the one causing the anguish."

Jesse doesn't say anything. When I stop there, she gives me a push, "Lily, nothing you say will surprise me. I've survived the ugliest of men. Your dad is not you. You have nothing to be ashamed of."

"But I do. I should have done something."

"How old were you the first time you remember hearing them?"

I shrug. "I don't remember a time when I didn't hear them." I rise from the floor to get a better look at the mural behind Billie Rose's bed. "Jenny was the first one I ever saw though. My dad was good at keeping them hidden."

"What was she like? Raffe told me she was beautiful."

"She was." I sit back down on the floor, wrapping my arms around my legs. "Jenny loved Raffe. She kept going because they said they would hurt him if she didn't. When they sold her to my dad, I think she thought she was free. She was going to end it all, but I stopped her."

I groan quietly. "God, Jesse, she suffered for so many years after that. I was so selfish. She stayed for me."

Jesse lays Billie Rose down before sitting on the floor beside me. "It helps when you have someone to live for. She had Raffe, then she had you. If she didn't think you were worth it, she would have split."

"This is all so crazy," I say quietly.

"Not going to lie, it is." Jesse flips her hair over her shoulder.

My eyes roam over the ink on her skin, then back to the mural on the wall. "I don't like that Raffe is hurting."

She hums in agreement.

"Will you help me with something?"

Jesse cocks an eyebrow. "Hell, yeah." She stands, pulling me to my feet. "What do you need?"

"Your artistic ability."

211

She grabs me, excited as we make our way down to a small room in the basement. She flips the light on. "This is my painting room."

Spinning in a circle, I grin widely. Jenny would have loved Jesse. Both strong, free souls. Jenny was free even though she wasn't if that makes any sense. She never let anyone steal her essence.

"So, what are we painting?"

Taking my phone out of my pocket, I flip it open slowly, remembering the day we bought it. We took a selfie in front of my bedroom windows before she tucked it away for safe keeping. When the image pops up, I cover my mouth. I hadn't been able to open it until now.

Jesse wraps her arm around my shoulder, taking the phone from me. "Oh, wow, she was beautiful. Raffe is going to love this, Lily."

"I thought he might like to see what she looked like as a woman."

She hugs me tight. Wiping tears from her face, she backs away, setting the phone down so she can see the image while she paints. I move to sit in a nearby folding chair. "Oh, no. Come here, we're doing this together." She snaps her fingers, beckoning me to her.

When we emerge from the basement several hours later, Dan rushes to me. "Goddammit, Lily." He hugs me to him.

"Chill, big guy. We were downstairs painting."

Dirk smirks as he sits down to his breakfast.

Dan walks with me to the table, forcing me into a chair gently.

"Tonight, six o'clock, we meet here for supper," Dirk informs all of us.

Jesse sits down beside him. "That should work. Dan and I have a few clients today, but we should be done by five."

"I'm cancelling," Dan chimes in as he leans into the refrigerator.

"No, you're not." I swivel in my chair to look at him.

"Baby, you had a rough day yesterday. I want to make sure you're okay."

"I'm fine and JD is coming to the house today to help me on a project."

Dan brings a gallon of milk to his lips, draining half of it in seconds. He caps it and puts it back in the fridge. *Why was that so hot?*

"Seriously, Dan. I'll be fine. You can pick me up after you're finished at the shop." I fan myself; the temperature having risen several degrees in the last few minutes.

Dirk and Jesse both laugh under their breath, neither taking their eyes off their plate.

"Okay. Okay, I'll go to the shop, but you call if you need me." He wraps his arms around me from behind, kissing me on the head.

"Did you find Raffe?" I ask Dirk. "Is he okay?"

Dirk nods, standing to rinse his plate. "He's chill. Like I said, once the shock wears off, the anger will fade. He's not mad at you. He's upset with the situation."

I pick at the eggs and toast in front of me. "We painted a portrait of Jenny this morning. If he's ever ready to see it."

"He will be. Eventually." Dirk gives Jesse a quick peck on the cheek. His eyes run a quick assessment. "You good?"

"I'm great," she smiles at him. He leans in and kisses her for a long minute. I sit back in my chair afraid I might catch fire from the sparks they emit. These two are combustible.

When they finally pull away, I hide my face, certain I'm all sorts of red. "See you all tonight," Dirk says before leaving the room.

Jesse cleans up and leaves a few minutes behind him. "I need to go get Billie Rose up for the day."

"Thank you for helping me with the portrait."

"No problem, hun. He's going to love it." She smiles assuredly. "I know I've said this before, but I'm really glad you're here."

"Me too."

Dan waits until she leaves us. "I didn't hear you leave the bed. I was worried you ran away."

"I heard Billie Rose crying." I go back to picking at my breakfast.

"Ah, Lily. Why didn't you wake me?" He runs his hand over the back of my neck, kneading away the tension.

I moan and relax my shoulders. "I need to learn to face my fears and I did."

214

"I'm happy you could do that but don't ever be afraid to ask for my help."

Smiling, I lean forward, tugging at his beard to pull him nose to nose with me. "You are my sun, and I am yours. When it gets cloudy, I will turn to you, I promise."

He visibly relaxes, giving my neck a gentle squeeze. Dan then drags me up to his room, showing me just how sunny living in his presence can be. He makes love to me slow and with so much intensity that he heals a little more of the damage done to my fragile heart.

Chapter Twenty-Eight

Lily

JD and I work the morning away. "Okay, she's ready," he says, standing back to appraise the job we did.

"It's so cool." I run my hand over the seat, the wood smooth beneath my palm.

"Give it a try."

Gingerly, I sit down on my new porch swing. I bounce a tiny bit, making JD chuckle. "It's not going to fall."

I lean back, pressing my back into the Ford tailgate we resurrected. He sits down next to me.

"Fuck, this is awesome." He gives us a gentle push.

A grin spreads across my face. "We should make more and sell them."

He grins at me. "You know, we should. I bet we could get at least a solid Benjamin out of one of these."

I nod, turning my face to the sun, closing my eyes. "Coming here was the best thing to ever happen to me."

He pats my leg. "I'm going to grab another glass of that lemonade you made."

"Help yourself." I keep my eyes closed, reveling in the comforting motion of the swing and the warmth on my face.

The screen door swings closed behind him. It's then I hear a car approaching. I peek my eyes open, shielding them from the sun to see who it is. A black car comes into focus.

A dark cloud slowly shifts over the sun, stealing the warmth and blocking out all the goodness I felt only moments ago.

Calmly, I stand and head into the house. JD is leaning against the counter. "Want a glass?" he asks.

"No. Um, JD, I need you to listen to me closely."

He straightens, hearing the car himself. His eyes dart from me to the window.

"I don't have much time. That car is here for me. It's my dad's men." He quickly shoots for his jacket, where I assume he has a weapon. "Stop, you can't fight them alone. They will have weapons too."

I glance out the window, seeing they're almost here. "Listen, tell Dan I will come back. Somehow, I will get back. Just please stay inside. Please don't let them see you."

"Lily." He hugs me to his chest. "You're scaring the fuck out of me right now."

My fingers lock around his back. I don't want to let go but I have to. "I'll be fine. Just please tell him I'll find my way back." Before I have time to change my mind, I rush out.

"Lily," I hear him yell before I shut the door firmly behind me.

I jog down the driveway to meet the car. It stops beside me, idling quietly.

Oh god. He found me.

The back door opens and Rudy steps out.

"Hello, Rudy," I say dutifully.

"Lily." He bows slightly. We stare at each other for a moment. His muscles tense as he prepares for me to run. He shakes his head sadly. "I've got to take you back."

"I know."

I glance over my shoulder, thankful that JD did not run out guns a-blazing.

My heart sinks as the realization of what is happening settles into my bones. Rudy holds the door open, ushering me inside with the swoop of his arm.

The drive back is quiet. I watch the world pass me by, stuck once again on the other side of the glass.

As the sun sets, we pull inside the gates of my father's estate.

218

Rudy opens my door and escorts me inside. One of the maids greets us. "He's in his office," she says politely, avoiding my gaze completely.

I glance up the stairs nervously.

Rudy places his hand at the small of my back and escorts me into my father's office. He doesn't look up from his work. "Lily, go to your room. Benjamin will join us shortly."

Stand up to him. Tell him you're done listening to his every word. Put an end to this so you can get back to Dan.

When I don't jump on his order, his fingers pause over the keyboard. I straighten my shoulders as his eyes meet mine over his laptop. "Did the jump off the bridge damage your hearing, Lily?"

"Can we please have a conversation?" I ask nervously.

"Take her to her room." He waves his hand over me in dismissal.

Rudy grabs my arm and spins me from the office. "What are you doing?" he hisses in my ear.

He drags me up the stairs, tossing me into my room roughly.

I spin on him. "I can't do it anymore."

"Lily, your father gets what he wants, you know this." He runs his hand through his hair, clearly upset by the entire situation.

My eyes roam around my room, the thought of spending another minute here makes my skin crawl. I need out of here. "How did you find me?"

He grimaces. "Your father got the FBI involved. They put two and two together and realized you dyed your hair and took the train to Reno. Then they found a bank account associated with the same name you bought your ticket with. They've been watching it." He runs his hand over his face.

"And when I made a transfer, they had me," I say softly, sitting down on my bed. Why did I think I could outsmart him?

The door to my room opens and the two men who haunt my nightmares step through. "That will be all for today, Rudy," my dad says, removing his jacket and draping it over the loveseat.

Rudy tips his head and backs out of the room. His eyes plead with mine before he shuts the door.

Benjamin sits down, resting his arm along the back of the loveseat, his mouth cocked in a lazy smirk. I look away from him.

My father walks slowly around my room, trailing his finger over all my things, his things. "Have you ever wanted for anything under my care?"

I begin to tremble, the answer I want to give him on the tip of my tongue. There's no going back from this. Everything is about to change. "Yes," my voice cracks as I push the word from between my lips.

He stills, his control slipping. It's this look that terrifies me. This is why I'm scared of him.

"What did you want that you did not have?"

I stand up and turn to face him. "Peace, love, safety." I lift my hands, gesturing around me. "All this... I didn't want any of this. I *don't* want this."

220

Just like I thought, everything changes. Two long steps and he reaches me, his hand rearing back before landing against the side of my face. My head whips violently, sending me skittering across the carpet.

I bring my fingers to my mouth as copper erupts over my tongue. When I pull my hand away, they are tipped in blood. Smiling, I laugh at him. "Finally, the monster crawls out of the shadows."

He flexes his fists, towering above me. He cracks his neck from one side to the other before taking a step away from me. Bringing his phone to his ear, he glares at me. "Get me a fucking hair stylist. Now!" he barks before hanging up.

"The wedding is tomorrow evening. We've moved it to a private ceremony that will take place here, at home." He walks over, snagging his jacket from behind Benjamin.

He shifts his focus to him. "It's time, son. Put her in her place or she will be a thorn in your side from here on out." My father's eyes roam over my face and he winces. "Learn from my mistake, boy. Stay away from her face." He flicks his wrist my way, regretting the mark he left behind, not the fact he put it there.

My father is a handsome man. A man with charm and charisma. A man who gets what he wants.

When will he get what he deserves?

For several minutes Benjamin and I sit in silence before he rises to his feet and comes to stand beside me. I flinch when he holds his hand out for me to take. He waits patiently for me to accept his offer.

He pulls me gently to my feet when I finally put my hand in his. He walks me into the bathroom, tipping my head to inspect my father's handiwork. The harsh light reveals the beginnings of a bruise. "Nothing a little makeup won't hide," he says, his voice void of emotion.

Someone just hit his fiancé in front of him and this is his response.

He turns the shower on. "Get undressed," he orders, blocking the bathroom door with his body.

"W-what?" My mouth falls open, stunned.

"Get. Undressed."

I stare at him. He stands with his arms folded across his chest. His clothes pressed to perfection. Not a hair out of place. So handsome yet so ridiculously callous. I can't marry him. I *won't* marry him.

"I'm not doing this, Benjamin. We can't get married. You don't even want me."

"I don't want you. You're a spoiled, boring, little brat. But…" he holds up a finger, stepping closer. "That doesn't matter because while I may not *want* you, I do need you. Being married to Senator Ramsey's daughter is like a golden admission ticket to the inner circle of politics."

I shake my head back and forth. "You don't need me. If you work hard…"

His laugh is loud and harsh and cruel.

"If I work hard," he shakes his head, amused. "Hard work isn't what gets you ahead. It's who you have in your back pocket, whose secrets you keep and whose you reveal. It's a game of chess, Lily. It's. A. Game. And you, my dear, are nothing more than a pawn."

Watercolor Skulls

He grabs my shirt and begins to lift it over my head. "No," I say softly, trying to pull it back down.

Benjamin backs me into the wall, ripping the shirt out of my hands and roughly tugging it off me.

"No!" I say louder, the panic I'm trying to control evident in the cracking of my voice.

He grabs me by my throat and slams me against the wall not once but twice.

While my hands are desperately trying to remove his from my throat, he takes the opportunity to unbutton my pants and shove them down my thighs. When he finally releases me, it's only to grab me around the waist and toss me over his shoulder.

He drops me under the spray of the shower. The oxygen scurries from my lungs as the stinging cold rushes over my face. Benjamin holds me there by his hand which is once again wrapped around my neck. I claw at him, trying to get out from the freezing cold water. My jeans tangle around my ankles as I struggle in his grasp.

Trapped. Shivering. Humiliated.

Benjamin is winning.

I am losing.

My mind.

Faith.

Hope.

He doesn't need to beat me to get me to submit. There are other ways. Ways that leave no marks. Not on the outside anyway.

I don't know how long he holds me there. My lips match my hair by the time he pulls me out. If the hairdresser hadn't shown up, maybe I would still be there.

My decision has been made. Now, I understand. Once you've lived in the sun, it's hard to accept the shade. I can't live in the shadows, too much light has been shown there. It's ugly and cold and not life at all. It wasn't for Jenny and it's not for me. If I can't have the sun, then I want nothing at all.

The hairdresser works her magic, transforming my beautiful carefree watercolor beginning into a restrictive black and white rendition of my demise.

Tomorrow, my father will force me to marry Benjamin. No one will stop him. My protests will fall on deaf ears. Why? Because he is either paying or blackmailing those around us for their selective hearing.

Just like all those poor girl's cries... they all fell on deaf ears, except mine. I heard them. I felt their hopelessness, their fear. All I could do for them was pray. Pray that it would be over soon and that someday, maybe they would get justice.

The Rebel Skulls were the first group of people I'd met that had banded together to raise money, to help victims get justice. I wish I could give that to the girls my father hurt. Just getting Jenny home would have been amazing.

I open the door to find not one but two security men sitting outside my door. They both turn their heads toward me. "Do you need anything Ms. Ramsey?" one asks.

"No. No, thank you." I close the door quietly, pressing my head to the cool wood. What am I going to do? I have to get out of here before Benjamin touches me. If he touches me, it's over. I'll never be able to look Dan in the face.

If I do find a way back, what prevents my father from coming for me again? What if he already knows about Dan? Would he hurt him? Them? This is why Jenny was so careful. *I* need to be careful. My father can never know about any of them.

I've never felt more alone than I am right now.

Chapter Twenty-Nine

Dan

Thirty minutes after JD sounded the alarm, was all it took to get everyone gathered around.

Dirk sits at the head of the table, Jesse, and I on either side of him. Even Bill is here. He semi-retired from the club after he bought the bar but for Lily he is here.

"So, what do we know?" Dirk asks, leaning back in his chair.

JD shakes his head. "We finished up her porch swing, I went inside for a drink, and she came in a few minutes later saying her dad's men were coming for her and to tell Dan she would find a way back." His sad eyes meet mine briefly before he continues. "I went for my gun, but she stopped me and said they would be packing as well."

Dirk focuses his intense eyes on me. "Do you know where her father lives?"

"I'm guessing San Francisco." I bang my hand on the table. "Honestly, I don't know a fucking thing other than I'm going to kill someone if she's hurt."

Jesse leans across the table, placing her hand over mine. "We'll find her."

"How? We don't even know her fucking real name."

Our resident computer geek, Travis, bops his head up over the laptop he's been furiously tapping on since we all sat down. "The name on her ID says Lily Gladstone but it's no surprise that's not her real name. Wait, I found something."

He tips his glasses down on his nose. "Looks like she made a large transfer from her bank account a few days ago.

"How large?" I ask.

"Over two hundred grand." Travis scratches his nose, before looking at Jesse. "The transfer went to your charity account."

JD's attention snaps to Travis. "Two hundred thousand dollars!"

"Yep." Travis whistles. "That's a hefty sum."

The room grows silent, all of us deep in thought.

Raffe speaks up first. "We go there, ask around. She has to be there somewhere. We know she comes from a wealthy family. What else do we know?"

"She was a teacher," Jesse pipes up.

"Her favorite place was the bay," I add sadly.

Dirk stands up. "Let's roll. Travis, call the Nor Cal Chapter and tell them we might need assistance. Book us rooms and keep digging." He claps his hands, sending everyone scurrying to obey his orders.

I shove my shit in my bag as quickly as I can. My mind is going over every detail of every conversation Lily and I have had. Where the fuck do we even start?

Dirk pokes his head into my door. "Got your shit together, man?"

"Yes and no," I answer honestly.

"What do you know about her old man?"

I pause after zipping my bag. "She's scared of him."

Dirk cracks his knuckles. "We haven't gotten to play in a long, long time."

Smiling, I toss my bag over my shoulder. "I'm going to destroy this motherfucker."

Jesse walks us out to our bikes. "I wish I could go."

Dirk picks her up, kissing her soundly on the mouth. He swats her ass. "You just take care of my baby girl."

She hugs me. "Be careful, big guy."

"I will."

"Tell her thank you. You know, for the donation." Jesse kicks a rock, sending it skittering across the pavement.

"You can tell her yourself because I'm not leaving San Francisco without her."

Jesse smirks. "You going to go caveman on her?"

"If that's what it takes."

"She needs us, Dan. She needs *you*. Don't give up on her."

"I didn't give up on you, did I?"

Jesse glances at Dirk before settling her gaze on me. "She's not me, Dan. Not that she's not strong. She is. Coming here took a lot for her. Going back must be a kick in the gut. Whatever she grew up with... it hurt her."

"I'll do what needs to be done."

She gives me a kiss on the cheek, then hands me my helmet.

When we get to San Francisco, we break off, going our separate ways. Bill and Raffe will start with the schools. We're hoping Raffe still has his charm. Dirk and I are heading down to the bay. The rest of the crew along with some of the Nor Cal Chapter are going to ruffle some feathers with the elite of this godforsaken city.

Dirk and I decided to split up to cover more ground. I walk out on the bridge, thinking we don't even have a picture of her. This is going to be tough. No name, no photo, we literally have nothing to go on.

Fuck it is beautiful here. It's no wonder it's one of her favorite places.

She told me she would never come back here but what if she changed her mind? What if discovering Raffe was Jenny's friend was too much for her. Lily is harboring a lot of guilt for her father's sins. Maybe it's more than she can carry.

An officer approaches me. "Are you doing all right today, sir?" he asks. Funny question for an officer to ask.

"Yeah, just looking for a friend. She told me she used to hang out around here."

The sun is setting, bringing a close to the day. We should have been having supper as a family, hashing this whole Jenny thing out. But now, I realize I know just as much about Lily as I do Jenny. Which is nothing. Both are a mystery.

"Ah, I saw the look on your face. I was worried you might be here to jump." His gaze roams over the others on the bridge before resting back on me. "What's her name? I've been walking this bridge for almost two decades, maybe it will ring a bell."

He thought I was going to jump? What the fuck? I peek over the edge of the bridge. No fucking thanks, it's a long way down a one-way street. Dirk walks up. He shrugs. No luck on his end. I turn back to the officer. "Yeah, my friend's name is Lily." If that's even her real name.

The man stares at the water below. "The girl who jumped a few weeks ago?" He blinks a few times as if he's seen a ghost.

"Well, if it were the same Lily, I would think I would have better luck searching the graveyard. I just saw my Lily this morning, so not the same girl. Thanks though." I start to head back the way we came, disappointed we didn't find anything.

"She lived."

I stop dead in my tracks.

Dirk lights up a cigarette. "You mean someone jumped off this thing and fucking lived?"

The officer nods, staring straight ahead. "Not many do. She is one of the one percent." He takes off his hat to wipe his brow. "I watched her for a few minutes before I approached. They get this far off look on their face. That's why I noticed you." He points at me before continuing. "She looked so lost, so alone. I reached for her. Told her I could help. She looked at me but then a dragonfly caught her attention. It was the darndest thing. She watched it land on the cable beside her, smiled and then she just let go."

Dirk grips my shoulder hard, pinning me in place. It can't be her. She wouldn't...

the bruises...

the dragonfly...

she said she had a fall...

a fucking fall...

"The girl who jumped, her name was Lily?" Dirk asks the officer.

"Yeah, Lily Ramsey, the Senator's daughter. Is she the one you're looking for?"

"Our Lily has a class A asshole for a father, so Senator's daughter sounds about right," Dirk answers, his fingers digging into my shoulder, keeping me grounded.

Everything slowly clicks into place. I force myself to look over the edge again.

She stood here, hopeless, alone and she fell. Oh god. I think I'm going to be sick.

"You know I've never liked that guy. He's disgusting. Everyone knows what he's about." The officer throws his hands up. "Pricks like him always seem to walk. You know he's been accused of some nasty shit, but not once has he ever been charged. He's got big names in his pocket." He taps the side of the railing. "Poor girl. I didn't know it was her until after they pulled her out. I tried to visit her a few times but didn't even get inside the gate. They told me she wasn't feeling well. She must be feeling better though. I read in the paper that she's getting married tomorrow."

Dirk drops his cigarette on the ground, stomping it out with his boot. "Let's go."

I thank the officer, shaking his hand. He gives me his card. "If you talk to her, let her know I've been thinking about her. I didn't get to her in time that day…" he sighs, "but, if there is anything she needs, you tell her to call me."

I tap the card in my palm before pocketing it. "Could it have been an accident? I mean did she just fall?"

He shakes his head sadly. "It wasn't an accident. I'm sorry."

Nodding, I turn away from him.

Dirk calls everyone back to the hotel. We gather in the attached restaurant. He explains what we know. I'm not listening. Hearing it once was enough.

"What are we going to do?" JD asks.

Dirk signals the waitress to bring another round of drinks. "Well, I guess that's up to Dan."

I down my drink, slamming the empty glass on the table. "I'm going to kidnap the bride."

Cheers ring out across the bar. The men are antsy for a fight. We haven't had one in a long, long time.

Later that night Raffe and Dirk find me sitting on the ground outside my room. They each take a seat beside me. Dirk lights up a joint and hands it to me, cocking an eyebrow. "You need to take the edge off, brother."

I take a hit, passing it to Raffe.

"Today at the bridge, that was some heavy stuff." Dirk leans over to take the joint from Raffe.

"I'm… I don't know." And I really don't know. Lily dropped into my lap and in a few short weeks became my everything. I miss her.

Raffe blows smoke rings above us. "I've been going to a therapist since my accident."

Dirk releases a huff of air but doesn't say anything.

Raffe continues. "After I got shot, I… I didn't want to live. Shit, I didn't even know where to begin." He runs his lighter over his jeans over and over again, the flame licking at the denim. "When we get her back, she needs to talk to someone."

Dirk tries to speak but Raffe interrupts him. "Not to us. She needs to talk to someone who is trained to deal with this sort of thing. Her wounds are deep. I know that we've all had our share of shit to deal with, but Lily was to the point where she couldn't see past it. She gave up."

"But she lived." I lean back against the cool rough bricks of the hotel. The thought of her not living almost too much to bear.

He nods slowly. "She did and I think she found the space to breathe with us. All I'm trying to say here is we cannot mess this up. We can't miss anything. She needs us no doubt, but she also needs professional help."

"I can't think past my need to have her in my arms." I bury my face in my hands.

"I know, brother. We'll get her back and then we go from there." He pushes off my shoulder as he rises, giving it a squeeze before he walks away.

Dirk snuffs out the joint. "He's right. Lily has a lot of shit to unpack. We can't risk missing something. A fresh pair of eyes, ears, whatever a therapist might offer is not a bad idea."

I run my hand over my face and stand. "I'll talk to her about it. Along with the five million other things we need to discuss."

"She's worth it. You know this. I know this. We all know this. It's like that shit she's been resurrecting from the junkyard." He jumps to his feet. "Her own fucking family left her to sit and rot. We aren't going to do that. One man's junk is another man's treasure. Do you think the prick she's being forced to marry tomorrow thinks of her as a treasure... fuck no. If he did, she wouldn't have jumped off that fucking bridge."

Jesus, he's right. She was so desperate to escape them, she tried to kill herself.

I knew she saw the world differently.

She looks past the exterior and homes in on what lies beneath. Like the way she talked with my mother. She didn't hide the fact that my mother didn't remember me. She rolled with the punches. She introduced me to my mother as her handsome boyfriend and my mother agreed. She thought I was handsome as her son, and she thought I was handsome when I wasn't her son. It made me feel good, like my mother still saw me and I guess she did… she does. Is one better than the other? Not really. It's all how you look at it.

Then there's Jackson. She didn't shy away from him when he broke her painting. She made sure he knew he was more important than any material thing. Then she went above that and took time out of her day to embrace Jackson's restlessness. She marveled in it and showed him how to turn it into something productive. She made an impact on him.

She sees the world differently because she knows what it's like on the other side. She said so herself. That she felt stuck on one side of the glass, watching others live. She's so good at it, she notices things others overlook.

I jump when I notice Dirk still at my side. He shoves me toward the door to my room. "Hit the hay, brother. Tomorrow is a big day. Smurf is going to see what being a Skull is all about." He waits for me to unlock my door and stumble inside.

"What if she doesn't want to go with me?" I hate being insecure, it doesn't look good on me.

"Dan, that girl looks at you like you're some kind of knight in shining armor. Tomorrow, she's going to have proof of it." He lights up a cigarette, backing out of my room. "Don't you ever fucking tell Jesse I said shit like that."

I laugh, then slam the door in his face. Fucking asshole. I fall face first onto the bed, the last couple days finally catching up. *I'm coming for you, baby. Please don't worry. I'm coming.*

Chapter Thirty

Lily

I spent the last night I'll ever spend in this room, staring at the ceiling.

I'm grieving. For him.

His big arms. I miss them. His beard. I miss it. My hand rises to my cheek, remembering the scratchy feel of it against my skin. His voice. God, how I miss the sound of his voice.

I know you must think I'm the biggest doormat on the planet and maybe I am.

What do I do? Stand up to him? I've tried. Plead with someone to help me? Yep, done that.

My entire life has been molded by my father. Until I fell.

He didn't plan for that. He didn't seem surprised though. Maybe because of Jenny, he expected it.

A knock on my door begins a rush of chaos that I can't even wrap my head around.

It's my wedding day.

My heart digs its heels in the ground, skidding against the gravel as I'm drug through the sham of the day.

The hair stylist that "fixed" my hair last night is back and she's pinning and pinning until all my hair is away from my face, trapped in a tight chignon at the base of my neck. I watch her in the mirror as she animatedly talks to the girl who's here to do my makeup.

Both are oblivious to the horrors that have taken place in this house.

When I was little, I loved it when my dad would have someone come to do my hair. I would watch the girl in the mirror just as I'm doing now. Sometimes, it would be the only touch I would get for weeks, months. I loved it.

Today, not so much. Not now that I know what being touched by someone who really cares about me feels like. A friend's arm draped around my shoulder, a high five given for a job well done, a hug from a little boy who appreciates my friendship. The touch of a man who loves me. Big warm hands, grabbing me around the waist, pulling me to him. His breath fluttering over my cheek as his body comes inside of mine.

The makeup lady scolds me, but I don't listen. "Girl, you're ruining your makeup."

Am I crying? I don't know. I'm numb.

She huffs, leaving the room. When she returns with my father by her side, she has a big grin on her face. I catch the wink he throws her way.

238

"See what I mean?" She points to my face in the mirror. I don't turn around.

"Can you ladies please give my daughter and I a minute?"

They both scurry out of the room. If only they knew.

He lays his hand on my shoulder. "Would you like me to have your mother come up and help you finish?"

"No, thank you. Is she here?"

"She is." His eyes search mine.

Figures. What kind of mother doesn't help her daughter get ready for her big day. I've seen movies of brides surrounded by their friends and family. The mother of the bride is always fretting over finishing touches, tears in her eyes.

He reaches around my shoulder, a tiny pill in his palm. "Take this. It will help."

I stare at it. Fear tingles up my spine.

My eyes meet his in the mirror. I had forgotten this part.

"I'm fine. I'll be fine." I drop my eyes. Every cell in my body screams at me to pull away. His hand is hot and heavy on my shoulder. Unrelenting.

"I insist." He pulls the glass of water on my dressing table closer to me. Again, opening his palm.

The pill sticks in my throat on the way down. I cough lightly. He pats me on the back. "There's my girl," he says softly. "Benjamin bought a home a few miles away. You will be comfortable there and once you meet some of the other wives your age, you'll see it's not so bad."

"You want me to have a life like my mother's?"

"It's not a bad life."

I shake my head sadly. That's not life at all.

My eyes meet his again. This man has so much power. He could have used it for good. He could have chosen to help people like Jenny. Instead, he used it to hurt her. I sigh loudly, ready for him to remove his hand and his presence.

"Good?" he asks.

"Yes, sir."

He leans down and brushes his dry lips across my cheek. I close my eyes, swallowing the bile that rises up my throat.

The girls come back in, giggling. I'm sure my dad said something charming to them. Smoke in mirrors. All smoke in mirrors.

I let them do their worst. My body relaxes as the pill my father gave me kicks in.

After my father found me in the hall as a child, with a hand full of vomit, the tiny pill became a bedtime snack. I think he gave it to me to keep me in my bed and most importantly away from the other wing.

Watercolor Skulls

I'm not sure when the practice ended. I suppose when Jenny came. He didn't hide her because she was so wonderful, even he saw it. He wasn't content with only one night. His greed to have her, ultimately led to his demise with me.

Jenny told me I could have more.

And then a group of Skulls showed me just how much more.

More wonder, more magic, more love…

I can't live without it.

The girl who did my makeup snaps in front of my face. "Hello, earth to Ms. Ramsey."

When I focus on her, she laughs.

"You act like you're going to a funeral. It's your wedding day. You're marrying one of the top ten most eligible bachelors in the country. Smile for god's sake."

"Fuck you," I say blandly.

Her mouth falls open. The other girl pulls her away from me. "We'll tell them you're ready."

I walk to the window, sliding it open. My eyes take in my father's beautiful flower garden with brightly colored bird feeders scattered amongst the blooms. It's his little space, no one else is allowed to feed the birds. Yet he never sits out there to enjoy them.

My hands shake as I bunch this stupid dress in my fist and lower one leg and then the other to the ledge outside my window. I sit down and scoot so that I'm out of reach, my feet dangling over the edge. Tiny wisps of hair tickle the side of my face, but I don't brush them away, scared I might fall.

You're wondering if I'm going to jump. I don't know what I'm going to do. This is my only escape. Maybe I'll just sit here till I waste away.

"Lily!" My mother's shrill voice screeches to my left. I turn my face toward her. "Lily, get back in here, right now!"

I smile at her. "Hello, Mother."

"Lily, right now."

"Have you ever been free?" I ask her, kicking my feet back and forth, my fingers locked around the cool cement of the ledge. Euphoria sets in from dad's little pill. It's working its magic.

"Lily. You're leaving me no choice. I'm going to have to go get your father."

I laugh. "So, that's a no then?"

She stares at me, her lips parted.

"It's wonderful mother. Have you ever let your hair whip in the wind while driving down a lonely road? Have you ever had a man whisper dirty things in your ear while bringing your body the most pleasure it's ever known? Have you looked in a child's eyes and wondered how the world could get any more perfect?" She stares at me like I've grown two heads.

I chuckle sadly. "No? Hm, didn't think so." I continue to swing my legs precariously. "Well, I have. I lived more in the last two weeks than I have in my entire twenty-five years."

She pulls her head back inside.

My imagination must be playing tricks on me. The rumble of bikes calls to me. I imagine myself on the back of Dan's bike. Home. I want to go home. I let myself slip into my memories of the past few weeks. The best weeks of my life and even if this is it… I can now say I've known what it's like to have had a friend, a lover, a family.

Chapter Thirty-One

Dan

Dirk really came through last night. He got another three chapters to ride with us today. I thought I would be nervous but I'm not. I'm here for one thing. Her. I don't give a fuck about anything else.

When we pull up to the gate, two guards stop us. It only takes two seconds to disarm them and drive right on in. That was easy.

Looks like we're just in time for the festivities. It's a small affair. Maybe twenty or so guests. They all stand from their white fold up chairs, shocked expressions on their faces as we park in the grass behind their little gathering.

Two men stand out to me as I swing my leg off my bike, reaching into my saddlebag for one thing, her jacket. I grab it and walk up to the man standing at the end of the isle, assumingly her father, as he waits for the bride.

Dirk whistles. "She must really love your dumbass to leave all this behind." He smirks, knowing the true evil behind the artificial beauty.

"What in the hell is this?" her father demands. A large bodyguard moves to his side.

I light up a cigarette. Haven't had one in years but I think the occasion calls for it. "We're here for the wedding."

He blinks, a confused look on his face.

A few of the guys take a seat in empty chairs, making women in big hats blush and quickly scoot away. Some of the others help themselves to the food that's spread out across a few tables to the side. A cake that stands at least three fucking feet high topples over as JD dives in with his whole hand, fisting a giant piece for himself. "Good fucking cake," he says, laughing, cake crumbs falling into his beard.

A woman comes running out from the side of the mansion. She stops dead in her tracks when she sees us. Lily's father glares at me before taking a few steps to meet her. "Where is she?" he asks angrily, his eyes darting over the bikers taking over his zillion dollar home.

"She's sitting on the ledge outside her window. I think she's going to jump again!" the woman wails.

I tip my head, studying her, this must be Lily's mother. The Senator snaps at her. "You had one job, Margaret." He storms toward the house. "Rudy," he hollers to the bodyguard who has been standing by quietly. "Call the police."

Dirk pulls out his pistol. "You don't want to do that, Rudy." He spins in a circle. "Everyone, please have a seat." He moves to the front, shoving a frightened minister into a chair.

I glance around, seeing some of the other Skulls pull their weapons to keep people off their cell phones. The groom rushes toward the Senator. "What the hell is going on?"

The Senator looks at me, ignoring the groom. "I don't know who you men are, but I need to get to my daughter. She's not well."

I motion for him to lead the way. He huffs not wanting the likes of me in his home but that's too fucking bad. "You stay." I point to the groom.

When he starts to follow us, JD grabs him around the throat. "I got him," he says, smiling like a kid in a candy store.

Raffe joins me as we escort Senator Ramsey and his wife inside.

"What is this about? Why are you here?" he asks, climbing the stairs. He still hasn't figured out we're not here for him or his money. It hasn't even crossed his mind we might be here for his daughter.

"Let's just say Lily is a friend of ours."

Both her parents stop to stare at me. Mrs. Ramsey grips the pearls around her neck. I continue up the stairs, taking two steps at a time. I can feel her. She's close.

Mr. Ramsey storms ahead of me. He pushes a door open and runs to an open window on the other side of the room. I scan it quickly. It's her room but it's not *her*. Not even close.

"Lily, honey, come here, please, please take my hand," he coaxes. The sentiment even sounds phony to me.

I don't hear any response from her. I snap my fingers, indicating he should get the fuck out of my way. He turns his head toward me and steps away from the window, whispering harshly, "You don't know anything about Lily. She needs help. She's a very unstable girl."

"Get the fuck out of my way, asshole."

A click sounds over my shoulder, Raffe's gun is pointed straight at the Senator. I cock an eyebrow. "Looks like it's decision or collision time, buddy." I toss my cigarette to the floor, stomping it out with my boot, putting a hole in the white carpet. Who the fuck has white carpet?

The Senator swallows and slides away from the window, grabbing his wife and pulling her in front of him. I roll my eyes at the chicken shit bastard.

Raffe motions for them to take a seat on Lily's bed.

I step to the window, popping my head out into the warm evening breeze. Lily is sitting just out of reach. God, she's a beautiful bride. Her eyes are closed, her knuckles white as she holds onto the ledge, her feet swinging lightly.

Kicking a leg out the window so I'm straddling the sill, I light up another cigarette to get her attention without spooking her with the boom of my voice. Her eyes pop open and her head slowly rolls to the side. Her eyes lock on mine.

"Hey, baby," I say softly, taking a drag off my smoke.

A faint smile forms on her angelic face. "This is such a good dream," she whispers, swaying slightly on the ledge.

Somethings off. I poke my head back inside. "What is she on?" I ask the asshole sitting nervously on Lily's bed.

"I... I gave her a valium. She had wedding jitters."

The mother's mouth drops open, but she clamps it shut.

These motherfuckers. I crack my knuckles, letting him know just how displeased I am about what he just said.

Chapter Thirty-Two

Lily

When the roar of bikes quieted in my ears, I filled the minutes watching birds dart from one feeder to the next in my dad's flower garden.

My dad was just here, trying to coax me from the window. I didn't even turn to look at him. I'm not coming down from this ledge for anyone. I'm not marrying Benjamin. Not today. Not ever.

The click of a lighter catches my attention. I turn to see a mirage of Dan, smoking a cigarette. "Hey, baby," he says to me.

I smile, happy that my mind conjured him. Even if it didn't get it quite right. Dan doesn't smoke. "This is such a good dream," I tell the mirage.

He ducks back inside before returning to me.

Dan leans forward, holding the cigarette out to me. I've never smoked but why not. I snag it from him. My lips wrap around it, and I take a small puff. I cough a little. This seems….

Real.

The cigarette drops from my hand. I watch it fall to the grass below.

I turn back to the apparition. He smiles. He's real.

Oh god.

"You didn't think I'd really let someone steal my girl, did you?" He tips his head, running his fingers through his beard.

Immediately, my hand reaches out to him. He grabs me and holds on tight. I quickly slide my butt down the ledge toward him. He helps me inside, wrapping me up in his arms. The smell of man and pine trees envelopes me. Home. I'm home.

He pushes me back slightly, keeping my hand locked in his. He spins me around, whistling low. "You're so fucking beautiful," he says in awe. "But you're missing something."

I glance down at my dress. Fuck. What must he think? I hope he doesn't think I want to marry someone else. And then his big hands shove something black in my arms. My heart melts.

Never should I doubt anything with him. He knows me. He knows me. Tears stream down my cheeks.

Bringing the jacket up to my face, I place my lips over the patch that says *Property of Big Dan*. My eyes slowly roll up to meet his. He grabs me forcefully, crushing his lips to mine. "I love you," he mumbles against my mouth. "I love you," he says repeatedly as our teeth click together, his passion unleashed.

He's a man obsessed. A man searing his love into me, an everlasting imprint that leaves no room for doubt. I'll die with his love stamped across my lips.

"Um, not to interrupt this little reunion but can we get the fuck out of this creepy fucking mansion," Raffe says from somewhere behind Dan.

Dan quickly helps me slide into the jacket. He looks me straight in the eye. "You don't have to say anything to anyone. I'm getting you out of here."

I nod. The way Dan says this I know my parents must be in the room. "I need something," I whisper.

"Raffe, take the Senator and his wife downstairs. We'll be right behind. Lily just needs a minute to get herself together."

My mother sniffles and my dad says nothing. This is bad. This is so bad. He knows about Dan now.

When the door closes, I wait a few minutes before rushing to my dresser. I drop to the floor and pull the bottom drawer out, revealing my hiding spot underneath. I grab the journals, mine, and Jenny's. I hand them to Dan, making sure I have them all. When I stand, he is tucking the final one in the waistband of his pants.

I nod once. "I'm ready."

He kisses me again before grabbing my hand in his. We jog down the stairs. When we walk out onto the east lawn, I stop dead in my tracks. *Oh my god.* I double over, my hand over my mouth. I've never felt so loved in my entire life.

Skull men are everywhere. It's like a scene straight out of an action movie. My wedding cake is toppled over. Bikers have their feet kicked up on the tops of chairs. The smell of weed permeates the air. This is… this is fucking great.

My dad rushes over to me. "Glad you're finding this so amusing," he hisses. "Do you care to explain who these hoodlums are?"

Dan shoves him away from me.

"These *hoodlums* are my friends," I wave my hand out, my eyes stopping on JD. He has his arm wrapped around Benjamin's neck. He winks at me as he tightens his grip, making Benjamin dance on his toes.

I let my gaze land on my parents. My dad is glaring daggers at me.

"Goodbye," I say simply. What else is there to say?

My mother's eyes bounce from Dan to me.

"Lily. If you walk away, that's it. You'll never see a penny of my money." My father's threat falls flat. I've already told him. I don't want any of this. He remembers that as the words leave his mouth.

Dirk walks up, dropping his arm around my shoulders. "Hey, Smurf." He wraps a tattooed finger around one of my brown curls.

My dad bristles. Dirk leans forward, holding his hand out. "It's nice to meet you, sir," he says.

When my dad doesn't take his hand, Dirk laughs, turning to look at Dan.

Dan is studying my face closely, oblivious to what is going on around him. Dirk's gaze comes back to me, a scowl forms on his face when he notices what has Dan so shook up. His arm falls off my shoulder and he takes a step back.

Dan is in front of me in a flash, his fingers wrapping gently around my neck. He tips my chin from side to side as his eyes roam over every inch of my face. Even the best makeup money could buy didn't erase the bruise my father left behind. "Who did this?" he asks, deadly calm.

I shift nervously. Dan is really pissed.

"I asked you a question, Lily."

I nod my head toward my father. Seconds is all it takes before my mother is crying louder than I've ever heard her wail. People are screaming and all hell breaks loose. Dirk and Raffe struggle to pull Dan off of my dad. When they finally get him off, I glance at the ground. My dad is lying there, blood gushing from his nose. His handsome face is pummeled.

It happened. He finally got some of what he deserved.

Dirk hands Dan a white cloth napkin. Dan wipes his hands on it, his eyes never leaving my fathers. "Try to take her away from me again and see what happens." He tosses the napkin on my father's chest.

He wraps me up in his arms and walks us toward Benjamin and JD. Benjamin cowers against JD's chest, clearly not wanting some of the dish Dan just served my father.

"She's mine. You hear that, numb nut?"

Benjamin nods.

Dan looks down at me. "Ready, baby?"

I stare into Benjamin's frightened eyes for a second. They beg me not to tell Dan what he did to me last night. What he did to me in the past.

253

JD's eyes soften as he sees the turmoil play out across my face. He gives me an encouraging smile.

I turn in Dan's arms, giving Benjamin a full view of the back of my black leather jacket. Rising to my tippy toes, I tug on Dan's beard, pulling him to me. I kiss him with abandon, wanting everyone at this fucking fake ass wedding to see where my allegiance lies. Where it will always lie.

The entire club erupts in cheers, claps, and whistles. I don't give Benjamin or my parents a second glance. Dan scoops me off my feet and carries me to his bike.

Dirk yells, "Let's head out boys!"

Bikes roar to life one by one. My tribe… my family. They came for me. My heart bursts clean open as I wrap my hands around my man. My savior. My knight in shining armor.

Chapter Thirty-Three

Lily

We pull into a hotel on the edge of town, right off the highway. The men are beginning to gather, beers being cracked open. A party comes to life right before my eyes in the parking lot. I slide off the back of the bike, dropping the train of my dress onto the dirty pavement.

Dan sets his helmet down. His eyes are everywhere but on me. He grabs my hand and silently leads us through the throng of bikes toward the stairs. Once we reach what I assume is his room, he pulls a keycard out of his pocket, sliding it through the lock. When the little light turns green, I glance behind me, suddenly scared to be alone with him.

My eyes land on Dirk's. He's watching us like a hawk. Dan tugs on my hand, forcing me to follow him over the threshold. I catch him flip Dirk off before closing the door.

He turns on a light over the table, tossing his billfold and keys onto it. He drops his jacket in one of the chairs and then carefully pulls the journals out of his waistband, setting them gently on the table.

Only after all that does he allow his gaze to fall over me.

He reaches for me, spinning me so I'm facing away from him. His big fingers work deftly over the buttons on the back of my dress. Soon, it pools around my feet, a puddle of expensive white silk. He finishes undressing me until I'm standing bare for him.

His fingers brush down my arms. I shiver at the sensual feel of his warm hands on me.

"I'm sorry," I whisper, shifting to face him.

"Shhh." He wraps his fingers around my arms, stilling me. "No apologies."

My heart slows as he leisurely unpins my hair. The pins clink against the table as he tosses them one by one. When my hair falls, tickling the top of my bottom, he runs his fingers through it. "So, beautiful," he whispers over my shoulder. His breath is close and hot on my skin.

He walks us to the bed, giving me a little shove onto the cheap mattress. I lie perfectly still as I listen to him remove his own clothing. I'm thankful he's taking control and not expecting me to talk. My mind is still clinging to the ledge outside my window. If I think about everything that just happened, it will send me into a panic. I'm terrified of what my father might be planning.

The bed dips, Dan's knee pressing into the mattress between my legs. He reaches under and pulls me to my knees. His hands roam over my entire body. Gently, he caresses my breasts, my arms, my stomach, my legs. Kisses fall down my spine softly.

I groan into the bed when his hand finally lands over the ache he has stoked between my thighs. "Baby, you're always so wet for me."

His. His. His.

The world evaporates as his fingers sink into me. I try to glance at him over my shoulder, but he grabs my hair, stopping me. "I want you to listen to me, Lily." His fingers glide in and out of me, my need building with each stroke of his hand.

"I'm listening," I pant, lifting my bottom for him.

"The only fall I'll ever allow you to make is the one we are currently experiencing."

I still.

"Do you understand what I am saying to you?" He leans forward, his chest pressing into my back, his cock rubbing against my ass.

I nod, my hair still wrapped in his fist.

"Never again." He smacks my ass and I feel the sting clear down to my soul.

Tears rush to free themselves. Yes. I need this. To be exposed, flayed open so the poison can flow from my body.

Another smack and then another. I can feel his fear in the heat of his hand.

I scared him.

And he knows.

Somehow, he knows.

My eyes roam to the bedside table. A newspaper is carefully folded to an article.

LM Terry

Senator Ramsey's Only Daughter Jumps from the Golden Gate Bridge and Survives

His palm continues to lash across my skin. My pain hurts him. His pain hurts me.

An apology is on the tip of my tongue, but he won't allow it. That's not what he wants. He doesn't want an apology; he wants a promise.

"I promise," I cry. "I promise. I promise. I promise."

His assault stops and his fingers knead the sting away, dipping lower, stirring my desire to a combustible level.

"Never again," he rasps, struggling to regain his control.

"Never again," I repeat.

He releases his grip on my hair and I turn to look at him over my shoulder. His amber eyes reassure me that he is with me. He's always going to be with me. "I love you, Dan."

He slides into me in one smooth motion, dipping down to capture my mouth with his.

Dan makes love to me. Fucks me. Ravages me. The entire night. What was supposed to be my wedding night. I'll never doubt this man. Never.

Dan is a real man.

And he is mine.

All mine.

Chapter Thirty-Four

Dan

My hand runs through her hair mindlessly as she sleeps, draped across my body. I didn't want to talk last night. I wanted her to feel what I had to say. I think she got the message loud and clear.

Sunlight slips in through the curtains, dancing across us. I let the ray cut through the strand of hair between my fingers. Her natural color. I didn't mind the blue, but this is the real her and I love it.

I bring the strand to my nose and groan.

She stirs, wiggling her little button nose. Her ass flexes as she stretches. Hot. So. Fucking. Hot.

Her eyes open to mine.

I hold my breath. Last night was… intense and I'm not quite sure how's she's going to feel about it today.

She smiles, making my own mouth pull up at the corners. What she feels, I feel. She's happy. Content. Mine.

"Morning, baby." I run my foot over the back of her calf.

"Morning." She lays her hands on my chest, resting her chin on them.

"Want to go for breakfast and then do a little site seeing?"

Her smile falters and she sits up. "Yeah, sure." She shrugs as her eyes roam over the newspaper I left lying out on the bedside table.

I ignore her reluctance. "I'll go see if I can find you something to wear. One of the local wives might have something." I slip my legs into my jeans.

She nods, heading into the bathroom. The door clicks quietly behind her. I know she doesn't want to do this but it's time.

Shoving my keys and billfold into my pocket, I eye the journals on the table. I want to pull the cover back and peek inside, but the angel is on my shoulder whispering feverishly, *"Show her she can trust you, you big, dumb fuck. Don't even think about it."*

The little bitch on my shoulder is right. Lily will show me when she's ready.

I open the door almost tripping over a paper bag left on our doorstep. Scanning the parking lot, I notice Raffe sitting under a tree. He salutes me. I grab the bag and peer inside. Clothes. One step ahead of me. I shake my head and wave to him.

He stands and walks toward me, stopping at the bottom of the steps. "I called the coroner's office. Jenny's parents faxed her dental records." He drops his eyes to the ground, tapping his hand on the railing a few times. Eventually, he reigns in his emotions, his focus back on me. "I'm meeting him at four this afternoon if she wants to go along."

"I'll tell her."

"Be easy on her, Dan."

"I am."

"Are you though?"

"I needed her to know she can't…" a wave of nausea washes over me as I picture her sitting on that ledge, her eyes glazed over by the drugs her father gave her. How easily she could have fallen.

"Dan, for what this is worth, I think yesterday was her putting herself out of their reach in the only way she knew how. She doesn't want to leave you." His gaze shifts behind me.

Tiny hands slide around my mid-section. Her face presses against my bare back, her cheek wet with tears. I grab her hands, giving them a gentle squeeze. "I never want to leave you," she whispers against my skin.

I turn, forgetting all about Raffe. She is standing behind me in a towel, freshly showered, and oh so beautiful. Placing the bag in her hands, I lean down and kiss the top of her head.

"I'm sorry I scared you," she says, self-consciously running her free hand over her hair.

Pushing her hand away, I run my own down the length of it. I grab a strand, reveling in the softness. "I lost my mind when JD called me, but that was not your fault."

She watches my fingers lovingly caress the lock of hair. "That's not what I mean."

"I know. Will you help me understand?"

Lily sucks her bottom lip between her teeth, nibbling on it for a brief moment. "Okay."

We ride down to the bay, stopping at a little bagel shop for breakfast.

As we walk toward the bridge she slows. Logically or not, I grip her hand tighter. My fear of her running and plunging herself over the edge is increasing the closer we get. She stops. Her eyes sweep the entire area.

I've decided to let her lead from this point forward. There is nothing worse than being dragged toward your greatest fear. Her father has done plenty of that. I will not.

"When I was sixteen, my dad came to my room and told me that there was a young woman who would be staying with us." Lily stares at her feet. "She was the first one he acknowledged."

She takes a few steps before stopping again. Her eyes raise as she looks down the length of the bridge. "I waited six days for her to leave that room." She turns to face me now. "When she did, she walked out of the house, and this is where she came."

She takes a deep breath and pulls us forward a few more steps. Her fingers tremble in mine as she continues to walk slowly.

"I remember being struck by her beauty. A fresh face just like on the cover of a magazine. An All-American girl. When she swung her leg over the railing, I froze. I didn't understand what she was doing." Lily stops now and stares at a section of the bridge. Ghosts of the past reflect in the pools of her eyes.

Bravely she walks us forward, hand in hand and then she stops abruptly and turns to face the water. We both stare at the spectacular view.

"When she lowered herself, I rushed forward, leaning over to see her perched on the pipe below." Her hand trembles as she lays it gently on the rail. I place a hand on each side of her, standing with my chest pressed to her back. Cautiously, she leans over, we both stare at the churning water below.

Her hand dangles over the rail, reaching. "I didn't know what to say." She wiggles her fingers in the air. "It was then I noticed her necklace. I asked her about it."

She pulls her hand back quickly.

"You saved her that day."

Her face rises to the sky, she closes her eyes. "No, she saved *me* that day."

We stand quietly, the world rotating around us.

"My father sent me away the week she died. Demanded that I accompany my mother on a trip to Paris." Her body trembles against me. "She… she…" Lily cannot get the words out. Her heart is exposed, bloody and raw.

"She came back," I finish for her.

She nods, her hands scramble along the railing seeking mine. I lift my hands and place them over the tops of hers, pressing them securely over the rail.

"I've got you, sunshine," I reassure her.

"We had a plan... we had a plan. I don't know why she changed her mind."

Lily breaks down in my arms. I protect her from onlookers with my body. No one really pays much attention except for one person. The officer I met yesterday. He watches from afar. A frown upon his face. The man must have the soul of a saint, to walk this bridge every day, looking for broken ones.

I tip my chin to him in reassurance. He nods back.

"After she left, I tried to follow through on my own, but I just couldn't do it. The thought of running alone was too much. And then my father announced my wedding." She sucks in a ragged breath. "I begged him to reconsider and when he wouldn't..."

"You came here," I finish again.

Her head turns left, then right as she takes in the length of the bridge. "I came here," she repeats, she straightens her shoulders. As the salty breeze nips at her hair, I sense a shift in her demeanor.

"I came here," she says again. "And I lived. I lived." She tilts her face to the sun, a beautiful smile pulling at her mouth. "I lived." She laughs. And then she surprises me by turning in my arms. "I lived." She wraps her tiny hands in my beard and pulls me close to her. She mumbles over my lips, "I lived."

Lily kisses me, her tongue diving into my mouth. She kisses me with the kind of sheer abandon that only someone who has hit rock bottom can. The wind picks up, whipping her hair around our heads. She giggles as she pulls away.

My shoulders drop, the sun suddenly shining brighter, warming me from the inside out.

She stares into my eyes as I drown in hers. It took twenty shades of brown for God to come up with the sheer perfection of her eyes. Warmer than a cup of cocoa in the dead of winter, richer than a sip of coffee first thing in the morning.

"I promised her that I would let you love me." She blinks, and a tear rolls slowly down her cheek. I brush it away with my thumb, then press it against her plump, bottom lip. I drag my thumb across her mouth before leaning down and kissing her.

When I pull away, I ask, "Are you going to let me?"

"Yes." She smiles before turning back to look out over the bay. "The minute my hands left the bridge, I regretted it." Lily drops her head. "I don't want to die, Dan."

"But you did?" I ask sincerely, no judgement in the question.

Her gaze roams over the glittering water. "I wasn't thinking about dying." A crease forms between her brows. "I just couldn't figure out how to live."

Sighing, I hug her from behind.

"When I *fell*," she stumbles on the word. "I realized I had made a terrible mistake. One I didn't think I would come back from."

"I'm so glad you got a second chance."

"Me too." She lays her head back on my chest, relaxing fully into me.

I let her take all the time she needs as she processes everything. Several hours pass before she looks at me. "I need him to pay for everything he's done."

"We'll find a way."

"I'm ready to go." She tucks her hair behind her ear shyly. "Thank you for coming here with me today."

I drink her in. My beautiful little fairy. "I don't think you see it."

Her brow wrinkles as she tries to decipher my statement. "You are a splash of color in a dark world. That's why they want to keep you. It's why I want to keep you."

She tips her head to the side, pondering my words.

I reach out and trail a finger down the side of her face, over the bruise that bastard left behind.

"They don't deserve you."

"Do you?" she smirks.

"No," I answer honestly.

Her eyes soften. She places her hand over mine as I cup her cheek. She turns her face and presses her lips to the center of my palm. "This hand would never hurt an innocent human being." Her eyes lift to mine. "But it is strong enough to hurt those who are evil. When you came for me," she pauses, blinking back tears, "when you came for me, I thought I was dreaming." She closes her eyes. "I feel safe with you, Dan."

We leave the bridge behind. A chapter laid to rest. From here on out, we are together. There is more to discuss, much more but I think I understand her better now. She didn't want to die; she just didn't know how to live.

We stop for lunch before heading back to the hotel. I watch her carefully as I bring up the next topic of discussion. "Raffe contacted Jenny's family." She freezes, a french-fry paused mid-air. "They sent her medical records to the county. He has a meeting with the coroner at four today."

She sets the fry down before slouching against the booth.

"He wanted me to ask if you'd like to go with him." I comb my fingers through my beard as I wait for her response. The click of silverware and soft murmurs of other patrons is the only thing breaking the silence.

She scratches her head and leans forward, then back again. She wants to say something but doesn't know how to say it.

"Lily, just say what you're thinking."

"I'm scared," she leans forward, whispering, her eyes dart around the café. "He…" she shakes her head. "He is very powerful." She makes a fist, banging it on the table. "I don't want to see you or anyone in the club get hurt."

I lean forward too, our faces inches apart. Her eyes search mine as I speak. "You listen to me. I made a choice and so did the club. We chose you, Lily. This isn't the first time we've faced a threat and I'm sure it won't be the last. We get mean, Lily. We get mean and we protect what is ours. It's our motto. Never forget that."

She felt that.

I felt it.

We definitely understand each other now.

I close the distance, stealing her breath. When I pull back, I give her a final warning. "I will kill for you. I will die for you."

Her bottom lip trembles. "I love you," she whispers.

Chapter Thirty-Five

Lily

I'm shaking all over, a bead of sweat slowly rolls down my spine. Looking to my right, I watch Raffe's knee bounce. We haven't had a chance to really talk but he isn't angry like the last time we were together.

A man with grey hair combed over a bald spot takes the seat across from us. He pushes his glasses up on his nose as he opens the folder he brought with him. "I've had a chance to compare the dental records of our Jane Doe to your friend, Ms. Jenny Martin."

He tips his head slightly, peering at us over the rim of his glasses. When neither of us say anything, he continues. "They are a match. Please accept my sincere condolences. I hope this at least brings you and her family some peace. I see she has been missing for many years?"

My head turns toward Raffe. He glances at me before focusing on the coroner. "Yes, she was fourteen when she went missing."

The coroner frowns, deep wrinkles creasing the sides of his mouth. "How very sad." He steeples his fingers in front of his face. "If you give me a minute, I will gather the paperwork for her family. There is a process we must go through to have her moved."

Raffe nods and the elderly gentlemen rises and begins rifling through file cabinets.

"I need a minute," Raffe tells me, standing and excusing himself.

I wait for the door to close behind him. "Sir?" I quietly interrupt the man in his search.

He looks at me briefly before focusing once again on the files. "Yes?"

"Was… I mean was she pregnant when she was found?"

He stops, his fingers paused on a bright blue folder. "No." His brows furrow. "I thought she had been missing. Why would you ask about a pregnancy?"

"She was missing, yes, but not to me. I had met her a few times, here in San Francisco."

"I see." He pulls the file from the cabinet and takes a seat, not taking his eyes off me.

"You look familiar. Do I know you?"

"Perhaps. I'm Senator Ramsey's daughter."

He taps the folder on the desk.

I need to be smart here, so I offer him the best explanation I can. I don't need him getting suspicious and alerting anyone.

"I met Jenny while I was working with a charity. My hopes were to reunite her with her family. She was pregnant at the time. We lost touch before…" I leave my thoughts there. It takes longer to tell a lie than to tell the truth.

He smiles at me sadly. "No need to explain. I understand. It's too bad she couldn't have held on a little longer."

Raffe walks back into the room. His eyes wandering from the coroner to me. The coroner stretches an arm forward. "If you could get these to her family. We cannot start the process until they are returned to us."

"Thank you," Raffe tells him. The coroner rises from his chair to shake Raffe's hand.

Dan and Dirk are waiting for us outside, leaning against the building. Both are smoking.

"Get it all squared away?" Dirk asks.

Dan stomps his smoke with his boot before wrapping me up in the safety of his arms.

"Yeah, it was a match." Raffe slaps the papers the coroner gave him against his thigh.

Dirk grabs the back of Raffe's head and pulls him in for a hug. Not a quick bro hug but a real one. One that tells me they've been through a lot together.

"You okay?" Dan asks me.

"Yeah, fine." I'm not. I'm far from fine. There are so many questions. So many.

Dirk releases Raffe.

Raffe walks over to me and tugs me out of Dan's embrace, pulling me into his. My arms hang awkwardly at my side. "Thank you," he whispers against my hair, tucking his face into my neck. I stare at Dirk over his shoulder. He nods his head. Slowly, I bring my arms up and wrap them around him. When he pulls away, he brushes tears from his eyes. "Fuck, I'm ready to go home." He folds the papers in his hand in half, shoving them in his back pocket.

"Hell, yeah. I miss my girls." Dirk pats him on the back as they walk toward their bikes.

My eyes drift after them.

"What about you?" Dan asks, spinning me to face him. "You ready to go home?"

I nod shyly.

He smiles bright, making me feel like all is right with the world. It's not. Everything feels wonky and uncertain but that smile, it's my bright spot. Jenny used to tell me that I was hers. She had definitely been mine. As long as I have one, I think I'll be okay. No, I know I'll be okay.

We follow Dirk and Raffe out of the parking lot back toward the hotel. When we get close, I see the others waiting for us on their bikes. We don't pull in but as we pass, they file out one by one behind us. This will never get old, being part of a group like this. It makes me feel warm and safe.

Long hours pass before we finally arrive back at the warehouse. Some of the guys broke off earlier, headed to their homes. Soon, there are just a small group of us, those who live at the warehouse. Dan helps me off the bike. Everyone else heads inside, excited to hit their beds.

He tilts his head, studying me. "What's wrong?"

"I… I thought maybe we would go to my house," I admit, wrapping my arms around myself.

He cradles the side of my face in his big palm. "I'll get you home, eventually. I promise. But for now, I think it's safer if we stay here."

My gaze roams over the building. It's not that I don't like it here, it's just… my dad is still controlling my damn life.

Dan reads the emotions I'm battling in my head.

"The security here is probably better than what your dad has set up at his estate. We had some shit go down years ago. Raffe was hurt badly. We are safer here than anywhere. Dirk spared no expense."

"It's not that I don't believe you, I do. It's just… I simply wanted to go home but I understand. I trust you."

He leans in and kisses me on my forehead, letting his lips linger there for a moment before pulling away. "We'll go back to your place as soon as I'm sure it's safe."

I nod as he takes my hand, ushering us inside. The warehouse is quiet. Again, I'm struck by the beauty of the place. That warm, cabin in the woods feel, makes me sigh in relief. He steers us to the kitchen, loading my arms with snacks and drinks. It makes me giggle.

"I'm sorry but I'm hungry."

"Me too," I admit.

When we get to his room, we shower, washing away the dust from our travels. He inspects every inch of me, looking for more bruising. When he doesn't find anything, other than the one on my face, he drops his shoulders. Tension eases from his muscles.

He gives me one of his white t-shirts to sleep in. It smells like him and it's soft and warm. I smile to myself as I slip it over my head. Dan watches with an appreciative glint in his eye.

"I promised myself no funny business tonight," he says, biting his knuckle. "Jesus, help me."

I laugh, plopping down on his bed. It's nice to have a man who appreciates my body. "I don't mind your funny business," I say shyly, hiding behind my hair.

He chuckles as he begins unpacking his bag. "I don't mind it either, but I think we need to talk, then we should get some sleep."

Collapsing back on the bed, I roll to my side to pick through the snacks we brought up. "All we've done today is talk," I pout.

The bed dips as he sits down beside me. Dan lays the journals in front of me. "Out of everything in that house you could have taken, you chose these. Why?"

My gaze flits across them, landing on the two that have doodles all over the covers. I sit up and pull them to my lap. "These two were Jenny's." My finger traces over a smiley face she drew.

Dan pulls his legs up on the bed, sitting cross legged in front of me.

"The rest are mine. I've journaled for as long as I can remember." I pick one up and hand it to him.

He flips it over in his big hands. I break out in a sweat, seeing someone else hold my thoughts, my dreams. His eyes roll up to mine. Slowly, he hands it back.

I don't accept it, pushing it away from me. "I want you to know everything."

"Lily, you don't have to do this," he says, tapping the book on my knee.

Setting Jenny's journal in front of me, I pull my legs up to hug them. "I know I don't have to. I want to share them with you. That is the first one. My mother gave it to me on my tenth birthday. I want you to know me. The good, the bad, the ugly. You said you wanted me to help you understand. This is how I can do that." I motion a hand over the journals.

"If you're sure."

"I'm sure." I nod.

He smiles at me before leaning over and claiming my lips. My eyes fall closed. I wasn't sure I would ever see him again, but he came for me. He really does love me.

When he pulls away, he frowns. "You're crying again."

I laugh and wipe the tears from my face. "It's a happy cry. I promise."

"What were you thinking about?"

"You, and how much you love me." I tuck a piece of my hair behind my ear before gathering the journals and placing them on the nightstand. "You're the first man to tell me that you love me." I busy myself, turning all the binds so they are lined up and facing the same way.

He reaches past me, shutting the light off, then he grabs me and pulls me to lie down beside him. Once he has us in a spooning position, cuddled under the covers he whispers in my ear, "I love you. I love you. I love you." He squeezes me tight.

God there is no better place in the world than right here in his arms. "I love you too."

"I'm going to make up for all the times you should have heard it but didn't." His beard scratches against my cheek.

I raise my hand and hold his face to mine so he can't move away. "I missed you so much and we were only apart one night. How can that be?"

"We are just one of those lucky *love at first sight* couples."

Turning in his arms, I snuggle into his broad chest. "I was scared I'd never see you again."

He kisses me slowly and deep, making my toes curl before pulling away from me. "I wouldn't have let that happen." He kisses me once more before running his hand over my face. "Let's sleep. I'm fucking beat."

Laughing lightly, I close my eyes, drifting into a peaceful sleep.

Chapter Thirty-Six

Dan

I keep my eyes closed, forcing myself to go back to sleep, fighting the urge to get up and take a piss. Lily's head lands on my stomach, making me grunt lightly. My hand roams down to cup the back of her head. "It's still dark out," I murmur sleepily.

She giggles, turning her face to press a kiss against my stomach. I flinch and stifle the grin that is forming on my face.

"You haven't even opened your eyes," she teases.

I peek one eye open, then the other. "Why are you up so early?"

"I don't know." She traces circles lightly over my chest. Suddenly, she jumps to a sitting position. "Oh, I know what I could do." She climbs off the bed, scrounging around for her clothes.

Propping myself up on an elbow, I watch her, amused. "What are you doing?" I ask.

"I'm going to go down and make everyone breakfast." She shimmies one leg into her jeans and then the other, tugging them over her ass with a little hop.

Shit, that was hot. I lick my lips as I stare at her, my fingers itching to touch her. My eyelids droop right before I lunge for her.

"Dan, no, I've got to get started," she says breathlessly. I suck the sensitive skin under her ear into my mouth. "Please, I need to thank them somehow," she pleads.

I release her neck with a pop and sigh. "Fine, but you can show me your thanks after breakfast." I smack her ass before pushing her away from me. "I'll come downstairs and help you."

She bites her nails, shifting anxiously on her feet. "How do you want me to thank you?" she asks shyly. I'm not fooled, she's not that shy around me anymore. Maybe a little. But right now, I think Lily is messing with me. She likes these little games we play.

Tipping my head, I pretend to think about it. I tap my finger over my lips, when it stops, she squeezes her thighs together. She is getting turned on. "How about you let me do something to you that no one else has ever done."

Her lips part, a tiny puff of air escaping her. She shivers and her nipples poke delightfully against my white t-shirt. "Like what?"

"Well, sweetheart, what *haven't* you done?"

She opens and closes her mouth. I'm sure there are things that come to mind but she's a little scared to voice them out loud. My cock swells. Fuck, we are never going to get downstairs at this rate. A thought comes to me. It's a little evil. Should I?

Watercolor Skulls

Another shiver runs up her spine as if she can read my thoughts.

"I don't know what you want me to say?" She shifts nervously.

I shrug. "Well, there's no hurry, I guess. Maybe you can think about it through breakfast."

It's then she realizes what I've just done. She whines as she rips my shirt over her head. Oh, she did that on purpose.

Her eyes meet mine, checking to see if she has any chance of winning this round. Nope. Not a chance. Hey, I know my balls are going to ache over this too, but a little anticipation is good for the soul.

She huffs a stray piece of hair out of her eyes as she leans over to snag her bra from the floor. She glares at me but in a playful, yet I want to kill you, sort of way. I chuckle as I begin getting dressed myself. This is my Lily. She's back. With each passing minute, she is morphing back into the Lily I met at the tattoo shop, leaving the Lily I found clinging to that ledge behind.

"I'll meet you down there," she says, standing on her tiptoes to give me a peck on the cheek.

She bounces out of the room. An evil smile forms on my face as I grab the little clit vibrator I bought out of my nightstand. I was going to torture her with it the night of the run but that all went to shit after she almost dove headfirst into the lake. Pocketing it, I whistle my way downstairs.

She's washing her hands in the sink. I walk up behind her and press her against the counter. She grunts, instantly pressing her ass into my groin. When she turns her head, she's smiling. "About time you showed up. I thought you were going to ditch me," she says over her shoulder.

"I'd never ditch you." I pull the vibrator out of my pocket. "I've got something that might help stimulate your mind. Maybe it can help you think of something that has never been done to you." I lean in and nip at her earlobe.

She stills in my arms as my hands slide around, popping the button on her jeans. I shove the rubbery stimulator inside her panties, completely covering her clit. It has a tail of beads that I align right down to her asshole. She hisses, making my cock jump in my jeans.

Once I'm content with the placement, I gently pull my hand out of her pants and button her back up. I kiss her cheek before taking a step away.

She doesn't move. Not an inch. "Dan," she says, unsure of what is happening.

I slide the bar on my phone, giving her a little buzz. Lily jolts forward, grabbing the counter tightly. "Oh. Oh shit." She starts to double over, so I pull back on the control.

Slowly she rights herself, cautious for it to begin again. She spins toward me. "W-what is that?" she asks unsteadily.

"This?" I shake my phone in my hand. "Just a little item I picked up. Thought we'd give it a try." I put it in my pocket, wash my hands and head to the cupboard to retrieve the griddle. "Should we make pancakes?"

She rotates in place, her eyes not leaving my pocket. "Dan, everyone will be up soon," she warns, her eyebrows raised to her hairline.

"Well, then you better come before they do."

"Dan," she squeals, stomping her foot.

Buzz.

"Oh. Oh." She leans back then forward again, trying to get the thing to ease off her.

Buzz. Buzz. Buzz.

She is glaring daggers at me now, but I see the lust... so we continue to play.

I hand her a dozen eggs. "You can whip these up and I'll start on the pancakes." My eyes trail over her ass as she leans over the counter, cracking an egg in a bowl. I drag my gaze away and focus on the task at hand, which is making her squirm.

"So, have you ever given anyone a blow job?"

She stills, bracing herself for the kick to come. And it does.

She nods her head feverishly, answering quickly, hoping to escape the vibration. "Yes. Yes, I've given a blow job."

I pull my hand from my pocket, pleased she answered truthfully. Leaving the griddle to warm, I grab the bacon out of the fridge. Lily is eyeing me nervously.

Setting the bacon on the counter, I turn toward her. "It's been scientifically proven that the first sizzle of bacon causes Raffe to wake from the dead." I cock an eyebrow and she swallows hard, getting my message loud and clear.

I run a knife along the package. "Okay, blow jobs are not a first for you. Hm, let's see? Have you ever had your pussy feasted on?"

When she doesn't answer, I swivel my head toward her. She's biting her lip nervously.

"Well?" I think I know the answer and suddenly I want to beat her ex into the ground. What kind of man takes pleasure without giving it? Asshole.

Deciding to let her off the hook on this one because I feel like shit for even asking, I pop off another question. "Ever have someone fuck your ass."

Her eyes go wide, the previous question forgotten. Good. She blinks slow, her lips parting. This question intrigues her.

"No," she whispers.

Her answer sends a surge of blood to my cock.

Buzzzzzzz.

She thrashes against the counter, turning to face me. Her eyes beg me to stop, beg me to keep going. "Jesus, oh God, Jesus," she pants. Arousal kisses her skin, making it glow, and look so fucking sexy.

I shut it off.

Chuckling, I drop the bacon in the skillet. My eyes are on hers as I go back to the pancakes. She reluctantly breaks eye contact and stumbles to the stove, pouring the eggs into a pan. She reaches for the salt and pepper on the rack over the stove. A portion of her creamy skin is revealed to me. God, my fucking balls ache more than I thought they would. I hope breakfast goes fast.

She rubs her legs together, obviously trying to ease the ache between her thighs. I give it a few short bursts to keep her going. Lily lets her head fall back. "I… I can't do it here," she grits out.

I walk over and swat her ass with the spatula. "Yes, you can."

The first sizzle of bacon crackles on the griddle. Both of our heads turn toward it in unison and then they go to the ceiling as footsteps sound the alarm.

I smirk as she presses her back into the counter, staring at me. "Please," she begs prettily.

Holding the phone up where she can see it, I slowly slide the bar higher and higher. Her eyes open wide as she rises to her tippytoes. The sound upstairs gets louder. A bead of sweat runs down her neck. Fuck that's hot.

Taking two big steps toward her, I press my hand against her jeans, pushing the vibrator firmly against her. "Come," I growl low in her ear. She instantly convulses against me, throwing her head back. After a long minute, I let off the control, bringing her back down. She breathes heavily, dropping her head to my chest. Once I'm sure she won't fall over, I step back.

"Goddamn, I love bacon," Raffe says as he steps into the kitchen.

Lily's eyes dart to mine, a flush still kissing her cheeks and rushing down her neck. She swallows hard, struggling to control her breathing.

Raffe pats my back as I flip the pancakes. His eyes roam from the bacon to Lily. She turns away, sticking her head in a cupboard. I laugh out loud. She throws me one of her, *I'm going to murder you in your sleep,* looks before promptly sticking her head back in the cupboard.

Raffe shakes his head in amusement, pulling a piece of bacon off the stove and chomping on it.

Lily huffs when she realizes she can't hide in the cupboard all day. She stomps her foot and turns to face Raffe. "I'm making you all breakfast as a thank you," she says, tossing her hip into him to get him to move away from the stove.

He chuckles, pointing his bacon at her. "She's been spending too much time with the dark one."

Chapter Thirty-Seven

Lily

They both laugh as *the dark one* walks into the room. Jesse cocks an eyebrow, making them quickly smother their enjoyment.

I smile to myself. Jesse is badass. I love her.

Everyone has a wonderful breakfast. All the tension from the past few days, washes away. My eyes fall over each of my new friends, lingering longer on the one who makes my heart beat faster. Dan makes life fun. He's never in a rush. He truly lives in the moment. Sensing my eyes on him, an ornery grin spreads over his face. He winks at me before turning back to listen to Billie Rose who is babbling in the chair next to him. She's so tiny compared to him. My chest gives a little squeeze.

Jackson happily chomps on a piece of bacon as he sits on my lap. His focus is on the little chrysalis hanging on the branch in his bug catcher. Raffe nudges me. "Hey, I was going to ask if you wanted to drive down to Vegas with Rachel, Jackson, and me? I wanted to give Jenny's parents the news in person, you know?"

I bounce Jackson on my leg. "Oh, I don't think I'm ready for that," I answer hesitantly.

Raffe doesn't push me. "Hey, that's okay." He rubs his hand over my shoulder. "They are interested in meeting you. But no rush. We can take it slow." He leans back in his chair.

"I guess I hadn't thought of meeting them."

"Like I said, no hurry, okay?"

I nod, grateful he isn't pushing this.

"One more thing." He glances around as if he's making sure no one is listening to us. He turns back to me. "I don't want you to take this the wrong way. It's just a suggestion. I… well, I was once where you were, on the bridge." He tips his head, silently asking if I understand what he is trying to tell me. My eyes dip to Jackson before rising to his. I nod. I understand.

"Anyhow, I started seeing someone. You know, to talk."

"Like a therapist?" I wrinkle my nose, not liking the idea.

He takes my hand in his. "Could you go just once? If you don't like it, you don't have to go back. Please, give it a chance. For me?"

My eyes glide over his blue ones. Blue and still and genuine. Just like Jenny said.

My mind chants this is a bad idea as my head bobs a yes.

He smiles and suddenly it's worth it. It's just one time. It's made him so happy. Just once. For him. For Jenny.

"Thank you. I'll set it up. I'll even drive you to your first appointment," he says enthusiastically.

286

"My only appointment," I reiterate, making sure he's clear on the terms.

"If you don't like it," he adds before changing the subject. "Jackson did you tell Lily you're going to the big city?"

Jackson turns to look at me. "Grandpa and grandma live there," he tells me.

My eyes go back to Raffe. He answers my question before I ask.

"My parents have passed, so I've kind of adopted Jenny's parents as my own."

My heart swells and my thoughts leave my mouth without thought. "Jenny would have loved the thought of you keeping in touch with her parents, let alone claiming them as your own. You don't know how happy that makes me," I gush. Jenny would be ecstatic with this bit of news. She always worried that they would never get the chance to be grandparents, being she was an only child.

He taps his fingers over his heart. "Awe, Lily, it makes *me* happy to hear you say that."

Jackson's little fingers turn my face toward him. I chuckle. "Grandma and grandpa don't like bugs but they like birds," he informs me.

"Birds, huh." I tip my head, an idea coming to mind. "How about you and I build them a birdhouse on Wednesday? We can paint it and everything," I tell him.

He bounces on my leg. "Yes, I want to make a birdhouse." He jumps off my lap, running over to Rachel to tell her all about our plans. She looks up and smiles at me.

"You're amazing," Raffe says.

I shake my head humbly. "I'm far from amazing, Raffe."

I almost come out of my chair as the little vibrator erupts, torturing me with a lazy hum. My eyes dart to Raffe. He didn't seem to notice, his focus on his wife and son.

My gaze slides to Dan. He points a finger at me. Shoot, he overheard me putting myself down. I grit my teeth as he gives me another warning buzz.

Raffe looks at me. "The fact that you don't recognize how amazing you are, is something you probably need to talk to someone about."

Well, I guess he has me there.

After we finish breakfast, Dan and I rush upstairs. As soon as he closes the door to his room, we are all over each other. "You are such an asshole," I mumble into his mouth as we both fumble with our clothes, trying to get naked as fast as we can.

I'm so wound up I want to climb him like a tree. So, I do.

Once our clothes are off, I scramble up his frame as he grabs me under my ass and walks us to the wall. My breath leaves me for a moment as he slams me against it. "You love this asshole," he grunts as he thrusts into me, effectively shutting me up. And I do love him. I do. I do. I do.

He fucks me fast and furious until I come undone. Tension builds and builds and builds until I'm….

Spiraling down…

down…

down.

"Holy, fuck," I clench my teeth, clinging to this big beast of a man like he's my salvation. "I hate you and I love you," I speak into his mouth, grabbing his face in my hands.

He chuckles as he continues to pound into me. The small of my back presses into the wall with each thrust. "Oh, oh, fuck, don't stop," I grit.

"I bet you're loving me right now," he grunts, his muscles tensing. His head drops to the crook of my neck as we come together, our bodies vibrating from the explosion.

"We're going to kill each other." His breath is hot on my skin, his voice raspy.

"In the best of ways." I lay my head against the wall, sighing heavily, feeling light and airy.

We spend the rest of the day lying around lazily. Dan has started reading my journals. He flies through them. It's as if he's binging a series. I guess he is.

I take a bite of my apple, staring at Dan. I could stare at him for days and days. I've had time to inspect all the ink on this side of him and I'm contemplating asking him to come lie face down beside me so I can inspect his backside. My eyebrow raises at the thought of his tight ass.

"I love you," Dan calls my eyes to his. When they make contact, he smiles. I blush shyly. He stops every once in a while, to tell me he loves me. Sometimes, he doesn't take his eyes from the page when he says it.

It's like whatever he read broke his heart and he can't bring himself to show me the pain in his eyes.

"I've got a question for you?"

Leaning over, I drop my apple core in the little trash can on the floor, my mind racing. Question? He's going to ask me a question. I swallow down my panic.

"Lily."

When I turn to the sound of my name, amber eyes keep me tethered to the shore. I bob there nervously; afraid I'm going to drift into full blown panic.

"You wrote this so…" He suddenly jerks out of the chair, coming to sit beside me. He talks excitedly. "You wrote with such detail. It's like you were dropping breadcrumbs."

I shake my head, confused.

"You left clues, Lily, clues. You mention several times that the day after you heard the crying your father would flip something black between his fingers."

My mind instantly conjures my father, his fingers threading a piece of black plastic between them effortlessly. Mindlessly.

I always watched him closely after a night of hearing them. He reminded me of the lions I used to see in the zoo. He would grump around for days, throwing things, slamming doors and then I would hear them and the next day he would be calm. Just like the lions after being fed. It was as if he was finally satiated. It scared me.

Oh god.

"What was it he flipped in his hand, Lily?"

"Why?"

"Because this is how you get justice."

"You mean *they* get justice."

"No. I meant exactly what I said."

I blow him off. I don't need justice, they do. "It was a flip drive." And the minute the words leave my mouth, I understand where he's going with this.

"He recorded it, Lily," he says, cupping my tiny hands in his.

I blink quickly as images flip through my mind like a rolodex. Yes. Yes. The morning after, he always had one. Always.

Jumping from the bed, I spin to look at Dan. "It's proof."

He nods his head slowly. "It would be proof, baby."

"But where would he keep them? He's been accused before… law enforcement searched."

"He's either got a hell of a hiding space or he has someone high up in his pocket."

"I'm going to find them." I stand taller, determined.

"We, baby. We." Dan stands, running his thumb over my bottom lip.

"Thank you," I whisper.

He smiles before leaning in close. "Breadcrumbs, baby. This was all you."

I let him kiss me slowly, our tongues agreeing that we make a surprisingly good team. When he pulls away, we smile at each other. This man has my back and he's going to have it while I tear my father's world down around him.

Chapter Thirty-Eight

Lily

I'm not sure why I agreed to this. My eyes dart to Raffe who is sitting on the couch beside me. The therapist's eyes bounce over the two of us. "So, Raffe tells me that Jenny is a mutual friend of yours."

"Yes." Keep it short and sweet and this will all be over soon.

He smiles. He has kind eyes. But kind eyes aren't always kind. Sometimes, they're tricky. He will try to trick me into saying something I shouldn't. I glance at Raffe again. He's smiling too.

Maybe they are both going to trick me. I mean, sure Raffe is here because I said I couldn't or maybe it was that I wouldn't, do this without him.

"It's an amazing story," the young therapist says.

I mean, shouldn't he be older? I was expecting someone older. Wiser.

Narrowing my eyes at him, I don't say anything.

He chuckles. "Lily, I'm not here to trick you. Relax, please."

Oh, he thinks he's so good he can read minds. I cross my arms over my chest. Unsure why I'm being so bratty. Why am I being a brat?

The answer makes me drop my eyes in shame. I'm scared and I don't know if I can trust him.

Again, the fucker reads my mind. Did I just think the word fucker? I don't have time to contemplate my mind's use of profanity at the moment.

"Lily, did you hear me? Whatever we talk about, it stays in this room. You have my word. And Raffe can stay if you like. If you decide you're ready for him to leave, that's fine. Just ask him to leave."

I rub my hands over the top of my jeans, my palms sweating. "I don't really know why I'm here."

He nods. "Well, Raffe is concerned about the attempt you made at taking your own life."

Facts. No bullshit. Fuck. I don't like the facts. They suck.

"I did but…" I pause. "I did."

"He said you jumped off the golden gate bridge?"

I nod, wiping a bead of sweat from my temple. It's so hot in here.

"It's amazing you survived. I'm curious to know your thoughts after you jumped."

My eyes dart to his. "I regretted it. I immediately regretted it."

"That's what I've read. You know there are only a handful of survivors, but they've all said the same thing."

Maybe this guy will understand me after all. I rush to explain, "I… god, I thought I had made the biggest mistake of my life. When I realized the fall didn't kill me, it was like I had been born again. I knew I had to do something drastic."

"What did you do?" he asks, his pen scratching over the notepad on his lap.

I turn to Raffe, reaching over to squeeze his hand. "Thank you, but I think I'm okay now."

He smiles wide and stands. "I'll wait in the lobby."

When the door closes behind me, I turn to the therapist and purge myself of the day I jumped, the day I ran, and the day I met Jesse.

He shakes his head. "I think it's a very lucky thing you met her that day."

"Me too. She's amazing. I'm sure Raffe's spoken about her."

He gives me what I'm assuming is a rare smirk. "He has."

"Then you already know how amazing she is. All of them. They're the family I've always dreamed of. Well, not exactly." I laugh lightly. "Truthfully, they are more than anything I could have imagined."

"You must be something special too, for them to take you under their wing the way they have."

"Oh, I don't know about that," I say, embarrassed. "I'm nothing like them. I would love to be brave like Jesse but I'm nothing like her."

"You don't think of yourself as brave?" he asks, setting his pen down and focusing all his attention on me.

I laugh. "Um, no. I'm the farthest thing from brave there is."

"Why do you say that?"

"Because it's true. If I would have been brave, I would have been able to help those girls."

"What girls?"

Oh.

I tap my finger on my leg. He is a trickster. I thought maybe Raffe had told him about them.

I take a deep breath and give him a quick non-descript version, my eyes glancing up at the clock. My time is just about up.

He picks up his pen and points to the clock. "I've scheduled you for two hours today." He tips his head. "I find first time patients need a little extra time."

I drop my head against the loveseat. Great.

"If you could go back, what would you do differently."

My mind clatters around as I look for an answer to his question. What would I do differently?

When several minutes pass, he speaks. "The reason you can't answer that is because you aren't the same person you were then. You were a child when this started. Experiencing something as a child is completely different than experiencing the very same thing as an adult."

His words roll around in my head. Some of the guilt eases a bit. A tiny bit but it's a start.

"We all have our strengths, Lily. You are not Jesse and Jesse is not you. You are brave in your own way."

"I'm trying to find a way to give them justice… to stop him if he's still doing those things." I glance out the window, watching white fluffy clouds glide over the bright blue sky.

"That sounds brave to me."

"Well, I have help now."

"Having help or even asking for help doesn't negate the bravery."

We spend the next hour talking about my dad and the flip drives. The time flies by as I voice my fears, my hopes.

"Do you feel better than you did before you came?"

"Yes," I admit.

"Good. I'd like to see you again next week." He stands, setting the pen and pad on his chair. I rise with him, taking a few steps toward the door.

"I guess that would be okay."

"I'll have the receptionist put you down for the same time next week." His hand rests on the doorknob. "Could you promise me one thing?"

I shrug. "I never like to promise anything before I hear what it is."

He laughs. "Smart." Tipping his head, he studies me. "When you feel anxious, promise me you will let Raffe know."

"Why?"

"He will be able to relate, and he will alert me if he thinks you need more help than he can give. We're going to explore your anxiety next week but for now just promise me. I don't feel comfortable prescribing anything at this point, but I would like to part ways knowing you will reach out to him. I don't want you suffering unnecessarily. Anxiety is no fun."

"No. No it's not." I've always hidden my anxiety, running off by myself, which only intensifies the sensation. I look him in the eye. "I promise."

Smiling, he opens the door for me. "I'll see you next week, Lily. Thank you for trusting me today."

Raffe is ecstatic that I stayed for the entire session. "I'm so glad today worked out."

"Yeah, I guess it wasn't so bad." I tuck my hair behind my ear, glancing out the window, excited to be going to see Dan at his shop. Raffe is dropping me off there and then I'm going to ride with Jesse to the bar. Dan will take me home after my shift. They are all being overprotective after what happened with my father.

It might look stifling to some but to me it's wonderful. It shows me how much they love me.

I wave to Raffe as he waits for me to go inside. So sweet.

When I get inside the shop, my happiness quickly turns to unease. Dan is bent over a girl with long blond hair. He's tattooing something on her chest. She is looking over her head, speaking to a girl that looks just as perfect as her. Her friend is swinging her legs back and forth as she sits on a stool, watching Dan work. They both laugh and he glances at them briefly before going back to his design.

The blond winks at her friend and wiggles her eyebrows before allowing her gaze to settle back on Dan.

Jesse looks up from the guy she's working on. Her gun pauses. "Hey, Lily." She smiles, flipping her dark hair over her shoulder. "I'll be ready in a minute."

Dan glances up when he hears my name, giving me a sexy smile. My heart squeezes and I push my ugly thoughts about the two girls to the side.

He nods his head for me to come to him. His eyes go back to his work, not waiting for me to obey. He knows I will.

Slowly, I saddle up to his side. The blond gives her friend a questioning look. They are trying to decide who I am to him.

He pauses the gun. "How did it go today?"

"Good," I tell him, looking over his shoulder at the tattoo he is doing on this bimbo.

I roll my eyes. Typical.

Dan catches my annoyance and chuckles. Hmph. I saunter away from him, going over to inspect Jesse's piece. She smiles at me. "Going to let me lay stake to some of that flawless skin you have," she says, smacking her gum between her teeth.

The blond huffs behind me.

Jesse winks, fueling me to play along with her.

"What spot do you want?" I pull my shirt up, giving her and the guy that she's working on a glimpse of side boob.

Jesse's eyes light up, a mischievous grin on her face. "Oh baby, yeah. I'll take it all."

"Girls," Dan warns.

We both giggle.

Jesse wipes the excess ink off her current canvas, finishing up.

"You know your skin belongs to me, right?" Dan says. The blond literally lets out an exasperated sigh.

Good, she's getting it now.

I turn around slowly with my shirt still raised. "Can't she have this little spot right here?" I let my finger trail over the side of my breast, running down my ribs.

"No," he says, firing up his gun and going back to work.

I pretend to pout. The blond shoots daggers at me as I fight the smile trying to curve my lips upward.

Jesse's customer pays and she grabs her keys. "Ready?"

"Sure." I turn one last time to Dan. "So, I guess I'll see you tonight?" I can't help but look at the blond and her friend, making sure they know he has plans for the rest of the evening.

Dan shuts off his gun and sets it down on the tray and removes his gloves. He stands up and all eyes slide to him. His body takes up so much space he towers over all of us. And then, quick as a goddamn viper, his hand strikes, his fingers wrapping around my neck. He drags me to him, making me dance on my toes. When we're chest to chest, his mouth crashes down on mine.

Every woman in the shop groans out loud.

My body jolts as he claims my mouth. White sparks break behind my eyes as my core clenches hard. I find myself grinding against the thigh he shoved between my legs. He pulls away slow and deliberate, his eyes telling me that I'm the only woman he wants. Jesus. The corner of his mouth tips up slightly. "I'll be seeing all of you, tonight." His voice rumbles all the way down to my cunt. He releases me with a smack on the ass, before sitting back down, focusing once again on his work. I sway slightly before Jesse grabs my hand and pulls me from the shop.

I don't even look at the faces of the two girls I was jealous of. Dan effectively chased the green-eyed monster away.

"Jesus Christ, you two are making me horny," Jesse says, rubbing her hand over her groin, not giving a fuck who sees her.

Quickly, I slide into the passenger seat of her rod. My ass feels like it's dragging on the ground as we peel out.

"Dirk better be on his A game tonight." She laughs, lighting up a cigarette. "You bring out a side of Dan I've never seen and goddamn it's hot."

The bar is only a few minutes from the shop, so it takes us no time to get there. The bar is hopping tonight. When we get inside, I see a lot of the club members here tonight. Jesse leaves me as I clock in behind the bar. I watch as she walks over and wraps herself around Dirk. I smile, he looks happy she's all wound up.

Bill comes out from the back, setting his sights on me. "Lily, I'm glad you're back." He kisses me on the cheek. "I'll only need you a couple hours tonight. Susan is coming in at eight."

"However long you need me, I'm yours," I tell him, grabbing a towel to wipe down the bar. Sliding easily into my normal routine, I hum, happy to be working again.

The evening is going great, and everyone seems to be enjoying themselves. I glance at the clock. It's almost time for Susan to come in and relieve me. Dan should be here soon too. My tummy does a little flip, thinking about the night to come.

The door opens and a group of people walk in. They look… my heart plummets. It's Benjamin, his friends, and their whores. I don't know if they're hookers but some of his friends are married and none of the women with them are their wives. Benjamin's floozy is hanging on his arm. Fuck. Me.

"You okay, sweetie?" Bill sidles up beside me, looking from me to the group, back to me.

"It's…" I turn to face him. "It's the guy I was supposed to marry."

Bill pulls his head back, craning his neck to get a look at the group as they shove two tables next to each other so they can sit together. "I'll take their orders," he tells me.

"No. No." I hold my hands up. "I refuse to let him win."

JD has noticed the group as well and sits down in front of me, forcing me to look at him. "You got this, girl?"

"I got it."

I grab my pad and walk over to them. They all look up and the entire group bursts into laughter.

Smile. Remember to smile.

"What can I get for you?"

The girl with Benjamin squeals, "Oh my god, I thought you were lying. She really does work here. In a biker bar."

"It's not a biker bar," I inform her. My eyes dart around the room. Okay, there are a lot of bikers in here and a biker does own it, but still. My gaze snags on Dirk's and his scary eyebrow pops up. I take a deep breath focusing on my customers.

Benjamin speaks for the group. "We'll start with four pitchers of beer since I doubt there is much else to drink here."

I nod, ignoring his insult. "Anything else?"

His eyes run over my outfit. I'm in black ripped skinny jeans and a white tank top. My hair is pulled into a high ponytail. My makeup is on point and honestly, I feel pretty damn good about myself. "That's it… for now," he adds in a creepy voice.

I'm pouring the pitchers when I overhear Bill on the phone. "She's holding her own, but you better get over here."

Great, he called Dan. I can handle this. I can. Dan will kill Benjamin. Especially, since he's now read my journals. I don't exactly remember everything I wrote but I'm sure it didn't portray Benjamin in the best of light.

I take the group glasses and four pitchers of beer. They waste no time gulping them down. Benjamin and his four friends rev up their asshole game as the alcohol settles into their systems. They keep calling me back to the table for little things, harassing me more and more by the minute.

I feel the guys from the club bristle, waiting for me to say the word. I know Bill would kick them out if I asked but I'm not letting them win. I just don't know how to one up them.

I'm standing by their table, waiting for them to decide what they want next. They're looking over the drink menu, making fun of some of the shot names. "You know you should add a drink called the runaway bride." Benjamin's best friend tells me.

My eyes narrow and I'm just about to lose my cool when a slender arm slithers around my neck. I look down, seeing a feminine, inked hand trace along the top of my tank top. Jesse leans into me, looking at the group over my shoulder. "Hey, Lily," she says seductively.

The assholes stop making fun of me, a much different look appearing on their faces. Her fingers continue to trail over my skin. I close my eyes, playing along.

"Susan is here. Why don't you let her take care of these…" she pauses to look at the group, "let her take care of *them*." She flicks an inked finger at them in disgust. The men don't seem to mind the insult, busy watching her fingers trail across my pale skin. The girls stare at their drinks. Yeah, Jesse isn't someone you mess with.

Jesse's other hand wraps around me, landing right above my pubic bone. *Oh.* I jerk in her arms. This feels… um…

"Let's dance," her green eyes sparkle with mischief. "Susan," she sing-songs over her shoulder. "Can you help these city folks out?"

"On it," Susan says, coming over, a no nonsense look on her face. Bill just hired her. She's a mom of five boys. I think she can handle them.

Jesse laughs, pulling me over to the juke box. As we look over the selections, I whisper a thank you to her.

She taps her fingers over the selections. "You dodged a fucking bullet, girl. That guy looks like an asshole."

"He is," I agree.

I notice Dan walk in. His eyes slide to mine before roaming over the group of intruders. He's tense, ready for a fight. Jesse watches him for a minute too. "Ready to show that asshole what he lost?" She starts to pull me out onto the dance floor. I say dance floor but her and I are the only ones out here.

The music starts and Jesse smiles. *American Woman* by Lenny Kravitz begins to play. I want to laugh but she's looking at me all sultry like, a flirty smirk on her face. She takes my hand and wraps herself around me like I've seen her do to Dirk.

I close my eyes and let her lead me into the rhythm. We move and grind to the music, our hands intimately roaming over each other. It's kind of weird to touch a woman this way. But it's Jesse and she's smoking hot. "Everyone is staring at you," I whisper in her ear.

"No, they're staring at *us*." She flips me around so that my back is pressed against her chest. Her nipples are hard. I glance down at my own, *shit*. Her hands slide up my thighs as I grind my ass into her. When the song is almost over, she releases me, shoving me toward Dan. "Show that prick of an ex what he can never have." She swats my ass. Our friends all clap and whistle when our little show ends.

I focus on one thing and one thing only. Dan. Jesse has my libido kicked up to an unbearable level.

Dan is standing at the end of the bar. I slide between him and it, picking up his beer and taking a big gulp. He leans down and chuckles in my ear. "That might have been the sexiest fucking thing I've ever seen," he growls.

Bill grabs two more beers, sliding them down to us. He tosses me a wink.

Dirk and Jesse disappear to the back somewhere.

Dan's eyes slide across the room with mine. Benjamin is staring at me. At us. Dan growls, a sound that only stokes the fire Jesse started. "Did dancing like that make you wet?" His breath is hot on my neck. I shiver in delight. I love his dirty mouth. He braces one hand on the counter as his other slides to the front of my pants.

I glance around nervously but no one can see us tucked behind the end of the bar. We're in a dark corner and Raffe is standing a few feet away, blocking anyone from taking the seat next to us, so…

The sound of my zipper pulls me from my anxious thoughts. I swallow hard. "Dan," I say, trying to hide the unease in my voice.

He chuckles low. His hand slides into my panties, finding the answer he seeks. I'm soaking wet. My cheeks heat in embarrassment but when his warm mouth finds the crook of my neck I relax. Dan loves me, no matter what. He loves my kinky side.

His eyes slide over to Benjamin. "He's still watching you. I want him to watch you come on my fingers, baby." His voice is hypnotic, and so I have no choice but to chase my orgasm for him. Only him.

I grind myself against the palm of his hand as he slides one, then two fingers into my drenched cunt.

"Keep your eyes open and on him. Let him see what he's been missing, how beautiful you are when you come."

"Only for you," I whisper, not wanting to look at Benjamin.

"Look at him," he demands. "I want you to have the satisfaction of witnessing the moment he's realized his mistake."

Dan pumps into me harder and I toss my head back against his chest, my lips parting. Oh, god. My eyes lock with Benjamin's. He has a scowl on his face. *Oh. Oh.* "Dan," I whimper.

"You ready, baby?"

I nod slightly and he curls his fingers. He's relentless in his pursuit to make me come and I do. I see a flare of lust in Benjamin's gaze before I allow my eyes to fall closed, riding out my orgasm.

"That's it, baby. Show him how good you come for me." He kisses my temple. "Such a good, sweet, girl," he praises, pulling his hand out of my panties. I open my eyes in time to see Dan slide his fingers into his mouth, licking my juices from them.

I glance around the bar, no one is watching except Benjamin. Well, him and his slut. She is literally seething by his side, but he doesn't notice, his eyes are still on me.

Dan's hands are braced on each side of me. I turn in the corral of them, and he finally drops his gaze to mine. My tongue snakes along my top lip and then slowly I lower myself to the ground, his eyes following me.

Quickly, I tug on his belt before popping the button on his blue jeans. His amber eyes burn with desire as I pull his monster cock from his pants. Gripping him tightly, I slide my hands up and down his length. I've never done this with Dan before, he's so big and I'm a little unsure how I'm going to manage.

His head bops up, his eyes scanning the room before they tumble on me again. I run my tongue over the tip of his dick, teasing him. One hand leaves the bar and wraps around my ponytail, subtly taking charge. I smile around him. A sound I've never heard falls over my ears, inspiring me to take more in my mouth. Inch by glorious inch, I push him in, until it reaches the back of my throat. I gag a little and he rocks his hips back. My hand pumps what I can't fit in my mouth, my tongue pressing against the underside of his hard smooth cock.

"Jesus, Lily," he groans, making my core clench tight. His voice alone is enough to make me come. My eyes raise, locking on his. His cock jerks and hardens in my mouth. I'm making him feel good. The power that comes with that knowledge spurs me on. I want his orgasm. I want it now.

His fist tightens in my hair, he's losing control. I never take my eyes off him, until he looks up, staring across the room. I have no doubt where his attention is. I flick my tongue over his tip when I pull back, then I slam him in my mouth as far as I can.

His entire body jerks once, twice. His eyes fall closed as his cum shoots down my throat. I hum, satisfied by his reaction. He opens his eyes and smiles at me as I let him slip from my lips. "Open your mouth," he whispers. I dutifully do as he asks, sticking my tongue out for his inspection.

"Fuck," he says hoarsely.

I quickly buckle him up before sliding up his frame. He grabs the back of my head and kisses me slow, tasting himself on my lips. His tongue licks the roof of my mouth, along my teeth, it's like he can't get enough. When he pulls away, we are both breathless.

"Go clean up, then we're taking this back to the warehouse. I'm not finished with you."

I shiver in anticipation. Yes. More. I need more. I'll never get enough of this man.

Not looking at anyone, I drop my head and slide behind the bar, heading for the bathroom. As I'm washing my hands, I smile at myself in the mirror. I look flushed, sexy, satisfied. Hurrying to get back to Dan, I hit the button on the hand dryer and rub my hands together.

I'm flying high until Benjamin's floozy steps through the door. We make eye contact briefly before she busies herself reapplying her lipstick. I'm about to walk out when she speaks. "You know your father is still planning on you marrying Benjamin, so you better get your kicks while you can."

Leaning against the wall, I inform her my father doesn't make decisions for me any longer. "I'm not marrying Benjamin." I cross my arms across my chest.

She eyes me up and down and laughs. "You do know who your father is, don't you? He's trying to get you committed as we speak. Sounds like the white coats will be coming for you soon."

My heart stutters. He wouldn't. Of course, he would.

"And you know this how?" I ask as unenthused as possible, not wanting her to know she is getting to me.

She drops her lipstick into her bag, turning to face me. "You know you're just as sick as he is."

I shake my head in confusion. "What the fuck are you talking about?"

"Your little public display of affection. You get your rocks off, knowing someone might be watching."

I blink at her, saying nothing.

"Benjamin told me about how your dad taped the two of you. Sick if you ask me."

310

A ring begins low in my ears, my heart skips a few beats. "W-what did you just say?"

She stares at me, realizing all this is news to me.

"Oh, honey, how sad. Poor little rich girl has a sick daddy. He likes to tape her and her boyfriend doing nasty things. Do you think he jacked off when he watched it?"

I grab her by the front of her shirt, twisting it in my hand. "What the fuck are you talking about?"

She smiles, her red lips pull back to reveal her lipstick-stained teeth. "He taped the two of you to make sure Benjamin was holding up his end of the bargain. When you ditched out on your wedding, Benjamin was furious and told your dad he was done with you. The next day he received a flip drive in the mail with the videos. He's blackmailing him. He told Benjamin he would get you to pull your head out of your ass and that you would still be getting married. Fucking weird… all of it." She throws her hands up in the air.

I back up against the wall, grabbing for something, anything to hold on to. I'm… I'm going to be sick.

The girl cackles as she witnesses my demise. "Do you and the big, dirty biker make videos too. I bet so…"

One of the bathroom stall doors comes crashing open and Jesse flies out, grabbing the girl by her throat, slamming her into the wall. Dirk wanders out behind her, a bored expression on his face.

Oh god, they heard. They know.

I push Dirk to the side so I can slide into the now abandoned stall and purge myself of everything I've eaten for the last week. I can't stop throwing up.

A commotion erupts outside the stall, but I don't care. I don't care! Dirk crouches beside me, hugging me around the waist. "I've got you, Smurf. I've got you."

I can't breathe. I think my lungs are collapsing. I'm dying. I should go to the emergency room. I'm dying!

Dirk wipes my mouth as Dan fills the doorway. When he looks at me, I die a little inside. I'm so… so… embarrassed. How could my father...

They all know. What must they think? Oh god, my chest hurts. I can't breathe. I need to get out of here.

I'm dizzy, and nauseous, and dying and… Raffe. I need Raffe.

"Raffe," I croak, hurling myself back over the toilet bowl for round two.

Dirk still has me gripped around the waist. "Go get Raffe," he orders Dan and surprisingly he listens.

I want to cry but I'm afraid if I start, I won't be able to stop. What if I never stop? Can you die from crying? My brain starts to roll an image of Benjamin and me… stop, don't think about it. Oh god.

Raffe skids to a stop in front of the stall as Dirk is trying to get me on my feet. "Come on, sweetheart." He tosses my arm around his shoulder, Dirk on the other side. Dan holds the door open. My pain is slashed across his face. My hurt is his hurt.

"Let's take her out back," Raffe suggests.

Raffe picks me up and sets me on a picnic table behind the bar. "Lily," he says calmly, taking off my shoes and then my socks. What the fuck is he doing? I'm dying. I need to go to the hospital.

Once I'm barefoot, he helps me over to the grass that runs along the fence line. "Deep breath, Lily."

"I can't," I cry, holding my chest. "I can't breathe, Raffe." I claw at his shirt.

He takes my hands in his. "Look at me." So, I do. "Wiggle your toes."

"W-what?" I gasp.

"Do it. Wiggle your toes."

The grass and soil are cool on the soles of my feet.

"That's it. Focus on the ground and the feel of it. It's solid beneath your feet."

I drop my eyes and stare at my toes in the grass.

"Deep breath," he says, holding my hands tight in his.

Taking a deep breath, I shift my foot, running it over the grass, letting it tickle the bottom of it.

"Another one," he orders.

After we do this for several minutes, Raffe instructing my every breath, I begin to feel better. My heart returns to a normal beat. My lungs inflate without restriction. But my mind still knows the news that set my body off and it's devastating.

I risk a glance around. It's just the two of us, both barefoot, standing in the grass. When my gaze stumbles on Raffe's, he smiles. "It's called grounding."

He seems proud of himself for talking me down. "Thank you," I mumble, dropping my eyes.

Raffe taps me under the chin with a finger. "Look at me. I know your world feels like it's spinning out of control right now. It's not. I promise it's not."

I choke back my tears, refusing to cry in front of him. We stand together, just breathing, for what seems like a long time. I hear bikes and cars leaving the parking lot. I wonder what is going on inside, but I can't bear the thought of going in to see for myself.

The back door swings open and Jesse steps out. She walks toward us, but Raffe stops her.

"Uh, uh, take off your socks and shoes," he tells her.

She looks at her feet before raising a questioning scowl to Raffe.

"We're grounding," I say softly, then I giggle.

Jesse smiles and sits down in the grass, leaning against the fence. She takes her shoes off, rubbing her feet over the earth.

Raffe motions for me to sit next to her, then he plops to the ground on the other side of me.

Jesse sighs before speaking. "I'm going to give you the low down on what went on inside. I'm going to be honest with you, Lily. Can you handle that right now?"

I glance at Raffe. He smiles sadly. "It's best to rip the band-aid off. I'll be right here. I'm not going anywhere."

"Okay, let me have it. It can't be any worse than what I just learned."

Jesse looks past me to Raffe. Their eyes transmit a silent conversation before she directs her attention to me.

"I, um, may have broken that bitch's nose," she starts.

I laugh, pinching the bridge of mine. God, how I wish I would have seen that.

"All hell broke out. Dad kicked everyone out except for a few members of the club and your ex."

My laughter faulters. "What? Why did he let him stay?"

"He didn't let him. They forced him to stay." She scratches her head, gathering her thoughts. "Dan had questions for him." She sucks her bottom lip between her teeth.

"What kind of questions?" I ask, not sure I want to know the answer.

"He asked him about the flip drives." She looks up at the stars. "And he asked about the video your dad took of the two of you. I'm sorry. I had to tell him."

"What did he say?" I ask quietly. So quiet I'm not sure she heard me.

"He wanted to know how a video of the two of you could be used as blackmail. Because you had been in a relationship, and you were of age. It wouldn't have been abnormal for the two of you to have had sex."

I cringe and curl myself into a little ball. "Well, because it's embarrassing, that's why. Benjamin wouldn't want everyone to see us together like that."

Jesse stares at me for a long, long, moment. She wraps her arm around me, pulling me close. "Lily, Benjamin told Dan the truth."

"What truth?"

She takes a deep breath. "That he raped you."

"He... he didn't rape me." I pull my head back, staring at her.

"He said that the first time you were together, you told him you wanted to wait. You fought him..." her thought trails off.

I shake my head back and forth, trying to stand up. "No, it wasn't rape. I just wanted to wait but we had been dating and..."

Jesse doesn't release her hold on me. Raffe scoots closer, wrapping his arm around me too.

"Our first time might have been a little rough, but it was just the one time."

"Dan asked him how many times he raped you. He said he didn't have to after the first time. He said after that, you just laid there, and..." She stops as I burst into tears.

"It wasn't rape," I tell them repeatedly, sobbing uncontrollably. It wasn't. It just wasn't.

Raffe speaks gently to me, "Lily, you told him you wanted to wait, he didn't wait. That is the very definition of rape."

I sniffle, looking at him. "We," he motions between him and Jesse, "we both know what it's like. I'm sorry it happened to you."

Jesse pulls me into her chest, letting me weep in her arms. She rocks me back and forth, holding me tight.

As my tears dry, a fat raccoon meanders out from behind a tree. It waddles over to the trash bins. Raffe laughs quietly. "Mama Bear has been trying to catch that damn thing for months."

Jesse laughs too. "Just wait. Dad leaves him sandwiches every night."

Sure enough, it reaches behind the can and pulls out a sandwich. He sits down and eats it leisurely.

"Well, I'll be damned," Raffe says. "I didn't know Bill was such a softy."

I roll my head, staring at Jesse. "You are lucky to have a dad like Bill."

She nods. "I am. My dad didn't come into my life until I was seventeen. I didn't even know who he was until then. But he came at just the right moment. It was after I had been raped by several men." She pauses, chewing on her bottom lip. "I tried to deal with it on my own, just like you." She runs her hand over the back of my hair. "It's easier if you let the people who love you help. Just because we're not your blood family doesn't make us any less family."

"I don't know what I did to deserve you guys," I say sadly, rubbing my hand over my eyes.

"Lily, you have to stop acting like you don't deserve to be here. You do."

"Where did everyone else go?" I finally ask. I've been dying inside, wondering where Dan is. Why is he not here by my side. Now that he knows what happened to me, do I repulse him?

"Dirk and Rachel went home to put the kids to bed and Bill and Dan went to the gym. I told him I would get you home."

My heart cracks clean down the middle.

"Lily, it took everything inside him not to kill your ex. He was trembling with rage. Dad took him to the gym so he could take out his frustration."

"I don't want Dan to get in trouble for me. I'm glad Bill took care of him." I sniffle.

"That's what we do. We take care of each other," Raffe says as he stands to get our shoes.

We drive back to the warehouse in Jesse's rod. She drives and I sit on Raffe's lap in the passenger seat. He hugs me around the waist. "We'll get through this, Lily. We're going to find those damn flip drives. For you and for Jenny."

When we pull in, I notice right away that Dan and Bill haven't returned. Raffe suggests we have a drink, but the thought of drinking makes my stomach turn. "I think I'm just going to hit the hay," I say tiredly. He nods and gives me a kiss on the cheek.

It's weird walking into Dan's dark room alone. I begged Jesse to take me to my house but with the threat of my dad coming for me again, she wouldn't budge. I'm so scared of what he'll say. How he'll look at me.

I decide it best if I just shut the lights off and pretend to be asleep when he comes in. Which he does several minutes later. He's quiet as he shuffles around. I squeeze my eyes shut, trying my best to control the tremor running through my body.

Chapter Thirty-Nine

Dan

Whentext Bill and I get back to the warehouse, we find Dirk waiting for us. "Hey, man." I try to slide past him. He places a hand against my chest.

"We need to talk."

"I'm sorry I left Raffe and Jesse at the bar with her." I drop my head in shame.

Bill walks past us. "I'm going to bed. You two hash this out and then get your asses to bed too."

"Yes, sir." Dirk salutes him.

Bill chuckles and jogs up the steps, disappearing down the hall. Dirk took over as president of the club a few years ago when Bill decided it was time for him to retire. But Dirk still looks to Bill as his president.

Dirk walks behind the bar and reaches in the fridge, tossing me a bottle of water. I gladly accept it, downing it in two seconds. He laughs, throwing me another. I catch it and lean against the counter. "I had to hit something."

"I know." He glances at my knuckles.

"Again, I'm sorry I left. Raffe and Jesse shouldn't have had to pick up pieces that were meant for me to collect."

He shakes his head. "You don't get it. That was part of their healing."

I dig my finger and thumb into my eyeballs. Too much fucking pain in this world. Sometimes, I forget what my best friends have been through. Fucking Christ, how many sick fucks are there in this world?

"They handled it. That's what we do." Dirk lights up a cigarette, blowing smoke rings over his head. "I get what you're going through. This talk is for you."

"I don't need any of your shrink shit, cousin."

His eyebrows crawl up his forehead, telling me I'm going to hear what he has to say whether I want to or not.

"Lily disagreed with what that scumbag told you," he says.

Blinking at him slowly, I try to figure out what that means.

"She said it wasn't rape," he deadpans.

"But…" I don't fucking understand.

"Dan, she doesn't get it. Or…" he holds up a finger, coming around the bar to stand beside me, "she doesn't want to get it. It's a hard word to wrap your mind around."

"I don't understand. The fucker admitted it."

Dirk's face softens, he gives me a rare glimpse at the man beneath all the dark ink and intimidating snarls. "Some victims blame themselves. Maybe she thinks she led him on." He shrugs. "It could be anything actually, but she doesn't see it as rape."

"How do you think she sees it?" I ask, confused.

"Honestly, I think she sees it as something that was expected of her, something that would eventually happen, and it did. She wasn't ready, but in her mind, she thinks her reluctance was some silly thing and that he had a right. Predators have a way of making their victim carry all the shame. Make them feel like they are being ridiculous and overreacting."

When I don't say anything, he straightens, preparing to go back to his room. "I just wanted to give you a heads up, cousin."

"Thanks." I don't know what else to say.

Dirk heads upstairs, leaving me alone to wallow in my thoughts.

I can't deny that Lily has brought chaos to my life. But she's also brought splashes of color that make my heart pump faster. I've never felt more alive. Tonight, that color was red. I was so angry that I couldn't see straight. I've never wanted to strangle someone more in my whole life. I hope I made it clear to the asshole that if I ever see him again, he's as good as dead.

I'm sure it will be fresh in his mind for a little while anyway. I smile, thinking of how humiliating it must have been for him to have stumbled out of the bar covered in his own blood and urine. He was a mess, but I didn't kill him. Oh, how I wanted to.

Finishing the bottle of water, I crumple it in my hand, the plastic making a horrible sound. I toss it in the trash as I make my way to the stairs. I take them slowly as my mind clears. Calm, I need to be calm.

As much as this sucks, I can't wish it to be any other way. I mean, I hate she had to go through all that shit but if she hadn't... if she hadn't, would she have fell into my lap?

It's these thoughts that make me quicken my steps. I need to see her. To feel her. I didn't want to leave her, but I had to. I wasn't myself. It would have frightened her. I've never felt so out of control in all my life. But my club came through. Just like always. We protect what's ours. They took care of me and her.

It's dark when I push the door to my room open. A tiny lump is buried under the covers, facing away from me, scooted as far as possible to the edge of the bed. As I undress, I watch as she trembles beneath the blanket. She's not fooling anyone.

"Have you showered?" my voice cuts through the silence.

She stills.

"Come shower with me, baby," I try again. My words are calm, hopefully soothing.

She takes in a big shuddery breath before pushing the covers aside and sitting herself upright. Another deep breath and she follows me into the bathroom, refusing to meet my eyes.

Grabbing the hem of her shirt, I tug it over her head. Then I slide her panties down her slender legs, letting my hands run back up them in a calming motion. After I get the water adjusted, I take her hand and pull her into the shower with me.

The minute the warm water hits her back she lets out a whimper. I pull her into my arms and hug her tightly. "Let it out, baby. Let it all out." I rub circles over her back as she cries.

After several minutes, I begin to slowly wash her. As I run my soapy hands over her arms, I notice she still hasn't looked me in the eye. I stop abruptly, gripping her chin. She inhales sharply, bracing for what's to come. I force her head back. "Look at me, Lily."

She pinches her eyes shut tight. "I can't. Oh god, I can't," she cries. "I'm... I'm so embarrassed, Dan."

"Nonsense. You have nothing to be embarrassed about. But I understand why you feel that way."

My understanding must be the magic key that unlocks something inside her because she opens her eyes. She opens them and they literally suck my soul clean from my body. How could anyone look into those big brown eyes and hurt her. It's unfathomable.

"Do... do you think I'm like him?"

This knocks me on my ass. I stutter, "Like who?"

"Like my father?"

Wait. I thought she was upset about Benjamin, but she's been living with that for some time. It wasn't as much a revelation to her as it was to me. But her father's involvement was. I take a deep breath, reigning in my emotions.

"You are nothing like him." I grip her chin tighter. I shove my nose to hers. "Nothing."

"But I like…" she closes her eyes.

"What you and I do is consensual. It's between us and if we like a little risk in our play, that's our business. What your father does is entirely different. Never compare yourself to him."

She cracks one eye open, then the other.

"I will not let you feel bad about what we do. It pisses me off to no end that you had to hear those things from that little bitch."

The corner of Lily's mouth tilts up into a small smile.

"Maybe she was jealous. I mean you did give me a pretty intense orgasm."

Oh, this little creature.

Her humor is short lived, the mood turning solemn once again. "I hate that we even have to talk about this. I… I just wish we didn't have all this hanging over our heads."

"It's not. It's under our goddamn feet and we're going to stomp the shit out of it. Mark my words, Lily, your dad's house is going to burn."

Her eyes sparkle up at me. "I've been racking my brain trying to figure out where those flip drives could be."

"We'll figure it out." I pull her to my chest. "So, not to change the subject but were *you* a little jealous today?"

She pulls back, giving me a warning scowl, shoving away from me. "I didn't like the way they were drooling over you."

"Now you see how I feel when the guys at the bar drool all over you." I laugh at the haughty look on her face. "But in all seriousness, you never have to worry about that. You're all I want. You're my sun."

A shy smile forms on her face. She twirls a piece of wet hair on her finger. "I don't know what you see in me."

"Well, I'll tell you." I take a step toward her, digging my fingers into her waist. "I see my girl, my future wife, the mother of my children. I see it all, baby."

She stares up at me. "You may be a little crazy," she chuckles nervously.

"Crazy for you." Then I drop to my knees, pushing her back against the shower stall. Her eyes open wide as my tongue swirls around her belly button. I'm going to show her just how crazy I am.

This is a first for her and I'm going to make it good. When my tongue teases her clit, she drops her head against the shower wall. "Dan," she breathes, her eyes rolling into the back of her head.

I swirl my tongue a few more times before sucking her clit into my mouth, she shudders, her legs going weak. I pull back. "Go lay on the bed, baby."

She hurries from the shower, quickly drying off and practically running to bed. I take my time. She's wound up, and like I said, anticipation is all a part of the process.

When I walk out of the bathroom, I stop dead in my tracks. She's laid out across the bed, spread open for me, a teasing smile on her face. I climb between her legs, lowering myself to the space between her thighs. I run my nose along the inside of one of them, making her shiver.

326

"Dan," she pleads. My name is like a prayer on her tongue.

"Do you want me to lick your pretty little pussy?" I ask.

Her face turns red, but she nods. A tiny nod. Not good enough.

She huffs, blowing hair from her eyes. "Please lick my pussy," she says quietly.

"You forgot something." I roam over to her other thigh, kissing my way down to that delectable spot where thigh meets the promise land. She giggles, oh yes, she's a little ticklish there. Mental note made.

"Say it, Lily."

She huffs again. "Please lick my *pretty* little pussy."

I give her what she asks for. I'm going to get this girl to love herself, eventually. I want her to realize just how much I love her. Every part of her. She has nothing to be ashamed of. Not her thoughts, her body, or her kinks.

She squeals, pulling me out of my head. I ease up a bit as she grips the sheets. "You taste so good, baby," I say, leaning back to admire her perfection. She watches me as I slide a finger inside her. Her eyes roll back into her head when I add another and then another. When my tongue touches her lightly, she screams. So sensitive. So, mine.

Her fingers slide into my hair. God, I love that. I tease her until her fingers tighten, pulling, pushing. She's lost now. There's nothing holding her back. She's completely submerged in what I'm doing to her body. Good. I'm going to fucking erase him from her mind. One orgasm at a time.

"Dan, oh, Dan, somethings, oh, god."

I'm curling my fingers, pressing, pressing till she's completely at my mercy.

Tears stream out the corners of her eyes, she can't move, she can't do anything but lie here and take what I'm giving her. I've found the magic spot and she can't do anything about it. Her eyes are wide as she stares at me. She wants me to stop, she wants me to go, she doesn't know what's about to happen.

Almost there. I don't let up, I rock my fingers into that spot, never letting up. A little flick of the tongue and holy shit, she comes. Her muscles lock up as she presses her cunt into my face, exploding on my fingers, drenching my beard. Fuck yes.

I sit up, grabbing the towel she abandoned on the end of the bed, wiping her arousal from my face. She blinks, her eyes unfocused as she struggles to catch her breath. Her cheeks are red with embarrassment.

I never want her to be embarrassed around me. "That was fucking amazing," I tell her. "I love that you don't hold back with me."

She smiles lazily. "I love that you don't let me."

Laughing, I crawl up beside her and pull her into my arms. I hug her to me. "I love you, Lily."

She tips her head, her fingers playing mindlessly in my beard. "Jenny told me one day I would find someone who loved my body, my mind, and my soul. I didn't believe her. I was never able to picture anything other than what I had been programmed for. But anyhow, she made me promise I would let that someone love me. I'm trying, Dan. I really am."

"I wish she were here so I could thank her for loving you."

Lily stares at me and I sense another shift in her. "Jenny was my angel," she says quietly.

"And you are mine." I drag my finger down her face and across her jaw before placing a gentle kiss to her lips.

Chapter Forty

Lily

I've spent hours agonizing over where those flip drives could be. Like I said, my father has had accusations made against him. They never went anywhere. It's like this sort of behavior is acceptable in the world of the rich and powerful.

It shouldn't be but it is.

Raffe startles me out of my head, wrapping his arms around me from behind. "Raffe, what are you doing here? It's not five, is it?" I look at the clock in the kitchen where I've been silently brooding over flip drives for the last three hours.

"I decided to come early and keep you company. Rachel is bringing Jackson over later."

"Oh, I have something for you." I grab his hand, dragging him down to the basement.

He laughs. "Should I be worried?"

Glancing at him over my shoulder, I giggle. "I'm not a serial killer if that's what you're worried about." I push the door open to Jesse's art room and drag him to the portrait Jesse and I painted. That seems so long ago.

"What's this?" He points to the easel, a sheet covering the painting.

Now, I'm nervous. "I… okay, so I thought you might like to see what Jenny looked like as an adult." He blinks at me. "But I've been thinking, maybe you could give this one to her parent's when you visit them tomorrow and Jesse and I can paint you another one." I pull the sheet off, letting it fall to the floor.

Raffe slowly turns his head toward it. He covers his mouth with his hand, taking a step forward. "Lily," he whispers.

"I… I have a picture too if you'd like to see?" I ask hesitantly.

He swivels to face me, his eyes lighting up. "I would love to."

I pull my phone from my back pocket and click on Jenny and I's selfie. Both of us are smiling brightly.

He takes the phone from me.

"She's just as beautiful as I remember," he says wistfully. "She looks happy."

"She was. We had just completed another part of our plan. Buying the phone." I point to it.

He flips it over in his hands. "Her parents are going to love the painting, Lily."

"It's the least I can do. Like I said, I'm sure Jesse will help me do another one."

"You don't have to do that." He runs his hand over his mouth. "Could, could I have a copy of this instead?"

He shows me the photo. I laugh a little. "Yeah, sure, but I'm in it."

"I know, that's why I want it."

My eyes rake over him. He's so beautiful and kind and exactly how Jenny described him. God, it should be her standing here not me. I drop my head unable to look at him any longer. Guilt creeps in like a virus, infecting me, unseen to the naked eye.

But he sees it. Because fuck, he's perfect just like the rest of them.

"Lily, she isn't here. You are and you cannot feel guilty about that. She wouldn't want you to. You know this. She made a choice. We have to go on without her. You've brought me so much peace already. I don't think you see how much we all needed you."

"I'm the needy one. All I've done is bring chaos and confusion."

"Stop. We all come with those things. It's called life. Do you think I came to this family all sunshine and roses? No, I came in full of self-loathing and you guessed it, my own version of chaos." He laughs, turning to stare at the portrait again. "And Jesse, my god, the chaos that girl brought. Sometimes, what begins as a chaotic mess turns into a beautiful love story. Mine did. Jesse's did and I'm sure yours will as well. So, please try to tamp down those feelings of guilt. Okay?"

I nod, picking up the painting and handing it to him. He gives the picture on my phone one last look before trading me. He hugs the painting to his chest as I click a few buttons on my phone. When his phone dings, he smiles.

"Thank you, Lily."

I brush him off with a wave of my hand. "We should go upstairs; I need to get ready for Jackson."

Raffe helps me compile all the stuff I'll need to help Jackson build the bird house for Jenny's parents. It's so sweet that he thinks of them as his grandparents. Jenny would be happy to know he's filling the void she left behind.

When Rachel and Jackson show up, he comes running to me. "Lily. Lily. Lily," he pants, trying to catch his breath. I laugh.

I hug him as he barrels into my legs. "I'm so happy you're here," I tell him.

He looks up at me with his expressive brown eyes. "Are we building a bird house today?" he asks excitedly.

"Yes, and a bird feeder."

"What's a bird feeder?" He pulls away from me to touch everything I have on the picnic table.

"We'll leave you two to it," Rachel says, wrapping her arms around Raffe.

"Yeah, you guys go on. Go to dinner or something. Dan and I can feed Jackson."

Rachel looks up into Raffe's eyes, hopeful.

Raffe smiles down at her. "That sounds wonderful." He kisses the end of her nose before turning to me. "You sure?"

"Of course, everyone should be home soon. You know how it is. They make enough food to feed an army."

They both laugh, nodding. "Okay, we'll be back in a few hours." He slaps Rachel on the ass, making her squeal. "See you soon." They turn, leaving Jackson and I to do our woodwork.

JD stops by and joins us. Jackson loves working with his hands. He listens intently to what JD tells him. Time passes quickly and before we know it, we have a brightly painted bird house and one bird feeder.

My mind wanders to my childhood and the flower garden at my father's. The bird houses were exquisite. But nothing compared to the one I just built with my friends. Jackson rests his chin on his hands, peeking into the little door on the bird house. He's so darn cute.

"This would make a great hiding place," he says in awe, opening one eye and then the other as he stares into the dark hole.

I blink at him, my heart beating wildly in my chest.

"It would but soon a bird will be living in there," JD tells him.

My gaze roams over the bird house not really seeing it. What I do see are my father's bird feeders. He never let anyone else put feed in them. It was expressly prohibited. All the staff knew this rule. He didn't even like anyone sitting out there. I thought it was just like the rooms my mom deemed "for guests only." Except the flower garden wasn't for guests, it was for him.

I stumble back, falling into one of the deck chairs.

334

"You okay, hun?" JD asks.

"Yeah, I'm fine."

Jackson climbs up on my lap, noticing my distress as well. "You okay, hun?" he mimics JD.

I look him in the eye. "I'm perfect. I'm just thinking about how happy your grandparents are going to be when you give them the gifts you made them." He smiles, jumping off my lap. "I'm going to go check on my caterpillar," he tells me, running inside the house.

"Come right back," I holler after him.

He waves to let me know he heard.

Once he's inside, JD kneels in front of me. "What's going on?"

"Jackson just helped me figure out where my dad might have hidden those flip drives."

JD turns his head to look at our projects. When his eyes meet mine, he smiles. "Looks like we're going on a run."

I nod numbly. If I'm right and my father hid those flips drives in his precious flower garden… my god, could it really be that easy? I cover my mouth as tears sting my eyes.

JD hugs me. "I got you, girl. We'll know soon enough."

Jackson comes running out with his bug catcher. JD pulls away from me slowly. Jackson yells, "Lily. Lily. Lily," in his usual excited way.

He shoves the bug hut in my face and inside is a beautiful Monarch butterfly. His wings open and then close as he shows off for us.

"Oh Jackson," I croak.

"Why are you crying?" Jackson asks, confused by the tears streaming down my face.

I hug him to me. "Sometimes, people cry when they are happy and spending the afternoon with you has made me so happy it's running over."

"I'm happy too." His hair falls over his eye. "But I don't feel like crying." He's still confused.

"It's a girl thing," JD tells him.

"Oh," Jackson says seriously. "Now, I get it. My mom does that too. Sometimes, she just looks at me and cries. She says it's because I'm the best gift she's ever gotten."

"You are pretty special," I say, wiping my face with the palm of my hands.

Later that night when everyone is there, we release the butterfly down by the lake. "He can be friends with the dragonflies," Jackson says, jumping up and down.

Dan pulls me into his side, hugging me tight. We watch it fly away over the water. Everyone cheers and pats Jackson on the back. He's so happy. Everyone is happy. Life is good.

Chapter Forty-One

Lily

"Why are we doing this again?"

Jesse cocks an eyebrow at me which is scarier than it normally is because she looks like a skeleton. "We don't want anyone to recognize us," she says like I should already know this.

I don't think this is her first time breaking the law. We are about to break into my father's estate.

"Hold still," she says as she draws a line across my face. "This is so exciting. Dirk hasn't let me out to play in a long, long time." She licks her lips. "I hope I get to knock someone out."

Chuckling, I shake my head and she scolds me again.

"We go straight to the fucking flower garden. If we don't find anything, we're leaving. Don't get any ideas while we're in there. I'm not going to risk my best friend getting locked up. If your father thought you were crazy before, he will definitely think you're nuts if he sees you like this." She stands back, smiling at her work.

I walk over to the mirror in the hotel room. Jesse joins me. Our faces match. The only difference is our eyes. "I used to paint myself up like this when I was a teenager."

"So no one would recognize you?"

"That and because it gave me bigger balls. Don't your balls feel bigger?"

I giggle. "Actually, I think this is the first time I've felt them."

She hugs me around the shoulders. "It's going to be okay, Lily. Whatever we find or don't find, it's going to be okay. We're never going to let anyone take you away from us."

Biting my lip, I swallow back tears, not wanting to ruin the bad ass makeup job she just did on me. "I love you."

She hugs me tight. "I know you think you only need us, but we need you too."

The door bangs open and Dirk leans against the doorway. His jaw clenches when he sees us. "Dan," he hollers over his shoulder. His eyebrow is cocked at an alarming level.

Jesse steps away from me. "We're going in." She tosses a thumb out, indicating the "we" are her and I.

"Is that so?" He lights up a cigarette. The doorway beside him is soon filled with Dan. He runs his eyes over my face, then Jesse's.

"No. Absofuckinglutely no."

I step in front of Jesse. "I'm going in. I don't *want* this, Dan. I fucking *need* it."

"Fine, but we all go in together."

"Sorry, big guy, we already decided that the men are in charge of watching the perimeter," Jesse says, resting her chin on my shoulder.

Dan looks at Dirk and shrugs.

"Dan, we will be in and out in minutes. It will be easier with fewer people. Jesse can watch my back while I search the flower garden."

He steps into the room, pulling a gun out of the back of his pants. A gun. A fucking real-life gun. Sure, I've seen them. My dad's guards have them, but I guess I... well, I don't know what I thought. Dan gives me a quick ten-minute tutorial on it before thrusting it in my hand. "Just in case," he says.

I swallow. This is becoming real. Can I do this? I have to. I just have to.

When we get to my father's estate, we circle around to the back side of the property. Jenny and I used to sneak in and out of here. It's the one weak spot in my father's security. We climb over the fence and then shimmy between the bushes, leaving the guys behind to watch the perimeter.

Now comes the risky part, we will have to move closer to the house where the cameras are. It's late enough maybe none of the security will notice. Jesse holds up one finger, two, then three. Go. We rush over to the flower garden. I immediately start searching the bird houses and feeders. Nothing, nothing, nothing. Goddammit, I can't be wrong. I can't be.

Then I notice a bird feeder that has a large metal bottom on it. It looks odd. I rush over and push it. Sure enough, it slides out. I glance back at Jesse, she is watching the yard, her eyes sliding left and right. Her hand is poised on the gun in her pants. Returning my focus back to the bird feeder, I reach in and pull out a wooden box.

When I get it in my hands, I push the metal drawer back in place. "Let's go," I say excitedly, turning to face Jesse only to find her in a headlock. Fuck.

"Rudy, please let her go," I plead.

"Lily?" He drags Jesse closer to me. "What the fuck?" he hisses.

"Please, let her go. We'll leave. I just needed to grab something."

He looks at the box in my hands. Jesse gives me a look of encouragement. She doesn't even look worried.

"I'll let her go but I'm sorry, I'm going to have to take you to your father. It's for the best." He shakes his head like even he doesn't believe that's true.

"You know it's not. Please, Rudy."

He takes a big step, dragging Jesse with him.

I pull the gun from my pants, pointing it at him. He stops dead in his tracks, his eyes wide. "Lily?"

"Don't make me shoot you, Rudy. Please, don't do that. I can't go with you, and I think you know why. This," I nod to the box under my arm. "this, is my freedom."

"But he says you need treatment," Rudy says in hushed tones. His eyes bounce from me to the house.

"Rudy, I'm not going to lie to you, I'm far from being fine but I'm seeing a therapist. I will get better, but I can't do that under my father's thumb and like I said, I think you know why. Everyone in this fucking house knows why."

He drops his head shamefully, letting go of Jesse. "Go. Go now before I change my mind."

Jesse and I waste no time getting the hell out of there.

Dan catches the box when I toss it over the fence, then he grabs my hips as I slide myself over. He hugs me tight before we climb in the truck and drive away. Dirk calls JD. "They're out."

Everyone heads back to the hotel. I'm quiet as I run my hands over the simple wooden box. Don't cry. Don't cry. Don't cry.

"You should have seen your woman, Dan. She pulled your gun," Jesse says excitedly beside me.

Dan swivels in his seat and Dirk glares at me in the mirror.

"It was nothing."

"A security guy had me in a headlock."

Dirk steps on the brakes right in the middle of the road. "What?" His head swivels to her.

"Fuck," she whispers under her breath.

His eyes slide to me. "Thank you," he chokes, before turning back to the wheel.

Jesse leans over to me. "I'm going to pay for this tonight," she whispers in my ear.

I mouth an, *I'm sorry*.

She shrugs, wiggling her eyebrows up and down.

My laugh comes out in a snort and both guys give us a warning glare. Neither find this near as funny as we do.

I'm not sure why Rudy let us go. I'm equally not sure if I would have shot him if he hadn't. I'm glad I didn't have to find out.

Back at the hotel, we all gather in Travis's room. He has a computer set up, ready to check the files. Everyone nervously waits as he slips the first flip drive in. I can't do this. Anxiety is tingling across my chest, making it feel tight. Raffe isn't here. He's in Vegas at Jenny's parent's house. Shit.

"Dan," I say anxiously.

He crouches in front of me.

"I… I can't be here."

Nodding, he pulls me to my feet. "I'm taking Lily back to our room."

"I'll take her," JD chimes in. "If that's okay with Lily."

I nod, smiling. "That might be best. One of us should see what we're dealing with."

"Okay." He kisses my head, looking me in the eye one more time to make sure I'm okay.

JD and I leave the room. We chat about the dresser I'm restoring. I found these old window cranks of all different designs and I'm using them as drawer knobs. It's going to be cool when I'm finished.

I don't know how much time passes. JD is good at keeping me company. He's easy to talk to. Before I know it, Dan steps through the door.

JD quickly excuses himself. "I'll see you tomorrow, Lily. Dan." He nods before leaving the room.

Dan sits down beside me, pulling a business card out of his pocket. He rests his forearms on his legs, flipping the card in his hands. He takes a deep breath before turning toward me. My world crumbles from the look on his face.

"I said I'd never lie to you, but I want to. God, do I want to," his voice cracks and there are tears in his eyes. "If we turn this over, it's going to be hard on you. It's… it's really bad, Lily."

My eyes bounce over his face, my heart fighting to break free of my body. "I don't care about me, Dan."

He nods in understanding. "It's your call, baby."

"I don't care." I repeat, swinging my arm across the table, sending everything including the lamp crashing to the ground. "I don't care. He has to pay," I cry.

Dan stands, hugging me from behind, holding my arms across my chest. "Shhh, it's okay. You're not alone. I'll be by your side every step of the way."

He sits down on the bed, pulling me with him.

"We got him, baby. He will go to jail for the rest of his life. I promise."

"But who are we going to tell? How will we know who to trust?"

He pushes the card he has been holding in front of my face. "We can trust this guy."

My eyes scan the card. "Who is this?" I ask, suddenly feeling like I'm in a fog.

"Do you remember the day you fell?"

I still on his lap. "What does that have to do with this?"

He shakes the card in my face. "This is the officer who reached down to you."

I pluck the card from his hands, studying the picture of the officer on the card. "How did you get this?" I turn on his lap, straddling him.

"He gave it to me. That's how I found you. I went there, hoping to find clues, anything. You had told me you loved the bay. Anyway, he saw me looking lost, sad. I was missing you… he thought I was there to jump. He approached me and we got to talking. I asked if he knew a Lily. He told me about you and your dad. He didn't seem to be a big fan of his. We can trust him, Lily. He even went to your house to check on you, but they never let him past the front gate."

"How can all this be… it's too… like it's weird, right?"

"Maybe life is pre-destined," Dan says, rubbing the back of my neck.

"This is going to work?"

"It's going to work but it isn't going to be easy or pleasant," he answers honestly.

"That's okay because it will be worth it."

"It's going to bring down others. Important others."

"Benjamin told me it was all a game. I'm ready for the game to end, but first I'm going to win."

Dan agrees with me by flipping me onto the bed. I laugh. "What are you doing?"

"If you think I'm going to miss an opportunity to fuck you like that, you're sadly mistaken." He points to my face.

Fuck, I forgot I still had the makeup on. My eyes roll up to his and holy hell, I think he likes it.

"Right now, we're playing *our* game," he smirks.

I jump up, making a dash for the bathroom but he snags me around the waist. *This is one game I'm willing to lose.*

Chapter Forty-Two

Lily ~ 2 months later

"Lily, you did a great job today," Jesse says.

My family sat with me as we watched the arrests play out on the news yesterday. Today, I had a press conference. Dan stood by my side the entire time. He's been my rock.

"I'm just glad it's over," I grumble, helping her set up Jackson's birthday party.

It's been a rollercoaster the past few months, but things seem to be working out the way they were supposed to. Not everyone was charged. Some of the video was disputable, it was either too dark or too grainy but most of the videos led to arrests. Now, we have to wait to see who will be convicted.

My attorney has told me my father will spend the rest of his life in prison. I haven't spoken to him, nor do I plan to. My mother called, wanting to come and stay with me. I refused. I can't allow any negativity into my life. Maybe I'm a terrible daughter but I have to look out for my mental health first and foremost.

I don't know what will happen with my father's finances. Right now, everything is frozen. If I do receive anything, it will all go to Jesse's charity. I've been helping her with that. She's made me the spokesperson. She says I have great public speaking skills which I guess is one thing I can thank my father for. Whatever helps, I'll do.

Anyhow, things are going well. Raffe drives me to therapy once a week. I'll admit that there were a few weeks I had to go twice. Our therapist always makes time for any emergency visits I might need. So far, I haven't had to take anything for my anxiety. Dan has been so sweet. He's bought me a weighted blanket, candles, oils, anything he can think of that might help. Like I said, he's my rock.

Jenny has been moved to a nearby cemetery. Her parents are moving here in a few months. They say Vegas is too much hustle and bustle for them. Yes, I finally found my balls to meet them. I thought they might hate me for what my father did to Jenny. I was wrong about that. They are grateful Jenny and I had become friends. I'll get to see them today. They are coming to Jackson's birthday party.

I spend a lot of time visiting Jenny. Most days I go and sit with her and talk. It's quiet there. I still haven't done anything with her journals. Maybe I should give them to her parents. I guess they aren't hurting anything. They are still on the bedside table in Dan's room.

My gaze falls on Dan. He is filling balloons with helium for the party. He turns my way as if he can sense my eyes on him. He smiles, winking at me. My tummy does a little flip.

The club is all here, and my mouth is watering as the smell of Mama Bear's cooking wafts through the warehouse all the way out to the patio.

JD steps out, his eyes roaming over the activity going on. When he spots me, he grins, rushing my way. "Guess what I have here?" he sing-songs, slapping some papers on the picnic table in front of me.

I jump up and down and squeal. JD and I are going into business together. We're renting the building right across the street from Dan and Jesse's tattoo parlor. The name of our business is Junkyard Creations.

He picks me up off my feet and swings me around. Bill grunts. "You stole my best bartender," he grumbles. But we both know he's only joking. He's happy for us.

Dan walks over. "What's going on here?" He pulls me out of JD's grip, giving him the hairy eye.

JD ignores him, laughing. Nothing can burst the happy bubble we're in.

"It's the lease papers for the shop across from yours. We're going to be neighbors."

Dan kisses me on top of my head. "Good, I can keep an eye on you there." He looks over my shoulder, giving JD a teasing scowl.

I'm so happy my heart is going to explode.

Once Jenny's parents show up, we're ready to get this little boy's party started. We are all sitting around, waiting for him to open his mountain of presents.

"Lily. Lily. Lily." Jackson runs up to me with a large envelope in his hand. "Will you read my birthday story?" I glance at Dan confused.

He laughs. "Jackson, why don't you tell Lily what it is first?"

Jackson climbs up on my lap. "It's a birthday story. My angel mom sends me one every year."

Now I am confused. Dan explains, "Jackson is adopted. After Raffe's accident he was unable to have children, but an angel sent Raffe and Rachel this little guy." He chucks Jackson under the chin, making him laugh.

"Oh, how lucky they are to have gotten you," I tell Jackson. "Of course, I'll read it. If it's okay with your mom and dad."

"My mom already said you could," he tells me as he excitedly opens it.

Everyone quiets down to hear the story as Jackson hands it to me.

It is written in beautiful handwriting like someone put a lot of love into it. I glance up to make sure everyone is listening as Jackson settles comfortably on my lap.

I clear my throat before beginning.

To my special little boy,

How exciting it is that you are celebrating your sixth birthday. Now, you'll have to use two hands to count the years.

We all laugh as Jackson holds up six fingers.

Today, I'm going to tell you the story of how I picked the perfect parents for you.

I glance up catching Raffe and Rachel smile at each other.

You see, I searched through dozens and dozens of folders, looking for just the right couple. But when I opened your parents' folder, I knew that the dragonfly had struck again. It had brought me two more angels.

I was lucky indeed, because a dragonfly had already given me one angel, my best friend. She was there the day I found out that you were in my tummy. We cried on her bedroom floor for hours, happy tears, because we knew you were going to be special. You were our bright spot.

My heart pumps faster as I continue to read.

A dragonfly will bring you an angel at just the right moment. It's why they have two sets of wings so they can carry them on their backs.

You're not going to believe this, but not only did that dragonfly bring me a best friend and two parents for you, he brought you an entire family. Isn't that incredible? That's why I chose them. You see, your parents showed me who they were in that folder. There was a picture of them, pictures of your grandma and grandpa, and pictures of your motorcycle club family.

I liked that they showed me everything. They held nothing back. The picture of your family radiated love. It exploded right out of that photo and struck me in the heart. I knew they were a perfect fit for you.

I hope you're getting to spend the day with them. Remember to cherish every moment. They may not be your family by blood, but they are your family by choice and that is even better.

I want you to know how much I love you. I hope you have the best birthday ever.

Love, Your Angel Mom

Tears are pouring down my cheeks. Jackson takes the letter from me and hugs it to his chest. "My angel mom always writes about dragonflies.

That's why I love them so much." He takes his chubby little hands and wipes my face. "It's okay, Lily. Don't cry. You are my family now too."

He hops off and runs over to his parents showing them the letter.

Dan wraps his arm around me. "I know that hit a little close to home with the dragonflies and all. Are you okay?"

Sniffing back tears, I nod. He keeps me cuddled by his side as we watch Jackson rip into his presents.

You know, this could all be just another one of those weird coincidences. I mean, I'm sure there are lots of girls who sit and cry on the bedroom floor when one of them gets pregnant. Right? Right?

Oh god. Jackson smiles at his dad as he helps him rip the wrapping paper off a package. His smile is like hers. No. No. It can't be. Because if it is, then that means Jackson is my....

"Dan, I'm not feeling very well. Could we maybe go up to your room for a minute?"

His face falls. "Yeah, baby. Of course."

"I... I don't want to take you from the party."

He waves me off, leaning over to whisper something in Dirk's ear. Dirk's eyes slide to mine, and he frowns, nodding his head.

Dan and I quietly leave the patio and head to his room.

When he closes the door behind us, I lose my shit.

Are they going to hate me for keeping her pregnancy a secret?

351

Oh, god.

Dan is sitting on his bed, leaning against the headboard as he watches me pace back and forth.

I pause at the foot of the bed. "I… I have to tell you something." Oh god. I can't lose Dan. I just can't.

"Baby, whatever is tearing you up, let it out. I'm reading you like an open book. You're never going to lose me. What's wrong?"

I tap my fingers over my lips. "Okay." I pace a little more, trying to find my balls.

"Come here."

My eyes roam up the bed. He's patting the spot between his legs. I shake my head. I can't be close to him, I'll cry, and I can't cry right now. I just need to tell him.

Or I could keep this a secret for the rest of my life. I mean, I don't know if I'm right about any of this.

Dan waits patiently for me to talk to him. "What can I do to help you, Lily?"

I plop down at the end of the bed, turning to face him. "God, I don't know where to start."

He sits up, looking a little nervous now.

"I've had a bit of a secret but please know I only kept it because I didn't want to cause any more heartache than necessary."

He slides down to the end of the bed, taking my hands in his. "I love you, baby. Whatever this is, it changes nothing between you and I."

"Jenny had been pregnant."

Dan doesn't flinch, he just listens, his thumb brushing over my knuckles. Calm and steady. My rock.

"I thought the baby perished with her but when the coroner didn't mention she was pregnant, I was confused. I waited until Raffe left the room and I asked him. He said she wasn't carrying a child. I... I didn't understand but the more I thought about it, I just assumed she had the baby while I was in Paris with my mother." I pick at a string on his comforter.

"Go on," he says quietly.

"My dad let her pick the adoption couple. We were both surprised he was even letting her have the baby let alone allowing her to decide where the baby would go." I rub my hand over my forehead, a headache pushing in behind my eyes. "Jenny was his one soft spot, if you could call it that."

I stand up, walking over to the window to look down at the party still going on. Jackson must have gotten a new kite for his birthday. He and Rachel are running with it trying to get it into the air. I laugh lightly before turning back to Dan, resting my butt on the windowsill.

"She was so happy the day she picked a couple. She told me it was as if the fates themselves had written the chapter."

Dan stands up. "You mean... you think..." His eyes roam to the window behind me.

"I don't know, Dan, but the math is right."

He walks over to the journals on the nightstand. He grabs them and hands them to me. "I know you've been reluctant to read her private words but... but Jesus, Lily, we need some answers here before we go to them."

I take the books. "I'm scared to find out. Because if it is what I think it is, how can I stay here?"

"What do you mean?" He dips his head, capturing my eyes.

"He... he can't know who I am because he can't know who his father is."

Dan stands up straight, running his hand through his hair. "Jackson would be your..."

I slide down to the floor, laying the books in my lap.

He joins me, pressing his body close to mine. "This isn't a bad thing, baby. Read, maybe she wrote about it in her journal."

Picking up the journal she last wrote in, I glance at Dan. He nods once.

As I open the journal an envelope slips out. It lands on my lap face up with my name on it and all I can do is stare at it.

"Lily, it's okay. Take a deep breath."

Dan takes the journal out of my hands that are paused mid-air. They shake as I pull the letter out of the envelope. My heart is beating painfully against my ribs as I unfold it.

Dear Lily,

I wonder how long it took for you to open my journal. I hope not long. There was no way I was leaving a letter lying around for him to find.

I'm sorry I left you behind, but it was always going to end this way. The only reason I stayed was for you. I let you pull me back over the railing because you needed me. I wanted to help you get away. We may have talked about running together but I knew that was never going to happen. My heart and soul are too broken. No matter how far we would have traveled, it would have never been far enough to hide from my memories.

But it's okay because I stayed long enough to fulfill two of my dreams. One, to leave something behind that was pure and good. Two, to make amends to my friend for the pain I caused him. I'm sorry I could never tell you his name. It's been the hardest part of all this. Not being able to share everything with you. Please know that I wanted to. I really did. But for his safety and that of my family I couldn't risk it.

My purpose has been served and it's time for me to go. I know you may never understand and I'm sorry for that. But, Lily, I need you to listen to me. You need to run. Go. The plan will work and if it doesn't, run again and again but don't stay here. Please don't stay.

You deserve a life. A life you choose. Go out and find love. Find a family. Make a family. Do whatever Lily wants. Just please, please do it. My greatest fear isn't what I'm about to do, it's that you will stay.

I also wanted to let you know that I had the baby. A boy. He's so beautiful, Lily. I got to spend two whole days holding him. It was the best thing that has ever happened to me.

He's going to have a good life. Please don't worry about him. Like I said, this chapter was written by the fates themselves. His parents are amazing. They wrote a letter, telling me about their past tragedies, their biker family, everything. They held nothing back, Lily. That's why I picked them... well, that and one other reason I can't share, but just know that it was destined to be.

I stole the picture of their family. I shoved it right down my pants when the adoption lady wasn't looking. I've stared at it for days, memorizing every face. I'm giving it to you so you can remind yourself how much our little boy is going to be loved. I hope you get a family just like his. Go. Do it now. What are you waiting for?

Follow the dragonfly.

Love always and forever,

Jenny

When I look up, I stare into space. I don't know what to think. How?

Dan wraps me up in his arms. "What did it say, baby?"

I pick up the envelope, unable to speak. Pulling the photo out, I hold it so we can both see it together.

"Holy hell," Dan whispers, his breath ruffling my hair.

It's her baby's family. My family. Or at least it was…

Dan takes the picture from me and flips me around on his lap so that we are facing each other.

"This changes nothing." He stabs his finger over the photo. "I'm not losing you, Lily. Not now. Not ever. You are mine. If you run, so help me god, I will find you."

"But how?" I choke on a sob.

"We talk to Raffe and Rachel. Tonight. We do it tonight."

"I can't."

"You can, baby. You can." He takes my face in both hands and places kisses all over it. "This is wonderful news. It's not bad."

"He can't know."

"We will let Raffe and Rachel decide what they tell Jackson. Jenny trusted them. We can too."

He pulls me into his chest, and I curl up under his neck, his beard tickling my cheek. I want to stay here forever and ever.

"This is amazing. It's a goddamn miracle, Lily."

His voice rumbles in my ear and the more I think about it rationally, I agree. I mean, it's like life has come full circle. She gave Raffe the baby he couldn't have. That was what she meant by making amends to him.

I lean back as everything catches up in my brain. "That means the people he calls grandma and grandpa are really his grandparents by blood." I cover my mouth with both my hands, trying to keep control of my emotions.

"I told you, this isn't a bad thing, Lily. Everyone loves Jackson. When Raffe and her parents find out Jackson is Jenny's son, they are going to love him even more, if that's possible." His hands rub circles over my back.

I pick up the photo, staring at it. "She saw you before I did. How crazy is that?"

"No one can resist the allure of a Skull, baby."

This makes me giggle. "Oh, is that right?"

"That's right. Now, let's go back down to the party. Jackson is going to wonder where we disappeared to."

My head drops. He chucks me under the chin.

"Even when it's cloudy, you can look to me. Let me be your sun."

I bite my lip and nod.

Chapter Forty-Three

Dan

My friends took the news as I expected. They were shocked sure, but they were ecstatic. Jenny's parents were through the moon. Finding out Jackson was their daughter's son had to have been an incredible feeling of joy.

I'm going to be honest here. Lily wasn't the one who told any of them. I did. She chickened out the day of Jackson's birthday party. She told me she would tell them the next day. No big deal, right? But then that day came and went. Along with the next and the next and the next.

She agonized over it. Lily paced back and forth while I watched helplessly, unable to get through to her. I thought she was going to wear a hole in the new flooring. So, after two weeks passed, I decided to take matters into my own hands because that's what I do.

We are planning a big party tomorrow to celebrate, so I guess it's time to tell her that I let the cat out of the bag. Honestly, I'm a little nervous about it now. I hope I didn't make a big mistake.

Lily comes bounding out of the house. We are going on a ride. Our first stop is the cemetery to visit Jenny.

"You want to stop out to the cemetery today?"

"Yeah, that would be nice. Maybe it will give me some insight on this whole thing." She wraps her arms around me. I pat her hands and take off. The closer we get, the more nervous I am. Did I overstep? I'm sure it will be fine. Yeah, everything will be fine.

We park and walk hand in hand to where Jenny's grave lies.

"I love it here. It's so peaceful," Lily says. A gentle breeze blows wisps of hair into her face, she brushes it behind her ear. So beautiful.

Lily walks up to Jenny's stone, kneeling before it. Her eyes trail over the flowers that others have left. And then they land on the framed letter and photo Jackson left for his mom. It's our most recent family picture. The one we took at Jackson's birthday party, one that includes her.

Dear Angel Mommy,

Thank you for sending me the best birthday present ever. I've always wanted a brother or a sister and now I have one. Lily is the bestest sister in the whole wide world. I love her.

I'm sorry you died but mommy and daddy said I will meet you someday.

Love,

Jackson

She stops breathing.

I crouch down beside her. "Lily, it's okay. Everything is going to be alright."

She stands abruptly, pushing away from me.

"What did you do?" she whispers.

"Lily, I keep telling you, this is not something bad. It's good, it's wonderful."

She shakes her head, retreating from me.

"You shared my secrets," she accuses.

I reach for her, but she backs up, almost tripping on a headstone. A storm of panic is brewing behind her eyes. Her hands shake as she glares at me. "I… I can't…"

Before I can grab her, she is gone. My big dumb ass tries to keep up but her tiny frame dodges stones much more easily than mine. The last glimpse I caught, was of her slipping behind a mausoleum. And then she was gone. Just like that.

"Lily, please come here. We need to talk. Running solves nothing," I yell as I search high and low for her.

After an hour or so, I realize she isn't in the cemetery anymore and I'm going to need help. It's possible she slipped behind the shelter belt of trees and headed into town or home or who the fuck knows where. God, I'm stupid.

I send a group text to the club, telling everyone how it went.

Dirk: You're telling me you let a girl out run you?

Me: Fuck you.

JD: I'll go check the junkyard.

Jesse: Girls can run fast too, Dirk.

Rachel: Raffe and I will check the house. Oh, and Jesse's right. Girls can even be faster than boys.

Dirk: Okay, ladies, you can get off my dick now.

Jesse: Not a chance.

Me: All of you shut up. We need to find her!

Bill: I've got her.

Me: Thank god.

Bill: No. Thank Jose Cuervo.

Bill: She came in for one drink. That was eight drinks ago.

Me: Don't let her leave.

Bill: Wouldn't think of it.

Jesse: Let us know if you need us, big guy.

Me: I got it. We'll see you all tomorrow.

Dirk: You sound confident about that.

Me: Because I am.

I stop at the warehouse to grab my truck and then head over to the bar but before I get there, I get a text from Bill.

Bill: She's on the move. I tried, man, but fuck, she's quick. I turned my back for one second and she was gone.

Fuck! I slam the palm of my hand into the steering wheel.

Me: Thanks for trying.

As I'm about to turn around, I see something, or I should say *someone,* up ahead.

Me: I found her. Thanks, Bill.

Dirk: Tie her up this time.

I'm about to type no fucking way but then I glance out the windshield.

Is she trying to hitch a ride? She wouldn't. She's carrying her boots in one hand and yep, her goddamn other hand is sticking straight out toward the road. Thumb fucking up.

After I pull up behind her, I text Dirk.

Me: Consider it done.

Jesse: Really, Dan?

Me: I'll spank your little ass too if you want to argue with me.

Jesse: I'd like to see you try.

Me: Dirk.

Dirk: I'm on it.

Jesse: I hate you both.

Lily heard me pull up behind her and is wandering toward the truck not even looking to see who she's getting in with. Her eyes are trained on the ground.

I lean over and push the door open. "Need a ride, little girl?"

She raises her head in slow motion, confusion gracing her beautiful face. Her eyes are unfocused but only for a second. Seeing me sobers her up real fast.

"I…" she glances behind her.

"Think you can outrun me with half a bottle of tequila in you?"

Her head whips toward me. "Can't anyone in this fucking town keep a secret!" she shrieks, throwing her hands up in the air as she backs away from the truck.

Quickly, I get out, slamming my door shut and rounding the truck. She rushes me, beating her tiny little hands on my chest. "Why did you have to go and tell them? Why?" she screams.

Damn if she isn't a firecracker when she's mad.

"Better question is why wouldn't *you* tell them?"

Her fists pause on my chest as she stares up at me. The stars reflect against the pool of tears in her eyes.

"Why, baby?"

She steps away, her gaze fixed on the ground. "I didn't want Jackson to know I was his sister."

"He loves you, Lily."

"It doesn't matter. Don't you see…" her teeth sink into her soft bottom lip.

"Help me see."

"If he knows I'm his sister, eventually, he's going to learn who is father is."

"Rachel and Raffe will help him navigate that when the time comes. They will be there for him. We will be there for him."

Lily hugs herself. "It's not that easy."

"It can be."

Her eyes flash with anger, the alcohol burning a fire in her belly. "It's not. It's fucking not!" she screams.

I'm stunned. I've never seen her so angry. But then I realize she has every goddamn right to be and maybe this is what has been holding her back. She needs to let it out.

"Jackson will be fine because he has loving parents, grandparents, uncles, and aunts. And once his sister wakes up to see she's not responsible for her father's sins, she will be able to help him too." I point a finger in her face.

She gapes at me, her mouth hanging open.

"I'm sorry you didn't have anyone by your side growing up, but Jackson will. He won't have dreams of crying girls. Your father won't drug him or use him the way he did you. Jackson will never see Senator Ramsey as his father the way you do. Raffe is his father."

"I hate him," she says quietly. And then her face raises to the heavens, and she screams, "I hate him. I hate him. I hate him."

Her face turns red, tears streaming down her cheeks. If her father were standing in front of her right now, I have no doubt she would wrap her tiny hands around his neck and squeeze the life right out of him.

A raindrop lands on my cheek. What the hell? It was clear just a few minutes ago.

Lily continues to berate the heavens as a flash of light races across the sky, a rumble of thunder following.

Soon, the entire sky lets loose. Rain begins to come down harder and faster. "Lily, we can talk about this in the truck."

She stops screaming and stares at me. Her body trembles as she falls to her knees. I walk over and crouch down beside her. It's hard to tell where rain begins and tears end.

Her hand reaches up and cradles my cheek. "You are my sun," she rasps, wet hair sticking to her face.

"Always," I promise.

"I'm sorry I ran... I wasn't running. I just needed..."

"A drink?" I smirk.

The corner of her mouth turns up, a grin slowly spreading across her face. "Or two."

I laugh. "More like eight." I tilt my head down, giving her a look that has her clenching her thighs together.

"Again, can no one keep a secret around here?"

"No. We have no secrets in the club. I'm sorry I told yours though. I didn't mean to hurt you. I only wanted to show you what I already knew. That my family, our family, would embrace you. You and Jackson are incredibly lucky to have found each other."

She places her other hand on my cheek, pulling me close. Lily presses her lips to mine, her tongue pushing into my mouth hesitantly. She tastes like tequila and rain.

When we pull away from each other, I smile. "I think that was our first fight."

Lily leans forward, burying her face under my beard. She nips lightly at my neck, licking and sucking her up to my ear. *Jesus.* "I guess it was. Can we make up now?" she purrs seductively.

"Let's continue this at home." I quickly try to jump to my feet, but holy shit it got muddy fast. I slip, falling back onto my ass. She laughs at me but when she tries to stand the same thing happens to her, mud splattering everywhere.

We both roar with laughter. I've heard Lily laugh before but this is different, it's free, unrestrained. It's… goddamn amazing.

I crawl to her, stopping when I'm hovering over her face. "You look good dirty."

She stares up into my eyes, my body shielding her from the rain. Those big fucking brown eyes blink up at me innocently. "Do I?" she says quietly. Other than our breathing, the only sound is the patter of rain against the earth and an occasional rumble of thunder.

"Oh, you look so good. So good in fact, I think I'm going to fuck you right here."

Her eyes widen, her lips part and those gorgeous hips rise to grind against me. I trace a muddied hand along her bottom lip, smearing the wet soil across her face. Lily is a wet dream come to life and she's mine.

"Please," she whimpers. She wants this as much as I do. I glance around, knowing anyone who drives by could see us.

Fuck it. I pull her up and flip her so that she is on all fours. Quickly, I tug her pants down, spreading mud all over that beautiful ass of hers. She looks over her shoulder. So dirty, so beautiful, so mine. I tug my aching cock out of my pants, rubbing it over her wet pussy before sliding in balls deep.

She cries out, her face pointed toward the heavens. I watch my dick glide in and out of her tight hole as she makes the sexiest noises I've ever heard. Lily pushes back against me, matching me thrust for thrust. So perfect. So. So. Perfect.

Her hands slip in the mud as I pound into her faster, my balls tightening. I grab her around the waist with one arm, my hand sliding down between her legs, I roll her clit between my finger and thumb. She cries out as she finds her release. Her head drops, wet hair hanging around her face.

I slam into her one, two, three times more before I come harder than I've ever come in my entire life. I drape my body over hers, panting into her ear. "I love you."

She drops to her forearms, exhaustion taking over.

That was… that was intense. The rain has all but stopped. Lingering clouds pass lazily over the moon.

Lily starts to tremble under me. Fuck, is she crying again?

She falls to the ground and rolls herself under me, staring up at my face. She's laughing. "Oh god, Dan. Life is never going to be boring with you, is it?"

I give her my best smile, leaning down to rub our noses together. She giggles. "Never."

God, what a mess we have now. Her pants are still bunched around her thighs. I stand, pulling her with me, helping her tug them over her muddy ass. She sways a little on her feet, so I leave her standing against the truck. I pull a tarp out of the back to drape over the seats. If you're wondering if it was worth it… fuck yes, it was worth it.

I help her into the truck and drive home. "There's a party tomorrow." I don't want to ruin our make-up session, but I need to tell her before we get home. I want everything on the table before we fall into our warm bed for the night.

"Do you guys throw a party for everything?" she asks, still in her teasing mood.

"Yes," I deadpan.

She laughs, running a muddy finger over her window, staring out at the dark trees passing us by.

When we pull into her driveway, I see Dirk's truck sitting in front of the house. We get out and walk up to the porch. Dirk and Jesse are swaying gently on her swing. Billie Rose is sleeping soundly on Dirk's chest, a thumb in her mouth.

Jesse laughs quietly. "What the fuck happened to the two of you?"

We both look down at our muddy clothes before looking at each other.

Dirk stops the swing. "Jesus Christ, you two are fucking something else." He stands, carrying Billie Rose over to the truck and placing her gently in the car seat. She smiles at him sleepily, rubbing her eyes.

He leans in and kisses her cheek, making her giggle. When he leans away, she is already sticking her thumb back in her mouth. Soon, her eyes drop closed again. He turns to face us. "We just wanted to make sure you didn't need any help with this one." He points at Lily.

She blushes prettily, muddy hair and all.

"Well, thanks for stopping by but as you can see, we're just fine."

Jesse laughs, tossing her black hair over her shoulder. "You might want to shower before coming to the party tomorrow," she teases, rounding the truck and hopping in.

Dirk walks over to Lily chucking her under the chin. "Don't run from him again," he warns, and trust me, it is a warning. He loves me and he knows how much she scared me. We may have jested earlier in our text conversation, but he knows it would kill me if I lost her.

370

"I'm sorry," she whispers.

His eyes slide to me before going back to hers. "Don't be sorry. Next time just fuck it out first. Don't run."

She nods, dropping her eyes.

"See you both tomorrow."

And then they're off, leaving us standing muddy and alone in the driveway.

"If I hurt you, I am truly sorry." She says, not looking at me. "I... I was just so angry. Not at you but at my dad. I'm sorry I took it out on you."

I grab her hand, accepting her apology. "I'm sorry too. I should have waited for you to come around to the idea of telling them."

She doesn't say anything, she also accepts my apology.

We strip our muddy clothes off on the porch before heading upstairs to shower.

The two of us stand under the stream, watching the muddy water swirl down the drain. She turns in my arms. I grip her waist, holding her close to me, our wet bodies pressed together. "I love you," she says, pressing kisses across my chest.

"I love you too." I place a kiss on top of her head. "Do you know I wished on a dragonfly for you? It was when I drew up the tattoo that Jesse first told you about."

She hugs me around the waist, brown eyes blinking at me slowly. "It was Jackson's fifth birthday. I was down by the lake, watching the dragonflies darting over the water, remembering what Raffe had told me years before." I run my finger over her bottom lip as it wobbles.

"I was surrounded by my family, but I was lonely. There was something missing from my life. So, I wished for that something to come to me."

She lays her head against my chest, squeezing me tight. I've never told her this. Never told anyone but tomorrow is a fresh start for us, and I want everything on the table.

"You… you are a wish come true, Lily Ramsey."

She sniffles. "Thank you for telling me that story. I really needed it."

"Tomorrow is a new start for us. Everything is out in the open. No more secrets. No more threats hanging over our heads. It's time to celebrate you, us, friends, family, Jackson… everything. It's time to celebrate our new life… together. Yeah?"

Lily lifts her big brown eyes, gracing me with a beautiful smile. "Yeah."

Chapter Forty-Four

Lily

The minute I step into the warehouse, Jackson is running to me. He throws himself in my arms, hugging me tight. Instantly, he melts away the last bit of doubt I'd been harboring in my heart.

I set him down, ruffling his unruly brown hair. His big brown eyes, much like my own, stare up at me. "Hey, little brother," I murmur quietly.

He smiles big. "I always wanted a sister," he says before dragging me away from Dan. "Aunt Jesse helped me paint a picture. You can hang it by the other one I made for you."

I laugh. "I love your paintings."

He makes me sit down in a chair and close my eyes. "Okay, you can open them."

It's beautiful. His gift to me is a watercolor portrait of Jenny and I laughing, it's the selfie from my phone. But in this painting, Jackson is between us, smiling big. Our little family. My mind wanders to Jenny.

"I bet the baby will have your eyes," Jenny tells me.

"And your craziness," I counter.

We laugh as I lay my head on her stomach, facing her. The baby shifts, making Jenny grunt. I smile at her. "This one's going to be a go getter, I can tell. Does it ever sleep?"

She rubs her hand over my cheek, brushing hair away from my face. "Not much."

I close my eyes and trace circles over her swollen stomach. "Shh, little one. You need to rest," I whisper. The baby seems to settle at my words. When I open my eyes, Jenny is staring at me intently.

Jenny and I stay like this for a long time. It's just the three of us. Trapped in this big house. Able to walk outside but not free in any true sense of the word.

We gaze lazily into each other's eyes, as comfortable with each other as any two people can be.

"Sometimes, I pretend this baby is yours and not his," she whispers.

My heart squeezes painfully. I sit up and she leans forward, pressing her lips to mine. She tastes like sunshine and rainbows. Fresh and soft and so unlike Benjamin that it makes my toes curl. "Thank you for loving me, Lily," she says as she pulls away. She tucks my hair behind my ear. "I never thought I'd be loved again."

"You're the only person I've ever loved."

"But you will love someone else, someday," she says, reminding me of the promise she forced me to make."

"I don't need anyone else as long as I have you," I tell her.

"There's a man out there for you. I know it. You'll feel safe in his arms. He'll laugh at your silly jokes. I bet he'll even put up with your snoring."

"I don't snore." I shove her leg lightly.

"And I bet he gives you the best orgasms."

I laugh, rolling away from her. "I'll never let another man touch me."

She gives me a serious look. "Take that back right now," she orders.

"Okay, fine. I take it back."

She sighs in relief, lying back against the pillows. "I bet he's out there right now, wishing for you."

"Do you like it?" Jackson asks, jumping up and down, pulling me from my memories.

I laugh. "I think it's the best gift I've ever received."

"Grandma and grandpa are here too!" he exclaims. "I'm going to go show them." He wraps his arms around the painting, toting it outside.

When my eyes turn to Dan, I find him, Rachel and Raffe all crying. What the hell?

"What?" I ask, wondering how long I had spaced out while thinking of Jenny. God, I miss her.

Dan stumbles on his words, "It's just… wow… the love in your eyes as you stared at him. It's a beautiful thing to witness."

Rachel and Raffe walk over, wrapping me up in their arms. It feels good and strange and everything Jenny promised having a family would be. "Can I call you both mom and dad now?" I tease, trying to lift the mood.

Raffe's body shakes with laughter as they pull away. "Fuck no," he says, his eyes bright with amusement.

I shrug. "It was worth a try." I pretend to pout.

Rachel hugs me one last time before her and Dan leave the room so Raffe and I can talk. Raffe's knee bounces a few times before he turns to me.

"You know, I had the biggest crush on her." He shakes his head. "That's why I gave her the dragonfly necklace."

"She had a crush on you too," I tell him.

He gives me a beautiful, boyish grin. "I always wondered." He shakes his head again.

"Jenny was so happy when she found you and Rachel. She didn't tell me who you were, but she did say that giving you her baby was going to make amends for all the pain she caused in this life."

Raffe inhales deeply. He holds it in so long I'm afraid he's going to pass out. When he finally releases it, his breath blows wisps of hair away from my face. "I never blamed her." His eyes shine bright blue with unshed tears.

"I'm sure you didn't but it doesn't change her regret. She was sorry for getting you into that situation. She didn't talk about it much. And I didn't ask. I knew whatever had happened, it broke something inside of her. Something I could never fix."

He nods, wiping his eyes. Raffe slaps his hands down on his thighs, shoving his emotions aside. "Okay, today is about moving forward." He reaches into his pocket.

Raffe takes my hand and slowly releases a chain, letting it pool in my open palm. "I've come full circle, Lily. You've given me closure I never thought I'd get." He closes my fist around the necklace. "I want you to have this, not because it was hers but to recognize something new. It's a fresh start. A new friendship."

I pull my fist to my mouth, pressing it to my lips. I nod, unable to speak.

"Let's go celebrate. It's what she would have wanted."

I drop my hand. "You're absolutely right."

We walk out to the patio, letting our gaze settle over our family. Today, I'm seeing them in a whole new light.

Jenny has not only been my angel, but she's also been Jackson's, Raffe's, Dan's…

His amber eyes snag on mine. My tummy does a little flip when he smiles at me.

Okay, you were right, Jenny. He's just as wonderful as you described.

I smile as a dragonfly flits by.

Oh, now you're just showing off.

Epilogue

Lily

My eyes dance in the mirror, taking in the people who are mingling behind me. Dan's mom. Jenny's mom. Candice. Rachel. And Jesse. I watch Jesse's fingers whip my hair around the curling iron. She cocks an eyebrow at me. "You sure you want to do this? I mean the guy is kind of an asshole."

"I'm sure." I smile smugly at her reflection.

I run my finger under my lip, straightening my lipstick line, smacking my lips together.

"Okay, if you say so." She shrugs, letting my hair fall away from the iron, a curl falling softly at my shoulder.

I watch as she runs her fingers through my hair. My mind wanders to the last time someone did my hair. Stop. Deep breath. Focus on something real. My eyes go to my dragonfly pendant. Deep breath. The wave of anxiety passes. It's getting easier and easier. My therapist and

Raffe have given me so many good tips to keep it under control. I control it, not the other way around. It makes me feel powerful.

"All done," Jesse says.

Jenny's mom is up next, her fingers fret over the tiny pearl buttons on the back of my dress.

Dan's mom walks toward me. She's been doing so good. We have her on a new experimental drug for dementia. It hasn't improved the disease, but it has kept it from progressing. That in itself is amazing.

"Is it your wedding day, dear?"

"It is," I reach out and take her hand in mine.

"Oh, I remember my wedding day. My husband and I ran off to Vegas."

I smile. She's told me this story many times. But I love it each and every time. Knowing Dan's parents love each other gives me hope for my own marriage.

"Where are we?" she asks, looking around as if she's just arrived.

"We are at the Harvest Festival," I tell her.

"Oh, Dan loves the Harvest Festival. He will be so happy."

I turn to Jenny's mom. "Go get Dan."

"The groom isn't supposed to see the bride…"

Cutting her off, I pull Dan's mom with me out the door and down the hall. I don't even knock; I just barge into the room that is set up for the groom and his men. Dirk raises an eyebrow at me in passing. Dan is standing in front of a long mirror, his chin lifted high as he tightens the bow on his tux. I stop dead in my tracks. Fuck me, he's sexy. His eyes drop to mine. Slowly, he turns. "Lily?" he rushes to me in concern.

I nod my head to the side, raising my eyebrows at him. His gaze shifts to his mom. Instantly, he smiles. "Hey," he says, not sure if he should call her mom.

"Hey, baby." She reaches up and pinches his cheek. "Don't you look handsome on your wedding day." Her hands slide over the front of his white shirt.

"Thank you, mom." He leans down and gives her a kiss on the forehead.

"And look at your bride." She pulls away from him, gesturing over me.

He turns in slow motion, realizing this is the first time he's seeing me in my wedding dress. The muscle in his jaw twitches.

"Jesus Christ," he whispers hoarsely.

His mom swats him in the stomach, making him flinch. "Mouth."

"Yes, ma'am." He smiles at me wickedly. "You look good enough to eat." He nips the air, earning him another swat to the stomach.

His mom pushes me from the room. "Enough of this nonsense. We'll see you at the ceremony." She stops to give Dirk a kiss on the cheek on our way out, making him blush. I don't think I've ever seen the man blush.

Amazingly, she remains lucid the entire day. Our angel must be looking over us. I'm sure she is.

Jenny's dad walks me down the aisle. I wanted to ask him, but turns out I didn't have to, he offered.

All I can say is that I thank Jenny every day for them.

The rest of the ceremony is a blur. I literally have hearts in my eyes for the man I'm marrying. He's all I see as we recite our vows.

Later that evening, Jackson finds me sitting on a bench alone, staring up at the sky. My feet are killing me. The guys have kept me dancing all night long. He sits down beside me, watching my face intently. I drop my eyes to him, and he smiles shyly.

"I made you something." He kicks his feet back and forth and I notice he's hiding something behind his back.

"You did?"

He nods. "JD helped me."

Jackson hands me his gift.

"Jackson, I love it."

I run my hand over the wooden frame. It's a map of the United States. There is a box attached to the side filled with push pins. One is already pinned on the map. It's a special pin, a tiny little dragonfly. It's stuck at home.

"You can put the pins in all the places you visit," he tells me, running a finger under his nose.

"Jackson, this is a very thoughtful gift. I love it."

"I'm going to miss you," he says, sniffling sadly.

Dan and I are taking a month-long honeymoon. We are road tripping across the United States. I know that seems excessive but soon, we won't be able to travel. We have a secret… well, two little secrets. Yes, I know Skulls aren't supposed to keep secrets, but Dan and I want to keep the news to ourselves for a while. At least until my second trimester begins.

"I'm going to send you lots and lots of postcards and we can facetime any time you want."

"Really?" he perks up a little.

"Really. I'm going to miss you just as much as you miss me."

He smiles, scooting closer to me. We both turn our faces back to the heavens. I'm hoping Jenny can see us. Maybe Jackson is wishing for the same thing.

Before I know it, it's time to leave. Everyone gathers around to wave us goodbye. I laugh, curls whipping around my face as Dan pulls me past the rows and rows of sunflowers to our vehicle.

I stop, skidding in the gravel. "Dan," I squeal, jumping up and down like Jackson does when he's excited.

It's a Volkswagen Bus. Holy shit! This is perfect.

"This is a gift from the club," he tells me as he scoops me up and sets me in the passenger seat.

I swivel, looking behind me. It's so amazing. We can camp right here in our own little world. I love it!

Dan slides in beside me.

"Where to first, wife?" He smiles big and bright. His amber eyes sparkle with an excitement that mirrors my own.

"Let's go to the Grand Canyon."

He shifts into gear. "That sounds like the perfect place to begin."

I bounce in my seat. This is our first drive as a married couple.

We drive all night, chatting the entire way. I don't think we will ever run out of things to talk about. We finally reach our destination in the wee hours of the morning. I brew a pot of coffee as Dan sets our lawn chairs outside the van. Instead of sitting in my own chair, I perch on his lap. We wrap up in a big blanket, sipping our coffee.

There's a peaceful quiet here. No traffic. No people. Just him and I and this magnificent canyon.

The clear sky turns pink, then yellow, then orange, gracing us with the colors that you can only find in the sun's unique palette. It's beautiful, making my heart sing with happiness. Now that I think about it, I can't remember the last time it was cloudy. Or maybe I haven't noticed since my sun is always by my side.

When the sun glints on the horizon, like the diamond in my ring, we both stop breathing. This feels like a dream. But it's not.

It's real life.

My life.

"I love you, baby." Dan snuggles his face in the crook of my neck, his hands wrapping protectively around me.

"Dan?"

"Hmm?" he hums, sleepy yet happy.

"Thank you for loving and protecting me."

"I'll always protect you, baby. You're mine and as a Skull…

I cut him off, laughing. "And as a Skull, you'll always protect what's yours."

"Always," he says against the shell of my ear, making me shiver.

Sometimes, the world in which we're born is not the one we're meant to inhabit. I'm lucky to have found the perfect world for me. All thanks to a dragonfly and the angel he carried on his back.

About the Author

LM Terry is an upcoming romance novelist. She has spent her life in the Midwest, growing up near a public library which helped fuel her love of books. With most of her eight children grown and with the support of her husband, she decided to follow her heart and begin her writing journey. In searching for that happily ever after, her characters have been enticing her to share their sinfully dark, delectable tales. She knows the world is filled with shadows and dark truths and is happy to give these characters the platform they have been begging for. This is her sixth novel.

Facebook: https://www.facebook.com/lmterryauthor/

Website: https://www.lmterryauthor

Made in the USA
Columbia, SC
23 December 2024

50556843R00238